Barbara

MORE . . .

"This was an impressive sensual read that will grab the reader from the first pages and not let you go until the very amusing and delightful end."

—TheMysticCastle.com

"A steamy, romantic, scheming, and totally enjoyable Regency romance."

—*Fresh Fiction*

"There's no disappointment from this author when it comes to the steamier side of romance."

—*Romance Reader at Heart*

"Pierce reaches new heights in this titillating, spicy romance as she plays upon our wicked fantasies while crafting a fine-tuned tale of revenge and sizzling desire."

—*Romantic Times BOOKreviews*

"Barbara Pierce's star continues to rise!"

—Gaelen Foley, national bestselling author

COURTING THE COUNTESS

"Pierce carries off just-simmering-underneath sexual tension like a virtuoso and keeps readers wondering just how these two dynamic characters will get together. This splendid read shimmers with the temptation of seduction and the healing power of love."

—*Romantic Times BOOKreviews*

"Pierce once again earns our appreciation for delighting us with her talent."

—*Rendezvous*

"A good story line . . . a nice read."

—*The Best Reviews*

"Impossible to put down . . . [Pierce is] a truly exceptional storyteller."

—*Romance Reader at Heart*

TEMPTING THE HEIRESS

"Pierce does an excellent job blending danger and intrigue into the plot of her latest love story. Readers who like their Regency historicals a bit darker and spiked with realistic grit will love this wickedly sexy romance."

—*Booklist*

"Masterful storyteller Barbara Pierce pens captivating romances that are not to be missed!"

—Lorraine Heath, *USA Today* bestselling author of *Love with a Scandalous Lord*

"I love everything about this book. The characters are like friends you cheer for, and the story draws you in so closely you will dream about it."

—*Romance Reader at Heart*

"*Tempting the Heiress* is the latest entry in the Bedegrayne family series and it is an excellent one. Known for the complexity of her characters, Barbara Pierce doesn't disappoint in this aspect of *Tempting the Heiress* . . . I should warn new readers to the Bedegrayne series that they will find themselves eagerly glomming the previous three novels in the series. Highly recommended!"

—*The Romance Reader's Connection*

"This story is so touching . . . an excellent read."

—*The Best Reviews*

"Pierce writes a captivating story full of passion and turmoil."

—*A Romance Review*

"Fans will appreciate this suspenseful second-chance tale, especially a final fiery twist."

—*Midwest Book Review*

"The Bedegrayne family . . . is unforgettable."

—*Romance Reviews Today*

"Another jewel in Pierce's bestseller crown."

—*Romantic Times BOOKreviews*

"This is one you shouldn't miss."

—*Rendezvous*

NAUGHTY
by NATURE

BARBARA PIERCE

St. Martin's Paperbacks

This is a work of fiction. All of the characters, organizations, and events portrayed in this novel are either products of the author's imagination or are used fictitiously.

NAUGHTY BY NATURE

Copyright © 2007 by Barbara Pierce.

Cover photo © Shirley Green

ISBN: 0-312-94796-8
EAN: 978-0-312-94796-5

Printed in the United States of America

St. Martin's Paperbacks edition / December 2007

St. Martin's Paperbacks are published by St. Martin's Press, 175 Fifth Avenue, New York, NY 10010.

10 9 8 7 6 5 4 3 2 1

Et spes inanes et velut somnia quædam vigilantium.
Vain hopes are often like the dreams of those who wake.

—QUINTILIAN DE INSTITUTIONE ORATORIA, BOOK VI, 2, 30

October 1808, Cheshire, England

Patience Rose Farnaly was rebellious, opinionated, and prone to lie.

Ah, her life would have been much simpler if she had been born a male!

Julian Phoenix's hand connected with the underside of her jaw and sent her sprawling on the dirt floor of the barn. She choked on manure-laced dust as several vexed hens flapped their wings in agitation and scurried away from the violence.

Braced on all four limbs, she turned her face away from him and spat into the hay. Freedom had a price and she was willing to pay for it in blood if need be. Her blue eyes glittered with hatred when she tilted her face upward to meet his cool, steady gaze.

"No honeyed words to gain my obedience, Mr. Phoenix?" she mocked through gritted teeth. Patience rose and slowly sat back on her heels. She gingerly fingered the throbbing flesh on the left side of her face. The duplicitous snake had not spared his strength when he had slapped her. "You must be desperate."

With swiftness she had not anticipated, he seized both her arms and dragged her onto her feet before she could dodge his grasp. "Not desperate, my lovely pigeon. I have grown bored indulging your high-and-mighty airs. Your tantrums no longer amuse me."

Oh, Julian Phoenix was the devil himself. Her life lay in tatters at her feet, and now the scoundrel was demanding her very soul. How she wished she had never set eyes on him!

She shook off his bruising grip. "I was merely a girl when you beguiled me away from my family with false promises. I am six and ten. No longer am I blinded by the misguided notion of love. For some time, I have seen through your flattery and handsome face, sir." Her upper lip curled in disgust. "A pity my father never discovered beforehand that you intended to run off with his eldest daughter. A single ball into your black, shriveled heart and hundreds would have been spared the misery of your association."

Phoenix took a step toward her, his face rigid with fury. "Impudent little witch! I'll—"

Patience agilely ducked, avoiding his hand. If her disobedience was worthy of violence, then an insult to his pride was doubly so. Although she was terrified all the way down to her dainty feet of the man before her, she refused to back down. He had cost her too much. "You are getting clumsy, Phoenix. Have a care or someone is bound to tumble you onto your arrogant backside." There was a defiant fire in her eyes as she circled him, keeping just out of his clawing reach.

Patience had made a fool of herself over Mr. Julian Phoenix from the first moment she had glimpsed him two years earlier while he spoke earnestly with her father, Sir Russell Farnaly. Mr. Phoenix and his merry band of players had been engaged for several performances by one of their neighbors. It had been a rare treat for the fourteen-year-old Patience. The family's country house in rural Devon was far from the thrilling stages of London, and rarely were the inhabitants of her parish gifted with true talent. It was apparent to all who encountered him that Julian Phoenix at nineteen possessed talent. Two years ago,

Patience had gazed adoringly on his handsome face twisted in feigned agony while he made his small audience weep over the tragedies in his life, and hungered. Mr. Phoenix and his players were experiencing an adventurous life the daughter of a baronet should have not dared to contemplate.

Still, a young girl could dream.

They were like the traveling minstrels of old, moving from one village to another, bringing news from the towns Patience would likely never visit, and for a brief moment these wondrous players filled her mundane world with excitement. There was more to life than dance lessons, recitation from dry, uninteresting tomes, and limpid hues of watercolors she tried each afternoon to perfect. Oh, how she envied the players' freedom, the fawning attention they had received after their performances from her family and neighbors.

She had almost fainted when her father had provided a personal introduction to Mr. Phoenix. Patience had shyly gazed up into his soulful brown eyes and sensed a kindred spirit. The subsequent meetings that took place without her family's knowledge had sealed her fate. She wholly offered him her tender heart, and Phoenix vowed to share his beguiling world with her. Even when he had revealed his true vicious nature, she had remained at his side. Heartbroken and slightly wiser, she understood better than

Phoenix that her actions would be considered unforgivable by her parents. She had nowhere else to go.

"Come now, love," Phoenix cajoled, realizing she was not cowed by violence. "Your skills for tragedy have been honed to a razor's edge since our dramatic escape from your family's lands. What I ask of you is no more than any sage miss would offer a prosperous gent who is willing to fill her greedy hands with gold."

Panting slightly, Patience steadied herself by gripping one of the wooden structural posts of the barn. "And you knew my answer, even as you accepted Lord Grattan's gold. I will not be your whore!" she shouted at him, feeling the tenuous control she had over her temper slipping from its tether. With a soft disgruntled sound, she squeezed her eyes shut and thumped her forehead lightly against the wooden post at her own gullibility. Slowly, Patience turned her face toward him as her eyes snapped open. She pinned him with a bitter look. "You swore this engagement with His Lordship was for theatrical performances. You assured me this was not one of your infamous swindles." She shook her head in disbelief. "I should have sensed you were up to ugly business when you told the others to wait for us at the inn. How much was my virtue worth, Mr. Phoenix? Was the value so high, it is worth the risk of a few bruises to gain my consent?"

Phoenix lunged suddenly and caught one of her arms. Wrenching the abused limb sharply behind her back, he shoved her against the rough post. Patience would have rather bit her tongue in half than cry out.

"What virtue, little pigeon? I distinctly recall the pleasure I took on your stiff little body when I relieved you of your fragile honor," he said cruelly. "Lord Grattan does not want a virgin. In truth, most are tiresome. What he desires is a pretty player who feigns virtue and yet is willing to pleasure him with the appetites of a Covent Garden whore."

"Send Deidra," Patience said, shuddering at the thought of being at the mercy of a man who viewed her only as a commodity that could be bought and sold. "She does not care who shares her bed, so long as she is compensated for the inconvenience."

He rewarded the insolent remark by giving the arm pressed behind Patience's back a painful twist. She squeezed her eyes tightly shut and endured. Like a translucent apparition, the young player's face wavered in Patience's mind. Deidra had no qualms about selling her body when the situation warranted. Although they had been discreet, Patience knew Phoenix and Deidra were lovers and had been so for years. When Deidra gazed at Phoenix, the blind devotion Patience glimpsed sickened her. Deidra was a constant reminder that love did not discriminate. It turned everyone into fools.

"Deidra is prettier, I grant you," he said, turning his face into Patience's hair and breathing in her scent. "And obedient, too. Regretfully, His Lordship is smitten with your fair young face, sweet Patience. Our bargain is nullified if I send another chit in your stead."

Patience trembled against him. This was simply business to Julian Phoenix. He was anticipating the warmth of the hearth and the succulent-smelling dinner that awaited him back at the inn. "I cannot do it," she said, shaking her head. "I cannot." She had little left to sacrifice. If she surrendered to his demands, he would wholly break her. Patience tensed, bracing for the pain that was to come for her defiance.

Julian Phoenix surprised her. He kissed the top of her head and sighed with resignation. "Somehow, I would have thought less of you if you had simply agreed." Abruptly he released her.

Still expecting some sort of trickery from him, Patience whirled around to confront him, but he had presented his back to her. "This is the end, then. You will refuse Lord Grattan's offer." As she rubbed her sore wrist, she tilted her head to the side, trying to deduce what Phoenix was doing.

"On the contrary, I have every intention of personally tucking you into His Lordship's bed." Although Phoenix's back was still facing her, he revealed a small dark glass bottle of laudanum that he must have kept in his inner pocket. "Past experience has taught me that even you can be amorous, even eagerly cooperative, with the proper inducement." He turned his head and smiled.

The calculated cruelty in his grin forced her to recall another time when he had forced the foul tincture down her throat. He had stolen her virginity from her that night. She felt something physically snap within her, freeing her from her frozen stance.

"No!"

Patience made a stumbling charge at Julian Phoenix, her arms stiff in front of her. If she could get by him and out of the barn, she had a chance of reaching the carriage just beyond the door.

Like a trap being sprung, Phoenix lunged for her in an attempt to catch her. What he didn't expect was that instead of dodging him, Patience collided with him in hopes of throwing him off balance. Both grunted at the bone-crunching collision, and Julian Phoenix staggered backward with Patience fiercely clutched to his chest. He fell against a wooden railing dividing the barn into sections and froze. A look of horror washed away his earlier anger and determination. Patience fell to her knees as he brought shaking hands to his side.

Something was terrible wrong.

Phoenix's face was ashen. Even his lips had a bluish gray cast to them. His stance also seemed awkward. He had yet to move away from the railing they had collided against. Getting to her feet, she watched him warily open the left side of his coat.

"Oh my God," she said, her voice high with fear as she brought her hand to her throat. "The blood!"

The unveiling revealed a bloodstained waistcoat. More disturbing were the evenly sharp tines puncturing his abdomen. A small helpless sound rattled in her throat as she circled around to glimpse the weapon of Julian Phoenix's downfall.

It was a long hay fork.

The angle at which the fork had entered his back left him literally pinned to the railing. Phoenix tried to straighten, but his movements lacked his usual grace.

"Pray, halt. Your floundering only makes what I have to do worse," she pleaded.

"I seem—I seem to be caught on something," Phoenix confessed, glancing about the barn in confusion.

"I know," she grimly replied. The end of the handle was buried in the strewn hay on the dirt floor. Phoenix was wiggling like bait on a hook. Patience's stomach roiled at the thought. Tentatively she bent down to pick up the handle.

He screamed at the barest movement. "Leave it!"

Phoenix looked horrible. His black hair was damp with sweat and his entire body was trembling. Patience hated him, but she discovered that she was not as heartless as she had thought. She felt no satisfaction in watching him suffer.

"You have impaled yourself on a hay fork," she said quietly. "I cannot remove it without assistance, and you are losing too much blood for me to summon help. Can you stand if I help you?"

"Spitted like a pig," he said through gritted teeth. "How you must relish my predicament."

"Immensely," she blandly replied, hoping his anger would give him strength. Patience placed her left hand on his shoulder blade as she threaded her fingers on her right hand through the tines. "Though it was another creature that came to mind. Now, try to stand."

He was tall, but his lean figure belied the heaviness of marble. Patience pressed her face against the hand on his back and pushed.

Phoenix chuckled faintly. "Which God's creature do you view me akin to, my cruel pigeon? A rat? A sss-skunk?"

His entire body was straining to obey her command to rise. Patience renewed her efforts to shove him onto his feet. She fully expected him to collapse the minute she removed the tines from his back.

"No," she panted, the irony that she was rescuing the very man who minutes earlier had planned to drug and sell her to some debauched earl not lost on her. When she had a moment to reflect on it, she could lament over her foolish actions. "More like a slimy squirming worm!"

Bracing herself for what was to come, Patience ruthlessly jerked the wooden tines out of his flesh.

Phoenix screamed and crumpled face-first into the soiled hay. Dropping the hay fork, Patience slipped through the railing and crouched down next to the unmoving man. Heaven help them both, there was so much blood. When she rolled him over, he did not even cry out. The front of him looked worse than his backside. She worried her lip as she pondered what she should do. She had no skill in the healing arts. The blood had soaked through his coat, and his breeches gleamed with the spreading wetness. Patience was so horrified by the blood, she started when he suddenly spoke.

"You've had your revenge on me, have you not?" he rasped, blood seeping from the corners of his mouth. Even the gaps between his teeth were tinged with blood. "You've killed me."

"No," she said, folding up the bottom edge of his coat and pressing the extra fabric to his wounds. "I will return to the inn and get the others. We will bring a surgeon and he—"

"Bloody stubborn," Phoenix said, speaking over her plans. "Never listens. Should have just tossed up your skirts, amused myself for a time, and left you to your bland life. You were never worth the trouble. *Never.*"

Patience's lip trembled at his deathbed lecture. She glanced away, ignoring the sting of tears in her eyes. After everything she had endured at his hands, she was not going to allow him to make her feel guilty over what was clearly an accident. "The laudanum!" On her hands and knees, she raked the straw around them with her fingers. "It has to be somewhere." The least she could do was ease his pain.

Phoenix watched her frantic search for the bottle dispassionately. "They'll likely hang you, you know," he said with some amusement in his inflection. "What will your precious family think when they learn that you are a murderess?"

Forgetting the laudanum, she slowly sat up on her heels. She had cut all ties to her family the night she had betrayed them by running off with a handsome player. Despite her best efforts to hide it from him, Phoenix knew discussing her family was akin to poking a fresh wound. "I have not murdered anyone."

He grimaced, keeping his hands tightly clenched to his side. "Not yet. But soon," he assured her. "Deidra and the others back at the inn know we were arguing when we left them. When my body is discovered, they will deduce I was attacked from behind—"

This was outrageous. A dying man was supposed to be truthful at the end. "You fell. I will tell them what you had planned . . . what you wanted me to do." She gestured helplessly, foreseeing several complications in her explanations to the authorities.

There was a disturbing rattle when he exhaled. "Perhaps. Either way, your fate looks grim, sweet Patience. If you convince the magistrate to believe your sordid tale of forced prostitution, he will believe you murdered me out of vengeance. If he doesn't, he will believe you merely killed your lover because he turned to another." Phoenix had the audacity to smile at her. "Deidra will verify that fact. The young lady loves me—and she certainly despises you."

Patience swiped at the strands of hair tickling her face. Where had all of this gone so wrong? He was the villain. She was just a sixteen-year-old girl who wanted her life back. "Cease talking about murder. I will ride on to the great house. I will bring back—"

He did not seem to hear her. His eyes glazed, he dreamily contemplated her hanging. "Your lovely neck—"

"No. Stop, I beg—" Patience brought her fingers to his lips, attempting to stem the flow of his cruel musings.

"Will snap and—" he continued.

She pounded her fists on her thighs in frustration. "Will you listen to me?"

Although his gaze was fixed on her face, he seemed to be looking through her. "Those . . . delightful graceful limbs will sway."

He was determined to break her, leaving her in madness. Losing control, Patience seized him by the shoulders and shook him. "Hear me, you black-hearted scoundrel! I am not a murderess!" she screamed at him. "I am not a murderess!" Her denial disintegrated into broken sobs.

This time, Julian Phoenix did not have a clever retort for her.

With his lips an unflattering blue and his chest eerily still, the ensuing silence made a mockery of her hysterical denials.

CHAPTER ONE

March 15, 1810
Swancott, country estate of the Earl of Ramscar

"If you insist on visiting Lord and Lady Powning, then you shall do so without me."

Fowler Knowden, Earl of Ramscar, scowled at his sister's back, noting the rigidity in her stance as he paced behind her. He had known even before he had uttered the suggestion that his younger sister, Meredith, would reject his offer to spend an evening with one of their closest neighbors. Still, he refused to give up.

"Meredith," he said, mentally preparing himself for her anger and tears. "You have been mistress of Swancott for eleven years. During that time, how many times have you called on Lady Powning? How many times did you invite her and Powning into your drawing room?"

She bowed her head. Her light brown hair was arranged high on her head, allowing him to admire the graceful curve of her nape. At nearly four and twenty, his sister lived like an elderly recluse. Guilt soured his stomach like an unpalatable dinner. He blamed himself for this sad business, and he was determined to rectify his neglect.

Ramscar strode over to her and placed his hands on her shoulders in a comforting gesture. She flinched at his touch. Her reaction cut him to the core. "It has been eleven years. It is time to let go of the past."

He felt the fragile bones of her shoulders quake before she shrugged off his hands. "Let go?" she echoed. "You might have the luxury of forgetting the past, my brother. I, however, must face it each time I look into a mirror."

Showing more spirit than he had glimpsed in six months, Meredith turned and faced him. She had grown into a beautiful woman. She was short in stature, the top of her head barely reaching his shoulders. Her shiny light brown hair was a legacy from their father, and her melancholy blue eyes reminded Ramscar of their mother. His sister never glimpsed her natural beauty when she used her mirror. All she saw was the awful scars marring her right cheek and neck, a permanent reminder of the house fire she had survived eleven years earlier.

Ramscar unflinchingly held her gaze. "I have never forgotten the past. I was there that night. If you recall, I was the one who carried you from the room, the one who extinguished the flames consuming your nightclothes." He stared down at his hands. Meredith was not the only one who bore scars from the fire that had claimed the lives of their mother and Meredith's twin sister.

Some nights, nightmares still plagued him over the choices he had made that night. Ramscar had been fifteen and arrogantly thought himself a seasoned gentleman of the world. His closest friends—Holt Cadd, Marquess of Byrchmore; Townsend Lidsaw, Viscount Everod; and the future Duke of Solitea, Fayne Carlisle, Marquess of Temmes—all belonged to the elite class of wealth, privilege, and refined bloodlines. They had been wildly reckless, prone to use their fists rather than their intellect, and feared no man or beast.

His father had not discouraged Ram's inquisitive nature that led him to adventure and mischief. The former Lord Ramscar was a traditional sort of gentleman, who believed a man's carnal exploits were connected to his well-being while a gently reared lady needed to be protected from her predatory nature. It was an opinion that Ramscar heartily disagreed with, because, well, simply put, he enjoyed ladies too much. If a young lady desired to explore her predatory nature with him, he would not be so cruel and deny her the pleasure. Ramscar meant no disrespect to the dead, but his father had never understood the workings of a lady's mind.

His ignorance had cost him his life.

"Meredith, it was Audra who died in the fire, not you." Ram cringed at the hint of tears in her eyes. He rubbed the back of his neck in vexation. "I have been a poor substitute for a mother and father, haven't I? I have allowed sympathy to overrule my concerns for you. You do not deserve the fate of a spinster, my loving sister. You should be dancing at balls and flirting with gentlemen."

"Look at me, Brother," his sister commanded, stepping closer so he could see her face. "See me not with the hazy veil of what was, but with the harsh truth of the waning daylight."

She turned her face to the left, exposing her scarred cheek. Most of her right cheek was ruined. The mottled rough pinkish flesh stood out in contrast to her pale complexion. The scarring began at her high cheekbone and disappeared along the line of her delicate jaw. There was more scarring on her neck that extended beyond her high collar. Meredith wore long sleeves year-round, so Ramscar was uncertain of the damage she kept concealed. It was a subject she refused to discuss at length.

Ram cupped her cheek and stroked the ruined flesh with his thumb. "Everyone has scars, Meredith. So yours are more visible than other people's. You are still beautiful to me."

She shut her eyes at his sweet words as if his compliment pained her. "You have a unique notion of beauty, Ram. I doubt any gentlemen I might encounter on the street or at a ball would view my countenance with similar generosity. Or any noble lady would gaze upon me with envy in her heart."

It was the same predicament every year. He tried to coax Meredith into polite society, and she rebuffed all of his arguments. After hours of tearful debate, he always yielded to her fears. Eleven years had slipped by. Ram knew another eleven could pass and her answer would be the same. "Come with me to Lord and Lady Powning's house. They are friends. No one would dare—"

"Pity me? Refuse to look upon my face?" With a sadness in her expression that always twisted his gut, she shook her head, her mind already made up.

"You are a good brother, Ram. The very best. However, I am reconciled to my seclusion. It is time for you to accept it as I do."

She was the only family he had left. Ramscar felt conflicted. He truly loathed hurting Meredith. Nevertheless, he was convinced that if he allowed another year to pass without a sincere effort to lure his sister away from Swancott, the damage would be irreparable. His visits to the rural country estate were usually brief. The family owned several houses, and the properties demanded his vigilance. He also preferred extending his stays in London, where friends and amusements awaited his return.

What he refrained from mentioning to Meredith was his selfish, less honorable motive for gaining her swift acquiescence so he might immediately depart for London.

Two days earlier, he had received a curt missive from his mistress impatiently awaiting his return to London. Miss Angeline Grassi was an impetuous creature who was prone to spectacular tantrums when she felt she was not being properly adored. Under normal circumstances, he was willing to indulge his little actress, but her latest threat to secure a new protector during his absence had Ramscar wondering if he had been too accommodating to the lady.

Angeline was not aware he had a sister. The intimate details of his private life were not something a man shared with his lover. It grated a little that his mistress thought him so enthralled that he would jump to her bidding.

His friend Everod would have advised him to offer the ambitious chit her congé and move on to a more agreeable lover. In spite of her threats, Ramscar found he was reluctant to coldly cut his ties with her. Angeline was an amiable companion, whether she was entertaining him in a drawing room or in her bedchamber. She had been the first mistress he had taken in several years, and his visit to Swancott had prevented him from fully enjoying his good fortune.

Ramscar sighed. A tryst with Angeline would have to wait. Meredith mattered too much to him to abandon her to her melancholy and solitude. "Do you recall meeting my good friend Solitea? Years ago, he once drunkenly proclaimed to all and sundry that he would not marry until he was in his forties. Last summer, he madly dashed off with his future duchess to Gretna Green. I have never seen a man so smitten with his lady wife or so blissfully leg shackled." He ignored the tug of envy at his friend's happiness. "Solitea was as blind to his future as you are, Meredith. Join me this evening at the Pownings'." Ram took up her hand and impulsively danced a few steps of a country dance, causing Meredith to giggle. Heartened, he pressed his advantage by saying, "Think of our outing as the first steps in casting off the self-imposed shackles you have chosen to don. Let me show you our world."

Ramscar arrived at the Pownings' estate alone.

"Why are you being so cruel, Ram? I wish I had died in the fire!"

With his sister's broken sobs echoing behind him as he walked out the door, the notion of an evening out held little appeal. He was in a sour mood, but the confrontation with his sister had left him restless. Ram suspected a few hours in good company would restore his earlier optimism. This business with Meredith was his fault. He had pushed her hard, too quickly. Although his intentions were honorable, he had overwhelmed his shy, reclusive sister. Ram was certain that given time, he could coax her from her sanctuary.

Angeline Grassi would not await his return forever.

He gnashed his teeth in frustration. It appeared the ladies in his life were determined to keep him in a state of perpetual agitation and physical denial. However, there was no visible sign of his inner turmoil on Ram's face when he approached Lord and Lady Powning.

"Lord Ramscar, you honor us," Lord Powning warmly greeted him, embracing him as if they were intimately connected. A stout gentleman in his mid-fifties, the marquess had more hair on his brow than the top of his head. He rubbed his hands gleefully, and Ram reluctantly found the man's joviality contagious. "I was just telling my wife at breakfast that nine months have passed without a visit from our esteemed neighbor."

Lady Powning extended her hand for Ram to clasp. She was ten years younger than her husband, and the passing years and birthing of ten children had softened her figure to matronly proportions. Her brown eyes twinkled with merriment as she glanced at Lord Powning. "And I had to remind the old charmer that we encountered you and your friends at some function last October."

The marquess snorted in disbelief. "You could not recall what you had for breakfast, let alone a banal gathering last autumn."

"On this, I am correct." She inclined her head regally and gave Ram a coy smile. "*Les sauvages nobles* tend to make an impression on a lady."

Ram rewarded her with a flirtatious wink. "Anything less and we would be disappointed, my lady." Laughing at his remark, his host and hostess moved on to greet some newcomers.

Les sauvages nobles, or the noble savages, was an amusing soubriquet the *ton* had bestowed on Ramscar and his friends Solitea, Cadd, and Everod years earlier when they seemed oath-sworn to stir up as much mischief as possible. Their wealth and family connections granted their every whim, while their endearing charm and good looks tumbled even the most intractable chit into their beds. Solitea, Cadd, and Everod were like brothers to Ramscar, and like all siblings, they had a tendency to annoy one another.

A pity his friends had not joined him at Swancott.

There had been some notable changes in their lives since his last visit to Swancott. Carlisle's father, the Duke of Solitea, had died last season. His death had been swift and occurred under some less than respectable circumstances. If half the speculation had been true, the old duke would have been proud. Carlisle had taken his father's death harder than most, and he had expressed his rage on numerous fellows who were idiotic enough to challenge him in his grief.

With true Carlisle luck, he had found the lady of his heart during his bleakest months. Ram was happy for the couple. Carlisle's duchess was an enchanting lady who was obviously besotted with her new husband. The new duke even managed to utter the words "marriage" and "husband" without hesitation. Yes, Ram, Everod, and Cadd were highly amused, witnessing the demise of one of London's notorious rakes. Ram could not fathom a lady having such a hold on *him*.

Absorbed in his private musings, he collided into a young woman dashing out of the ballroom. Ram grunted as the unrefined impression of female softness, ringlets of pale blond hair, and the scent of clove teased his senses. He caught her in his arms and then promptly released her.

"Oh my, I do beg your pardon, my lord," she said, her voice surprisingly low and strong for such a petite young woman. She had yet to meet his curious gaze. Distracted, she scanned the large hall for her quarry. "There is no shame in wearing your spectacles. I vow, it will spare you from future mishaps."

Without giving him a chance to respond to her outrageous suggestion, she walked away from him. Ram was speechless. He could not decide if he was bemused or insulted by her casual dismissal. As one of *les sauvages nobles,* he was accustomed to attracting a lady's interest. His looks were above passable. He gave his right shoulder a discreet sniff and pronounced his scent inoffensive. Ram was not a vain man, but it was rare for anyone to ignore him.

He sullenly watched the blonde greet and embrace a tall, slender brunette. His brows lifted questioningly at their affectionate exchange. Perhaps the lady favored female lovers. The explanation was a palatable balm to his wounded pride. Viewing her

only from the back, he watched the voluptuous
blonde as she nodded brusquely at whatever her
companion was whispering into her ear. The blonde
grasped the other woman by both wrists and gave
her a firm, reprimanding shake. Whoever the petite
blonde was, she was in charge. Glancing about to
see if anyone was listening, she dragged her agitated companion across the room and disappeared
through one of the open doors. Intrigued, Ramscar
decided to follow them.

The evening was turning into a debacle. All her
plans, the hours of hard work she had dedicated to
securing this engagement for their small troupe,
were evaporating before her grim gaze. Patience
pulled Deidra McNiell into a small antechamber of
Lord Powning's library. Did her companions foolishly believe legitimate employment was as easily
attained as a pot of beer ordered in a local tavern?
Oh, this was too much to bear!

Deidra sniffed into the handkerchief Patience
had pressed into the young woman's hands. At four
and twenty, Deidra's tall, gaunt figure towered over
Patience, emphasizing her own shortness and soft,
feminine curves. Her friend was a talented player
with straight black hair and wide liquid blue eyes
that seemed made for tragedy. At the moment, her

gaze was haunted with foreboding doom. "What are we to do?" she whispered, gesturing at the closed door. "All those people expect us to perform . . . something. . . . What a fine time for Link and Perry to run off."

"We have been a family too long for them to simply run off, Deidra," Patience said, trying to hide her growing concern.

It had been Julian Phoenix who had brought their little theatrical troupe together all those years ago. Long before he had seduced Patience away from her family with promises of love and dreams of becoming an actress, Phoenix had plucked Perry Kiffin off the filthy streets of London. The pretty twelve-year-old had been selling himself to anyone who fancied him to provide food for his invalid mother and younger siblings. Perhaps Phoenix saw something of his former life in the desperate young lad to offer him another means to fill his purse than whoring himself out to sodomites.

Deidra had been picking pockets in Dublin when Phoenix had encountered her. He bought her a pretty dress and vowed that she had the potential to be the next Mrs. Woffington. Deidra had been vastly devoted to her lover; that was, until the day when Patience had been forced to lie to the troupe about Phoenix's disappearance.

Finally, there was Link Stolker. He had been the

first to pair up with Phoenix. Patience did not know much about Link's earlier life. Once he mentioned that he had been an apprentice to a tailor before he ran off. Another occasion, he claimed he was the bastard son of a baron. Link was the oldest of the group, even older than Phoenix by four years. At seven and twenty, Link was a quiet, reflective man with curly, fiery red hair so contrary to his sober nature. His value to Phoenix was in his uncanny ability to quote from memory anything that was read to him. It was a convenient talent, since the man spent most of the day with a bottle of wine within reach. Link always boasted that he did his best work one step away from falling down drunk. Although there was no doubt the man could perform while inebriated, it was his temper that could be unpredictable. They had been forced to leave more than one village as the result of Link's drunken misconduct.

"We are too far from the nearest tavern," Patience mused aloud. "Besides, why walk miles in the cold weather when Lord Powning owns an enviable cellar?"

Deidra hiccupped and dabbed her eyes. "Oh, how I wish Julian was still with us," she lamented, her voice raspy from her tears. "Link was more manageable back then. He respected Julian."

Unlike me.

Deidra did not have to remind her that Julian Phoenix was a better tyrant than Patience. What providence, she thought with mocking disdain, that she turned out to be a superior liar. The pain in her temple was throbbing now. She resisted the urge to rub the painful spot.

Her friend's loyalty to Phoenix was remarkable, considering the lie Patience had told her companions two years earlier when she had walked out of the barn in Cheshire and Julian Phoenix had not. To this day, Link, Perry, and Deidra believed their arrogant leader had abandoned them. Phoenix had studied his fellow man thoroughly and knew all of Patience's private fears. He had known the dishonorable course she would be forced to take as he lay dying in the barn, even before she had. Had he not taunted her, provoked her into concealing his death from the others? It was fear that had kept her silent the day she had returned to the inn alone. She did not want to hang for his death. Neither did she relish pulling her family into another scandal. It was one of the reasons that she had stopped using her family name, Farnaly, and adopted the last name of Winlow.

"Julian Phoenix is gone, Deidra," Patience said tiredly. "So that leaves us to find Perry and Link or face Lord and Lady Powning's displeasure. I am weary of making all the decisions for the family.

For once, why do you not offer some constructive advice?"

Something akin to hatred flashed in Deidra's blue eyes as her thin lips quirked as if to deliver a scathing retort. Even though she and Patience had a tenuous alliance with regards to keeping the troupe together, their differing opinions of Phoenix would always prevent their being true friends.

"Forgive me for interrupting," a masculine voice interjected from the threshold. "Perhaps I can be of service?"

CHAPTER TWO

The blonde who had dismissed him so rudely whirled around at the sound of his voice. How fortuitous the young ladies were alone. Ramscar did not relish fighting off a suitor like his friends Everod and Cadd would have.

"I could not help noticing in the outer hall that something was amiss," Ramscar said smoothly, before either lady could respond to his intrusion. "I apologize for my boldness, dear ladies. Good manners were beaten into me with the flat side of a wooden spoon since I was in the nursery. I could not enjoy Lord Powning's hospitality without offering my assistance to the most enchanting lovelies I have encountered this evening."

Neither lady warmed at his compliment. In fact, the tension emanating from them seemed to increase. The dark-haired lady looked askance at her companion, while the blonde's suspicious gaze narrowed on his face.

Whoever she was, the lady was irritated by his presence.

Now that he could see her face, Ram was struck by her prettiness. There was symmetry to her beauty that encouraged the observer to study and admire. The dress she wore was an uninspiring white muslin, and she lacked the glittering adornments he knew most ladies hoarded like nesting magpies. Her heart-shaped face was fair and free of imperfection. There was an endearing softness to her chin, even though she had tilted her face upward in defiance. Long lashes framed eyes of a fathomless blue that revealed, on closer inspection, several flecks of gold. Her nose was straight and narrow, but it did not overwhelm her delicate features. She had a profusion of blond hair that was piled up high. The pale strands that were strategically left free rippled to the ends in a soft, appealing fashion. She was younger than his six and twenty years, probably fresh from the schoolroom. If she had enjoyed a season in London, Ram would have encountered her.

This petite mythical blond Diana cocked her head in curiosity. "How often do you succeed?"

He had expected coy gratitude or a flirtatious response. Her question befuddled him as much as his reaction to her beauty. Feeling simpleminded, he replied, "Succeed? How so?"

The blonde's full lips curled upward in triumph. "Why, with your rich flummery, my lord. Do ladies truly flutter and coo when you greet them with such tripe?"

The sting of her condemnation made his face heat, a sensation he had not experienced since he was a boy. The lady possessed a tongue honed for slicing a man's thick hide. If she expected an apology from him, she was about to be disappointed. "Usually," he said, giving her a cool nod. "Some even tumble quite easily into my bed," he added, hoping to goad her with his brazenness.

"Really?" The lady expelled a mocking sigh and exchanged a commiserating glance with her friend. "What silly creatures."

"Amazingly so," Ramscar agreed, attempting to hide his smile. "What a rare treat for me to encounter two remarkably intelligent ladies. Permit me to introduce myself properly." He inclined his head formally. "Fowler Percival Knowden, Earl of Ramscar. And you are . . ." He trailed off, giving the blonde a look that usually charmed most ladies.

The blonde laughed. The sound was not a polite chuckle or a girlish titter but, rather, the result of unguarded heartfelt amusement that beckoned anyone within hearing to share her mirth. "Honestly, do you ever give up?"

" 'Fraid not," he confessed cheerfully. He was glad he had not given in to his sullen mood and turned down Lord Powning's invitation, else he would not have met such an interesting lady.

She extended her hand and curtsied when he clasped her fingers. "Miss Winlow. Lord Ramscar, allow me to introduce my friend Miss McNiell."

"A pleasure, my lord," Miss McNiell said faintly, not meaning a single word. She looked nervously between Ramscar and her friend. "Patience, I must be off to . . . to look for—oh, I will speak with you later." She kept her gaze on Ram while she edged her way to the door.

"Soon!" Miss Winlow shouted before her friend could shut the door.

So he was finally alone with the impertinent young lady who had captured his interest. He was not the charmer like Cadd or as aggressive in his conquests as Everod was or Solitea had been before his marriage, but there was something about Miss Winlow that provoked Ram to be daring.

"Patience," he said, trying out her name. "It does not suit you."

His comment was so unrepentantly rude that surprise flared in her blue eyes. "Patience is a fine name. It is a family name and it suits me just fine." She stepped around him, intending to head for the door. "Besides, you do not have my consent to use it, so it matters not one whit whether you like it or not!"

"Settle down," he said, laughing and blocking her escape without touching her. "I did not say that I did not like your name. I just said that it did not suit a little spitfire like you."

His casual praise chilled the brilliant flash of temper. He supposed she did it deliberately just to be contrary. "You know nothing about me, Lord Ramscar," she said crisply.

"Perhaps not, Miss Winlow," he said, undeterred by the starch in her voice and stance. "If you would permit me, I would like to remedy that obstacle. We could start with you calling me Ramscar or Ram, if you prefer."

"I don't," she said, refusing to give him any opening of friendship. She pressed her hand to her temple and grimaced. Mumbling something under her breath, she shook her head as if she was having an internal argument with herself.

Intrigued, Ramscar calmly waited until she had hashed out her internal differences. Idly he wondered how Miss Winlow was connected to the Pownings.

She did not keep him waiting for long. "See here, my lord. I think a mistake has been made, and I am partly to blame. Miss McNiell and I are not Lord and Lady Powning's guests this evening." Miss Winlow took a fortifying breath. Her pained expression revealed her discomfort, though Ramscar could not fathom the reasons behind it until she continued. "We are players, my lord, hired strictly to entertain the guests. Though the sort of amusement you had in mind is not what we advertise on the playbills. So if you will stand aside, I can see to my business and you can . . ." She hesitated over her words, probably thinking it better not to wish one of Lord Powning's valued guests to the devil. ". . . can see to yours."

"So you are Thalia or Melpomene instead of Diana," he mused aloud.

She blinked, bewildered by his odd response. "I beg your—what did you call me?"

He waved aside her question. "It matters little to the subject at hand. I think you misunderstood me, Miss Winlow," Ram said quietly. "When I approached you, you could have been Powning's daughter, his mistress, or the scullery maid. Who you were mattered little to me. My offer of assistance, however, was genuine." Being alone with him was making her skittish. He silently wondered how often she was forced to fight off the amorous attentions of a male guest while trying to earn a living.

Ramscar moved away from the door.

The relief that flashed on her expressive face made his gut clench with regret. He had enjoyed teasing the feisty Miss Winlow, but he had no desire to terrify her.

She walked steadily to the door and opened it. With the spirit he was beginning to admire in her, she turned, saying, "Less charm flatters you, Lord Ramscar. I actually believe your original offer was genuine." She smiled at him, revealing pretty, white teeth. "Enjoy the evening's festivities."

She slipped out the door.

Ramscar crossed his arms and stared at the closed door. So the intriguing Miss Winlow was an actress. Fascinating. He was a devoted patron of the theater, and even if he weren't, the lady's spirit inspired him to offer himself as her personal benefactor. He threw his head back and laughed. Everything he had learned about Patience Winlow during their brief conversation warned him that she was protective of her independence. Such a lady would not allow herself to be owned by any man.

He left the anteroom, realizing belatedly that neither Miss Winlow nor her friend Miss McNiell had revealed what had upset them.

"Perhaps we should begin soon," Lord Powning said, frowning with uncertainty at Patience. He had caught her on the stairs as she debated whether she should search high or low for her male companions. "The marchioness and I were imagining our theatrical evening a bit less formal than the proceedings of a traditional playhouse. I would like our guests to participate in the performance whenever possible."

"Of course, my lord. I have not forgotten our earlier discussion on the subject," Patience assured him.

I only need to find Link and Perry before something goes terribly wrong.

Patience gave Lord Powning the practiced smile she reserved for stage managers and patrons. She had discovered while conversing with the marquess that he had once in his youth dreamed of becoming an actor. Unlike her, he had understood his responsibilities to his family and dismissed his frivolous aspirations. "We are merely here to support and encourage the true players of the evening, your guests. We shall not disappoint you, Lord Powning."

I hope.

"Very good. Very good." He clasped her hand

and gave the top of her hand a friendly pat. "Off with you, now. Gather up the others, and we shall create an unforgettable evening for everyone to discuss over their breakfast."

Her smile dimmed slightly at the older man's optimism. "I will send a footman to you when we are ready to begin."

Patience curtsied to the marquess before turning and starting up the stairs. There was little time to search the entire household for the errant gentlemen. If she had any sense, she would flee the Pownings' country house before anyone thought to look for her.

She did not want to be responsible for Deidra, Perry, and Link. They clearly did not respect her abilities as a leader. This evening's debacle was proof of that fact. Still, she could not seem to abandon them. Guilt over Julian Phoenix's death had tied her to them as thoroughly as the fear and violence Phoenix had used to keep her at his side when he was alive. Regardless, Patience was not a quitter. She was trying to make a better life for all of them, one that did not force them into the shadows. Her friends did not seem at all appreciative of her efforts.

Her approach to finding her missing companions was linear and methodical. She moved from door to door, peeking into each room. When she came across a locked room, she moved on, resisting the temptation to spring the lock by less than honorable means. A large old country house like this one would be the perfect assignation place for an amorous coupling. She tried another door and discovered it was locked.

Patience sighed. At this pace, she would be ducking in and out of rooms all night. A muffled sound from across the hall had her crossing the hallway to investigate the noise. If it were one of Lord Powning's guests, she would profusely apologize for her rudeness and abandon her search. With Deidra's assistance, Patience would give the Pownings an evening worthy of the money they had agreed on.

And then I shall take my time throttling Perry and Link for their incompetence!

Patience pulled on the latch and peeked inside. Gasping at what she glimpsed, she pushed the door open and charged into the room. "What the devil do you think you are doing, Perry Kiffin!"

The lean twenty-year-old whipped around so fast, he tumbled backward into the wardrobe he had been searching. She seized him by the edge of his frock coat and pulled him out, which was a testament to her anger, since the top of her head barely reached the middle of his chest. The relief she had glimpsed on his stunned pale features was quickly replaced with fury.

"God's sakes, Patience. I nearly jumped out of

me bleeding skin when you came rushing in like the militia." He yelped in pain when she reached up and pinched him on the earlobe. "Ow, or me cruel mum," he said, rubbing his abused ear.

Patience dug her fists into her hips and gave him a penetrating look. "Whatever you took from that wardrobe, I want you to put it back."

Perry feigned astonishment. She had known him long enough to recognize when he was trying to be clever. As he shoved back the long, straight blond hair that always seemed to cover his eyes, his smile was guileless when he said, "Honest, love. Nothing tucked in me breeches except what God blessed me with. On me oath."

"Do not be swearing oaths when I am standing within striking distance, Perry Kiffin," she muttered as she slipped her hand into his coat.

"Hold. Hmmf." Perry shifted, attempting to avoid her questing fingers. "Christ, that tickles." He collapsed against an inner shelf of the wardrobe and laughed.

"You promised," she seethed, her eyes burning with hurt and outrage. "You all promised. No pilfering. No trickery. We left that awful business behind when Phoenix discarded us. We are honest players, now, and I will not have you stealing from our generous employer."

Patience reached for the buttons on his breeches.

There was nothing carnal in her actions. Although he was older by two years, she thought of him as a younger brother. If she had to strip him bare to prove her suspicions, she would do it.

Perry realized he was soundly caught, too. He grabbed her wrist, and for a few seconds they struggled for domination. "Quit. I surrender. There is no need for you to be rummaging around in places that are no business but *mine*!"

"Fine, then." Patience shook off his grasp and held out her hand. "You return what you have taken or I will tell Lord Powning of your thievery."

Perry gawked at her. "Bleeding harpy! Selling out your own family, why, I ask you? To impress His Lordship, who will likely hand all of us over to the magistrate if he gets a whiff of our business." He dug into his breeches and slapped a garnet necklace into her hand. "Where is your loyalty, woman?"

"You want loyalty? Keep your promises!" she snapped, her fingers tight over the necklace. "What else is rattling around in your breeches besides your brains? It is unlike you to be so stingy."

His brown eyes flared at her insult. His full lips formed into a sneer as he sullenly slipped his hand back into his breeches. Patience saw the promise of retaliation in her friend's expression, but she was unconcerned. Unlike Julian Phoenix, Perry had never used his fists on a woman. He slapped a pretty gold bracelet and two pairs of earrings on top of the necklace.

"Is that all?" she said in a tone guaranteed to infuriate him.

"Yes," he hissed, clearly perturbed. "That's all of it. Though I don't see why you are being so fussy. A few trinkets tucked away for hard times fill not only my empty belly, but yours as well!"

"Not anymore." Patience gazed wistfully at the jewelry. It was not longing to possess such treasures for herself that nipped at her good intentions; it was the thought of one day being hungry. She shook her head in denial. "Return everything to its proper place. And be quick about it. Lord Powning is expecting us in the ballroom, and we still have to find Link and Deidra."

Perry snatched the jewelry from Patience's hand. "Patience, my lovely girl, honor is costly and not for the likes of us." He poked his head into the wardrobe to look for the pouch he had taken Lady Powning's jewelry from.

"I disagree." Patience closed her eyes and pressed her fingers against her temple. "You and I just never appreciated its value when it was rightfully ours."

CHAPTER THREE

"Where did you find the pretty Miss Winlow and her troupe?" Ramscar found himself asking his host several hours later after his brief encounter with the lady. She had reappeared at Lord Powning's side with Miss McNiell and two male companions.

The marquess had not taken his keen gaze off the lady in question. He had set up the ballroom to be reminiscent of a medieval great hall. Two exquisite stately chairs had been positioned in a place of honor so Lord Powning and his lady had a clear view of the players. Ram leaned negligently against the back of the gentleman's chair while they observed the two male performers juggling flaming torches.

"Are they not remarkable, Ramscar?" Lord Powning said; the reverence in his tone reminded Ram of a boy given his first sword. "I encountered the troupe nearly four months ago while we were off visiting Lady Powning's mother. They were performing at an obscure fair just outside Bath. A very depressing affair, mind you, but Miss Winlow and Miss McNiell stood out like fragile blooms in a conservatory."

"I noticed," Ram said dryly, though, truthfully, he had barely noticed Miss McNiell. "I assume you approached the players after their performance."

"Naturally." Lord Powning's expression revealed there had been no other rational choice. "It was later that I learned that the troupe had no commitments to a playhouse and they were willing to lend their expertise to private endeavors."

Ram raised his brow in doubt. "And Lady Powning approved?" Perhaps Miss Winlow was the man's mistress. It was an unpleasant thought.

The marquess finally pulled his attention away from the jugglers and gave Ramscar a startled look. Expelling a bark of laughter, Lord Powning slammed his fist down on the carved arm of the chair. "You savage rogue! Not those sorts of private endeavors. Are you serious? My lady would geld me for even contemplating such a fantasy."

The tension in Ram's stomach abated with the man's revelation.

Lord Powning did not notice Ram's discomfort. "The troupe is content to travel like the jongleurs of old. No audience, whether it is three or three hundred, is beneath them." The marquess smiled as he noticed Miss Winlow wending her way through the rapt spectators into the open area where her male companions defied setting their garments aflame. "An antiquated and charming tradition, I grant you. However, I predict our Miss Winlow is fated for greater things."

"My lord and lady," Miss Winlow greeted the Pownings, showing deference with a low and graceful curtsy. "The gentlemen behind me require a brave volunteer for their next feat. I leave it to you to name your fool—" She coughed delicately into her hand. "Uh, gentleman."

Everyone roared with laughter at her deliberate slight. She smiled sweetly at those around her while several names were shouted out in hopes of swaying the marquess. Ram sensed Miss Winlow was enjoying herself immensely.

"What say you, my lord?" she shouted over the din of the audience.

Lord Powning rose from his chair. "A brave man, you say?"

"Aye, my lord," she replied, willing to indulge her host. "The bravest. A man whose nerve will not falter when tested."

Lord Powning leaned down and whispered something to his wife. The marchioness nodded in agreement and smiled. Straightening, he said, "Well, my lady and I can think of no other man than the Earl of Ramscar!"

An encouraging cheer momentarily deafened Ram as Miss Winlow offered to him her hand. Her cheeks were delightfully flushed from excitement. "Do you like to play with fire, Lord Ramscar?" With a dramatic flourish, she gestured toward the jugglers.

Ram scowled at the flaming torches. "It depends," he drawled in her ear. He was not exactly afraid of fire. Nevertheless, since he had carried Meredith from the conflagration that once had been the nursery, Ram had kept a respectful distance from any open flame. "I'm rather particular on what I ignite with my hands."

Miss Winlow reacted to his saucy remark as he had expected. Giving him an amused side glance, she said, "How interesting. It has been my experience that fire is rarely tamed for long."

The screams of his mother and sisters still rang in his ears when he thought of that night. "I agree, Miss Winlow," he said grimly.

His trepidation increased as he followed her closer to those flaming missiles that shot out between the two men. Why, of all things, did it have to be fire? What was wrong with juggling several razor-sharpened knives? Or battle-axes? Ram could feel his skin heat under his clothing, and the trickle of perspiration as it collected along his lower spine. By God, he had no intention of being undone by a few lit torches. If word of this reached his friends, he would never hear the end of it.

"What will you have me do, Miss Winlow?" he asked, appalled at his behavior when he realized he was reaching up to tug on his cravat. "My skills as a juggler are abysmal, I can assure you."

"Never fear, my lord. I would never demand more than you would give willingly." She moved in front of him and offered him her hands with her palms facing upward.

He stepped forward, briefly wondering if the lady was speaking of more than this brief opportunity to humiliate him in front of his neighbors. The urge to loosen his cravat was as insistent as a hard-to-reach itch. The fire crackled and hissed with each practiced throw behind Miss Winlow. Entwining his fingers with hers, Ram was startled by the strength of her grasp.

"Did I happen to mention that I prefer my fires in a hearth?" he asked, his gaze following the arcing flames.

A glint of comprehension dimmed her smile. He felt like an utter fool for being so transparent to a complete stranger. Ram wanted to evoke any emotion other than pity in her lovely blue eyes. He tried to release her fingers, but she would not allow it. In fact, she tugged him closer. Ram raised a quizzical brow at her brazen actions.

Tilting her chin in a challenging fashion, she said, "Come now, Lord Ramscar." Miss Winlow made a soft chiding noise with her tongue and coaxed him to take another step forward. "You seem like a gentleman who likes to dazzle the ladies. What could turn a lady's head more than proving that you would walk through fire for her?"

Swallowing thickly, he focused on Miss Winlow's face and matched her measured steps. His initial appraisal of her was that she was pretty. He was wrong. On closer inspection, Miss Winlow was captivating. There was an inner radiance that enhanced her natural beauty. It added a healthy glow to her cheeks and a merry twinkle to her eyes as she beckoned him to pursue her. He was close enough to her now that he could count the gold flecks floating on a fathomless sea of blue. There were three flecks in her right eye and one star-shaped fleck in her left.

Ram was startled by the sudden burst of applause around them. It took him a few seconds to realize they were cheering for him. Miss Winlow stepped away from him and extended her elegant arm toward him, encouraging the guests to continue their clapping. He had been so focused on her face, he had not noticed she had positioned them between the two jugglers. The spinning flames seemed to leap out of each man's hands as they expertly caught and returned their dangerous missiles. Ram shivered despite the overly warm room.

"I-I had not realized—" He did not bother finishing the thought. Ram had not confessed his slight aversion to fire to his friends; he certainly was not going to reveal his fears to her.

Miss Winlow gave him a genuine smile, and the sheer power of it clouted him like a solid blow to his sternum. He felt his chest constrict as the air was squeezed from his lungs.

"Now, I *am* flattered, Lord Ramscar." She hooked her arm in a friendly fashion, and they strolled away from the jugglers. The level of relief he experienced heightened with each step. "Take your bow, my lord," she coaxed him with a nudge.

Feeling foolish, Ram gave an abbreviated bow and raised his right hand to silence the clapping around him. He must have been bewitched to permit Miss Winlow to lead him in an act of buffoonery. His sister, Meredith, had been wise to remain at home this evening.

"You have talent, my lord," Miss Winlow mused aloud. "I vow, no one noticed your discomfort earlier." She inclined her head as she curtsied.

"Except for you, Miss Winlow," he countered, his tone edged with a hint of unexpected resentment. Since others were watching them, he returned her show of courtesy with a bow.

She shrugged casually. "Observation is a useful skill for an actress, my lord. It is, however, of little consequence," Miss Winlow said, brushing by him.

Ram surprised them both by halting her departure by grasping her upper arm. "How so?"

The blonde gave him an innocent look. "I doubt we shall meet again. Your little secret is safe, Lord Ramscar. You have my word on it."

"You and the earl looked rather intimate earlier this eve," Link remarked to Patience hours later as Lord Powning's coachman drove them to their lodgings.

" 'Intimate.' " Perry made a rude noise. "Such a fancy word for a crude act. The gent wanted to tup some pretty miss, and thought our Patience was ripe for a tumble."

She grimaced at both her friends, although she doubted they could see her face clearly in the shadowed interior. "Not every gent has one hand in his breeches while the other is groping up some lady's petticoats!" she said crossly.

Deidra, Perry, and Link laughed at her naivety. The four years she had wandered the countryside with the troupe and Julian Phoenix had not completely eclipsed fourteen years of genteel innocence. Unlike the rest of them, she still believed there were a few notable individuals left in the world who were not self-serving. On the surface, Lord Ramscar seemed like a decent gentleman. Besides, he had been too preoccupied worrying about the proximity of the fire to think about seduction.

Why are my thoughts so troubled?

The marquess and his wife had declared their evening an out-and-out triumph, and the troupe had been paid handsomely for their efforts. Lord Powning had even given Patience a letter of recommendation, which she intended to use for procuring future engagements. Still, she could not shake off her edgy mood of discontentment.

"What were you and the earl chatting about?" Deidra asked while she rested her head against Link's shoulder. "He certainly seemed taken with you."

Patience wrinkled her nose at Deidra's suggestion. "If you had worn your spectacles, you would not be spouting such nonsense. Our brief exchange barely qualified as a conversation."

She was not going to admit that a tantalizing awareness stirred her senses whenever her gaze met Lord Ramscar's very direct hazel green eyes. Patience was too honest with herself to deny that she found the earl handsome. He was shorter than Perry and Link; she approximated his height at five feet, ten inches. His lean, muscular frame was likely honed by outdoor sports rather than the indoor variety suggested by the others. There was a confidence and arrogance in his bearing that drew one's gaze to him.

It was more than masculine beauty, although fate had not been stingy there. His chiseled oblong face was softened by hazel green eyes framed by long brown lashes, a straight nose, and full lips. Lord Ramscar's hair was much darker than her pale blond tresses, lightened only in places by the sun. Its thick length was slightly longer than what was considered fashionable to some. Nevertheless, he kept it neat and clean, the ends tied in a queue at his nape. The earl was not handsome in the classical sense, but his face reflected intelligence, humor, and vitality. If she were still Miss Farnaly, she would have found him charming and hoped to have partnered him in a country dance.

As Miss Winlow, she knew better than most that manners and a handsome face could mask the vilest scoundrel. Alas, she would never know if he were saint or devil. The troupe would not be in the parish long enough for her to discover the answer.

"Bah, you are evading our questions," Link said, slightly slurring his words. "We all saw him whispering into your ear. What did the gent do? Offend your fragile sensibilities by inviting you to his bed?"

Perry burst into a fit of laughter, and Link shared his amusement. Deidra gave Patience a sympathetic smile. Her friends knew that no amount of money would lure her upstairs with any man. She was still relatively innocent in matters of a carnal nature, and she was content to remain that way. Julian Phoenix might have taken her virginity, but her innocence would be given to the man of *her* choosing. The distinction was beyond her companions' understanding. The three of them came from a world where they bartered anything and everything. Patience's prim ways did not fit in their ruthless world. It was a quandary, since there was no place for her in the world where she was once Miss Farnaly.

So where do I belong?

She closed her eyes and rubbed her aching temples. Lord and Lady Powning's gathering had stirred up feelings Patience had thought were buried. It was so easy to imagine herself in her former life. Miss

Farnaly would have certainly sought a conversation with Lady Powning in hopes of attaining an introduction to Lord Ramscar. Would the earl have treated Miss Farnaly differently? Patience groaned. There was no place in her life for regret. Right or wrong, she had chosen this path when she ran off with Julian Phoenix.

For now, her place was with this small troupe of players. What they needed was a strong leader. Unfortunately, they would have to settle for her. "If anyone is evading a subject, it is you, Link," Patience said tartly. "You as well, Perry. Do not think I have forgotten you both almost ruined the evening by disappearing."

"Me? What'd I do?" Perry defiantly protested.

Anticipating a battle, Link shrugged off Deidra, who appeared to be dozing against his shoulder. "So I wandered off to share a bottle or two with the grooms."

"The number was closer to twelve," Deidra sleepily murmured. "They were opening five more bottles when I stumbled across them as they sat around a large bonfire behind the stables."

Link gave Patience a patronizing look that always seemed to raise her hackles. "I do not understand all the fuss, my girl. Deidra located my whereabouts before an alarm was sounded, and the fancy folk were pleased with their evening. You should be showing us some gratitude, rather than sniping at our faults."

Deidra gave Link's knee a sympathetic pat. She had been listening to her companions' complaints about one another for years and knew there was little she could do to stop them from arguing.

"Gratitude? For what, I ask you?" Patience yelled back. "If it wasn't for me, we wouldn't be able to pay for our lodgings, you ninny! I was the one who negotiated the terms of the engagement with Lord Powning. If we had left it up to you, we would still be performing at that filthy, pathetic excuse for a fair near Bath, while you and Perry drank and gambled away our meager earnings."

"We all earned our share. The blunt belonged to all of us," Perry argued. Sitting beside her, he turned his body so he could glare at her profile. "Who are you to tell us all how we spend our individual shares?"

"Shares of what? The shillings we collect from our performances at flea-ridden booth theaters from Dublin to Cornwall? We wouldn't have even them if I was not nagging you at each performance. Or perhaps you are referring to Deidra wandering off with every man willing to throw silver on her bed when he is finished with her—"

Deidra's eyes snapped open at the insulting remark. Her mouth thinned in anger. "Not *every* gent. I am not a whore!"

"Or Link. What did Phoenix call you?" Patience said, feigning innocence. "Oh, right, a handy ol' fool who will do anything for a bottle of blue ruin!"

"Enough!" Perry grabbed her arm and gave her a hard shake. "Your tongue could cut tough hide when you are full of bile."

"Oh, and what about you?" Her eyes burned with frustration and hurt as she scowled at him. "Stealing from our patron. How could you?"

"It's what we do, woman!" Perry slammed his fist several times against the side of the coach, causing the coachman to signal the horses to slow.

"Drive on!" all four members of the troupe shouted in unison.

Patience cleared her throat and strived to calm down. "You swore—no, we all swore an oath to live an honest life. We are not without talent. Phoenix's schemes would never have worked if we could not have presented ourselves as a real troupe. There is nothing stopping us from realizing our dreams—"

"Yours perhaps," Link said bluntly. "Not ours. I won't speak for the others, but my needs are simple—a dry roof over my head, a warm dinner in my belly, and a fat purse to pay for my pleasures. Why do you want to mess with what Julian set up for us?"

"Have you all forgotten what it was like to live under his tyrannical rule?" Patience asked, the past rushing into her lungs like foul air until she choked.

"The abuse, the hunger . . . the fear of rotting in some godforsaken gaol?"

Perry made a disagreeing sound in his throat. "Phoenix filled our pockets, too."

This was not the first time they had argued over their former leader or the last. Wearily she said, "No one should have to sell their soul to fill their bellies and pockets." Patience could never admit that she would never be free of the man. He haunted her in quiet moments. His words taunted her each night before she drifted off to sleep.

"You've killed me."

"What will your precious family think when they learn that you are a murderess?"

It was Deidra who broke the tense silence within the compartment of Lord Powning's coach. While she and Patience had formed a tentative alliance after Phoenix's disappearance, Deidra's loyalty to her dead lover was always apparent when his name was mentioned. It was a battle Patience had no hope to win. "Perry and Link were wrong to run off without a word." Deidra silenced both protesting men with a gesture. "Come morning, I am certain, both will be appropriately contrite for their actions." Her expression dared either man to contradict her.

She mutely blinked at Deidra's unexpected support. "I cannot do this alone," Patience said hoarsely, her throat raw with emotion.

Sharp, dark eyes glittered with undisguised malice at her confession. "It just sticks in your throat, doesn't it? Admitting that you need us." Deidra sniffed derisively in Patience's direction before giving both men conspiring nods to include them. "Gents, she sees us as the drunkard, the thief, and the whore. We do not fit in your grand lady's schemes, do we, Patience?"

CHAPTER FOUR

Ram had expected Meredith to avoid him in the breakfast room the morning after Lord and Lady Powning's gathering. He was surprised to find her sitting at the table, her plate already removed and an open book in its place. Distracted by her book, she did not notice him until he greeted the footman. Polite caution wiped away her blank expression when she lifted her head. "Good morning, Brother. You are up earlier than I had expected."

He resisted the urge to groan. Meredith was prepared to forget they had argued the previous evening. His usual response was to allow her to have her way. In the past, it had been easier than facing her tears. Unfortunately, their argument had not dissuaded him from his goal. In fact, the evening spent with the Pownings had only convinced Ram that he needed to take action.

He sauntered to her chair. "I have several matters that need my attention this morning. You look lovely this morning, Meredith," Ram said, bending down to kiss her on the cheek.

She stiffened at his proximity, and belatedly he realized he was about to kiss her ruined cheek. He was not repulsed by her scars, but he knew she was sensitive about anyone getting too close. Resigned that their day together would likely not be a pleasant one, Ramscar gave her a quick peck on the cheek before seeking his own seat.

"What are you reading?" he politely inquired, attempting to ease their discomfort resulting from his impulsive display of affection.

Meredith glanced helplessly at the book in front of her, seemingly flustered by his question. "Oh, this? Nothing important. Just an old book of poetry that belonged to our grandmother." She hesitated, searching for some equally polite subject to discuss.

Their mutual awkwardness was telling. They had

shared breakfast countless mornings over the years. Ram realized that although they had shared the room, had eaten breakfast together, they had never truly paid attention to each other. Meredith always had a book to hide behind. He usually read the paper or reviewed his steward's calculations in Swancott's household ledgers. With the exception of polite comments about the weather or plans for the afternoon, Ramscar and Meredith rarely spoke. The situation was worse than he had initially thought.

After he had been served his coffee he dismissed the footman. Once Ram and Meredith were finished, he doubted food would settle well in his stomach. "You missed a fine evening at the Pownings'."

She stroked the edge of the binding of her book. He usually did not discuss his outings with her. Ram had learned years ago that any subject outside Swancott upset his younger sister. His silence had been a show of respect, but it had also allowed her to hide from her fears.

"Did I? Mama always thought Lord and Lady Powning rather dull," Meredith said, her voice sharpening with defensiveness.

Ram took a tentative sip from his cup. As he had expected, he scalded his tongue. Grimacing, he set the cup down. "They are a charming, merry old couple who have always greeted me warmly. If you bothered to receive them at Swancott, you would know their kindness extends to you as well."

She glanced down at her book, feigning to read the page. Ram was not fooled. Nor would he give up so readily.

"They hired performers from a fair," he continued, watching her face for some kind of reaction. "Powning set up a mock royal court in their ballroom and encouraged his guests to take part in the performances."

Meredith made an ambiguous sound as she studied the page before her.

Ram waited a minute before adding, "I was even persuaded to participate."

Frowning, his sister slammed her book closed and gave him a gimlet look. "I cannot fathom you agreeing to anything as frivolous as reciting poetry or serenading Lady Powning with a romantic song."

"Nor I," he said, pleased Meredith knew something of his character. "I was coaxed into playing a small part with two jugglers who tossed flaming torches at my head." He had not been thrilled with the notion when he realized the distinctly uncomfortable predicament Miss Winlow had lured him into; nevertheless, he had endured and was no worse from the ordeal.

His sister's eyes rounded in horror at his casual

confession. She brought her fist to her heart as if pained. He had never spoken of his private fears of fire, but she had her own terrifying recollections of the nursery with walls of living flame.

"How could you?" she sputtered, amazed he was not distressed by his ordeal. "What was Lord Powning thinking to allow such a—"

Concerned by her tormented expression, Ramscar reached over and held her hand. She clutched his fingers so fiercely, he felt the edges of her nails cut into his palm. "Meredith, my sweet, Powning meant no insult. No one recalls a fire that took place in London eleven years earlier, and even if they did, it is old news. Look at me. I am unharmed. I will admit I did not relish the thought of fire so close to my hair and clothing—" He abruptly broke off his confession when she clapped her hand over her mouth and sobbed.

No longer caring if his touch upset her, Ramscar released her hand so he could circle around the table. He pulled her out of the chair and gathered her trembling body into his arms. "This is what I was trying to discuss with you the other day," he murmured into her hair as he rubbed her back. "You should not become so undone by the thought of fire."

Neither should I.

"Do not be silly. I am not a child," she said crisply. "I light a candle if I require one, and on cold nights I appreciate the warmth of a hearth." She delicately sniffed and pulled back to see his face. "Having flaming torches tossed at your head for the amusement of Lord Powning and his guests borders on lunacy!"

Her concern for Ram was so sweet, he could not help laughing at her endearing lecture. "No harm was done." If truth be told, the incident was entirely his fault. His interest in the enchanting Miss Winlow had truly placed him in his awkward predicament. Had he not been so wholly focused on her, he would never have approached the jugglers.

"Is this how you behave when you leave Swancott? Do you spend your evenings amusing yourself with reckless games, foolishly taunting fate, for what end?" Meredith asked breathlessly, her face a rosy hue from her impassioned outburst.

Ram cupped her chin, gently forcing her to meet his steady gaze. "Come with me to London and discover the answer for yourself."

Meredith froze at his challenging words. He saw her refusal even before the words formed on her lips. She pushed him away and stumbled backward into her chair. "No." She steadied herself with the chair and then moved around it to put more distance between them. "I sensed you were up to something. You planned this, did you not?" Her eyes glittered with tears and indignation. "Was it a lie? Did you make up that story about the jugglers and the fire to soften me to the notion of coming with you to London?"

"I am not a liar," he said, his face hardening into an unyielding mask. "Nor have I misled you. I told you last evening that I want you to join me in London."

"I beg of you, Brother . . . Ram . . . do not make me. I cannot." She shook her head, her demeanor collapsing into hysteria as he watched her dispassionately.

Meredith would never forgive him if he took her to London against her will. Still, if he surrendered to her pleas she would remain at Swancott until she died. At a loss, Ramscar knew he needed help. Suddenly he heard Miss Winlow's low, teasing voice in his head.

"You seem like a gentleman who likes to dazzle the ladies. What could turn a lady's head more than proving that you would walk through fire for her?"

He needed a blond angel who could tempt the devil into giving up his sinful ways.

Ram knew the perfect lady for the task.

CHAPTER FIVE

"You wish to offer me employment as a paid companion," Patience said, not quite believing her good fortune. "Here?"

When a footman from Swancott had arrived at the inn, inquiring after Miss Winlow, her initial reaction had been alarm. She had never heard of Swancott. Nor could she think of a single reason that someone from the estate would know her name. Only when she learned that the Earl of Ramscar was

seeking an audience with her had she allowed herself
to relax. The gentleman had been polite to her the
previous evening. He had not prolonged their conversation after the juggling demonstration or sought
her out later. She had overheard Lord Powning
speaking highly of the earl. Normally, she would
have never consented to climbing into a gentleman's
carriage. However, her curiosity regarding the earl's
summons and possibly employment for the troupe
lured her out to Swancott.

Lord Ramscar had skipped the formalities of the
drawing room and had ensconced them in his library personally. She had not viewed his actions as
untoward, since she was not visiting Swancott as his
guest but as a prospective member of his staff albeit
a temporary post. She had noted he had glanced ap-
prehensively upward as they strolled past the grand
staircase, and she realized she did not even know if
the earl was married.

"Our stay at Swancott is almost at an end," he
said, disrupting her private musings. They sat in
two large overstuffed chairs near the hearth to
compensate for the slight chill in the room. It was a
quiet, intimate setting, but Lord Ramscar was too
caught up in revealing his plans to question the im-
propriety of the situation.

"I have already begun to make preparations for
our journey to London for the season. Originally, I

had thought to travel ahead. However, Meredith will be difficult, and I fear it will take both of us to coax her off Knowden lands."

Oh dear. So the earl did indeed have a wife. Patience sensed there was a tragic tale involving his countess. What had happened to the poor lady that she was afraid to leave her own house? "Lord Ramscar, I am an actress of little acclaim. I cannot fathom why you think I would make a satisfactory companion for Lady Ramscar."

"Lady Ram—" He was startled by her deduction. Stroking his jaw, he gave her a chagrined look. "Miss Winlow, I have no countess. Meredith is my younger sister. She will be four and twenty in a fortnight. I intend for that celebration to take place in London."

His reasons for selecting Patience still baffled her. "You are aware that I have never been employed as a lady's companion."

He dismissed her concern with a flick of his wrist. "I am not concerned by the lack. In truth, you intrigue me, Miss Winlow. While the other guests enjoyed the various amusements Powning had provided, I found myself studying you."

Patience felt her face heat at his admission. A tiny flutter of excitement rose in her chest. Lord Ramscar had been watching her. She had been utterly unaware of his close scrutiny. Usually, her instincts were faultless. "If you were anxious that I might reveal your aversion to fire to Lord Powning or his guests—"

He silenced her with a piercing glance. "I do not care about the gossips. You caught my attention because you are rather good at your craft. You are lovely and have a quick wit. Your movements are graceful and your speech is refined. If we had met under different circumstances, you might have passed as a relation to Lord and Lady Powning."

The man saw too much. "I have a talent for mimicry," she said humbly. "Me mum would have been proud, hearing yer praise."

His hazel green eyes narrowed at her deliberate attempt to mock her gifts. "Your gifts have served you well, and now I intend for them to serve my purposes."

Lord Ramscar was offering her a chance to walk away from a life of wandering the countryside in hopes of finding a small parish or fair that might have use of her skills. She would have shelter, clean dresses, and daily meals. All that was required was that she look after his shy younger sister. It sounded heavenly. There had to be a catch.

If I accept the position, I will have to abandon the troupe.

Patience nibbled her lower lip in agitation.

"Perhaps you should engage one of your sister's friends to join her?"

"My sister has no friends, Miss Winlow," he said brusquely. He rose out of the chair and began pacing behind their chairs. "I am not comfortable sharing private family matters with anyone. However, I intend to make an exception. You will be spending most of your day with Meredith, and I think it is important that you understand certain details about my sister."

His expression revealed that he dreaded such a distasteful task. A surge of sympathy mingled with her curiosity about his sister. "My lord, you do not have to reveal anything to me."

"I disagree."

He paused near her chair and fiercely gripped the back. Suddenly, the heat from the hearth was stifling. Patience tried not to fidget. His keen gaze and proximity were unnerving her.

Lord Ramscar leaned down and growled in her ear, "I am trusting you with our family secrets, Miss Winlow. Do not make me regret my decision."

She heard the unmistakable menace in his tone. Pivoting in her seat, she quirked her right brow. "Are you trying to intimidate me, my lord?"

"Yes," he said, his teeth snapping together like those of a huge predator. "Have I succeeded?"

She laughed at his question. There was no doubt in her mind that the earl quietly and ruthlessly dealt with people who defied him. "Amazingly so. Proceed."

Ramscar stared down at Miss Winlow, suspecting that it would take quite a bit to terrify her into submission. She was remarkably poised for a young lady her age.

"How old are you?"

Choking on what he assumed was laughter at his amazingly rude question, she sharply retorted, "How old are you, my lord?"

He nodded, pleased with her reaction. As he had guessed, she was not easily cowed. She could hold her own with the curious and oftentimes vicious *ton.* "Twenty-six. And you?"

"Eighteen. Is my age imperative to gaining this position?"

"No." Christ, she was a prickly little thing. Ram could not help but admire her forthright disposition. It was a refreshing quality in a lady; however, he was certain her quick tongue had gotten her in all sorts of trouble. "In comparison to my sister, you seem ten years older than your given age."

She stiffened at his careless observation. "Oh, really?"

Ram's lips twitched in humor. He had not deliberately intended to insult her, but the results were delightful. So the little actress had a temper. If there had been more opportunity, he would have enjoyed provoking her to see how far he could push her before she surrendered to passions.

However, getting Meredith to London was more important to him. "If it soothes your vanity, you look younger. My observation was regarding your demeanor, not your beauty. Meredith has been sheltered at Swancott too long. Although she is older, you will discover she is rather fragile in spirit."

"Oh, I see," Patience said, her relief evident as she sank back into the chair.

"Do you?" He sauntered around her chair and walked to the mantel. Idly, his fingers caressed the painted head of a hawk made out of porcelain. "Eleven years ago, my father accused my mother of adultery. Naturally, she denied it. Enraged, my father decided to challenge the man he believed was my mother's lover."

"Was she?"

Ramscar glanced at Miss Winlow, who nervously moistened her lips. His eyes narrowed as he watched the tip of her tongue as it flickered over her upper lip.

"Guilty, that is. Had your mother taken a lover?"

It was a question he pondered on occasion. "I believe the speculation to be false. My mother was devoted to my father." Nevertheless, Ram's father had been a difficult, private gentleman who was prone to fits of jealousy. Ram had been fifteen at the time and he recalled hearing them argue behind closed doors. If his mother had faltered in her marriage vows, Ram believed his father had driven her to it.

"My father was mortally wounded during the duel. He was dead before he reached our London town house," he said dispassionately. Eleven years had passed since they had carried his father's bloodied corpse into the front hall. The grief Ram had experienced had dulled and eased with the passage of time.

Moved by his loss, Miss Winlow reached out and squeezed his hand. "It must have been horrible for all of you."

He marveled at the hint of tears he saw in her blue eyes. Was her compassion genuine or feigned? The ladies he had encountered over the years would have never shed a tear over the death of a stranger. They made the appropriate platitudes when they learned both Ram's mother and father were dead. Most ladies were interested in Ram's title and the lands he owned, not the tragic reasons why he had inherited the wealth of responsibility at fifteen. He stared down at Patience's sorrowful expression and gently disengaged her hand from his, recalling that she was a first-rate actress.

"My father has been dead a long while, Miss Winlow," he said, abruptly turning his back on her and gazing into the fire. "I have come to terms with my loss." Before he moved away, he noted a flash of pain in her eyes as if his rejection had hurt her. Ram was not dredging up the family history to gain her sympathy. He was telling her details he had not shared with another because he believed she could help Meredith.

"Your sister has not—come to terms, that is."

Ramscar gripped the end of the mantel, quietly testing its integrity. "No, she has not. Meredith is not weak-spirited. She just has suffered more than I. You see, the day my mother learned of my father's death, she was inconsolable. She blamed herself. He would have never issued the challenge if he had not called her faithfulness into question."

Ram heard a rustling noise and knew Miss Winlow had risen from the chair. She stood behind him. He stiffened, half-expecting her to try to soothe him with her touch. It was damned awkward making a confession to a stranger. Ram was not in the mood to be coddled. She must have sensed his rejection before he could offer it, because she refrained from touching him.

"You do not have to say anything more, Lord Ramscar. I think I understand," she said quietly, attempting to spare him.

"Not all of it. How could you?" He released the mantel and faced her with his arms crossed. "The guilt and grief drove my mother into the realm of madness. One night while the household slept, she carried an oil lamp into the nursery where my sisters were sleeping. Meredith had a twin. Audra."

He glanced away. If he looked too deeply into the open sincerity and compassion Miss Winlow's eyes reflected, it would be his undoing. "Many think what happened was an accident. I disagree. I cannot fathom the utter despair my mother must have felt. Why else would a mother douse a room and herself with lamp oil before igniting her night rail?"

Miss Winlow gasped. "Oh, the horrors your sisters must have endured to wake up surrounded by flames!"

The girls had not been the only ones.

Ram had not spoken the admission aloud, but Miss Winlow was too intelligent not to connect his aversion to the jugglers' ignited torches to that night eleven years earlier. "Dear God, small wonder you reacted—uh, were surprised by the juggling demonstration."

She was being kind. If she had not distracted him, he would have truly entertained Powning's guests by panicking in a very unmanly fashion. Everod and Cadd would have teased him unmercifully if they had discovered his weakness.

"I awoke to the screams of my mother and sisters. By the time I raced to the nursery, it was engulfed in flames. My mother was already dead. The girls were crying and screaming for help. The heat was unbearable. Somehow two footmen and I were able to reach them. I did not even know in that moment which sister I plucked off the bed. Suddenly, I was outside the room, gasping and choking from the smoke. Audra and the two footmen perished in that inferno."

Miss Winlow did not immediately respond. Swiping at a few errant tears on her cheeks, she finally said, "I doubt you want my sympathy for your family tragedy, but you have it just the same."

"Thank you." He slipped his fingers into an inner pocket of his coat and retrieved a handkerchief. "My intention was not to make you cry. I just wanted you to understand the obstacle you will be facing if you accept the position I am offering you."

Murmuring her thanks, she blotted the wetness from her face. "Lady Meredith is scarred?"

"Yes. Some scars are visible on her face and neck. Several more on her arms. After the fire, she was so ill from her burns that I feared I would lose her, too. It took years for her to recover. It is only in recent years that I have come to understand that I should have given the scars I could not see more attention."

There was no point regretting what he could not

change. He was paying attention now, and by God, he was willing to do anything to coax Meredith back to the polite society into which she had been born. His gaze shifted to Miss Winlow. He blinked at the fierce determination shining in her blue eyes.

Ram had chosen well. Revealing his family's past had not been pleasant, but his honesty had secured the lady he desired to befriend his lonely sister. He did not bother concealing his smirk. "So what say you, Miss Winlow? Will you accept the position of companion to my sister?" The question was merely a formality. He knew her answer.

She nodded, giving him a beatific smile. The impact of it was not lost on Ramscar. He reminded himself that he had a mistress awaiting his return to London. Nothing good would come of dallying with his sister's new companion.

"Yes. I believe I will accept you offer, my lord."

"Leaving!" Perry shouted after her, following her into the room she had shared with Deidra. He had been playing cards with several grooms in the inn yard when Patience had calmly announced that she was leaving the troupe. After he had gotten over his surprise, he had slammed down his cards and chased after her.

Patience ignored Perry as she crouched down and

dragged a satchel from under the bed. She wondered if she would get the opportunity to say farewell to Deidra. The young woman would likely be pleased when she learned of the news. At some point during the night, Deidra had disappeared after everyone had retired to their beds. When the summons to visit Swancott had arrived, Deidra was still missing. Most likely, she had a clandestine meeting with the vicar's son or, worse, the local magistrate.

From this moment on, Deidra was Perry and Link's problem.

Link appeared in the doorway. He was blurry-eyed, and his wrinkled shirt suggested that he had just crawled out of bed. "I could hear Perry yelling. What's this about you leaving?"

Perry stopped and glared at his friend. "Can you believe it? Our girl is running off on us!"

"Hardly running off, Perry," Patience said dryly. She began gathering up her meager belongings and stuffing them into a satchel. "I have decided to take the position the Earl of Ramscar offered me late this morning. His only stipulation was that I start immediately."

Perry made a rude noise. "Hired you for what position? Flat on your back with your legs spread? Me girl, I saw the manner in which he stared at ye. The man was wanting a mistress, not a new maid to polish his fine silver."

Patience reached for her spare corset and hastily stuffed it into the satchel before the men noticed the intimate garment. "This is strictly business, gentlemen. I have been hired as a lady's companion for his sister, Lady Meredith."

"Have you met this Lady Meredith?"

Patience frowned at Link. "Well, no. Lord Ramscar told me that she was indisposed in the mornings. I am to meet her later this afternoon." She whirled away from Link and returned to the unmade bed.

"My shoes!" Where were her shoes? She bent down and peeked under the bed. Popping up, she discovered Perry's angry face inches away. She straightened and tucked her shoes into the bag.

"Why would His Lordship hire a poor actress when his gold could purchase him an impoverished blue-blooded miss for his beloved sister?" Perry asked. The sneer on his face seemed to be a permanent affliction.

"He has his reasons," she replied vaguely. Lord Ramscar had trusted her with his family secrets, and she had too much honor to betray him, even to ease her friends' concerns.

Link scratched his head, fluffing his unruly red hair. "You didn't tell him about your family, did you?"

Her hands stilled at his question. *Tell Lord Ramscar about the Farnalys? Ha! Never!* Patience resumed rolling up her stockings. "No. There is no point to it, since the Farnalys would deny the connection."

"Give way," Deidra ordered from outside the room. She gave Link a push and entered the room. "What have I missed?" She looked from one to the next, grasping that she had interrupted a heated argument. "Oh, Perry . . . now what have you done?"

"It isn't me," the young man whined. He pointed at Patience. "Blame her. She's running off. Tells us the fancy earl she was cozying up to last eve has hired her to play lady's companion to a sister *she* hasn't even met!"

Deidra gave Perry a peeved look before she moved to stand beside Patience. Wherever the young woman had been last night, she had managed to bathe. Patience inhaled the scent of roses as Deidra picked up one of the dresses laid out on the bed and began folding it.

The young woman lifted an inquiring brow. "Is it true? You are leaving the troupe?"

Patience smothered her guilt with a soft, unladylike curse. "Yes." She rolled up a petticoat and stuffed the undergarment into the bag with more enthusiasm than warranted. "Why not? All of you should be thrilled by my departure. Last evening, you all made it abundantly clear that you do not need or desire me meddling in your affairs. Fine. So be it."

"Nothing has changed, Patience," Link argued, for once seeming sober. "We've always argued about how things should be done." He braced his long arm across the doorway as if blocking her way. "You get huffy. I bellow. . . . Perry whines—"

Perry naturally took exception to Link's assessment. "I don't whine!"

Link did not bother arguing with him. He nodded at Deidra. "She sulks."

"Creative individuals are slaves to their sensitive natures, you know," Deidra said, pouting slightly.

Everyone wisely refrained from comment.

Link became more animated as he summarized all the reasons Patience should remain with the troupe. He continued, "And the next day, we start anew. It all works out."

Patience glanced about the room, checking to see if she had forgotten anything. She did not own much. Anything of value had been sold off years ago. She picked up the satchel. "This day was coming, Link. I tried to keep us together after Phoenix left, since none of you wanted to take over the task. I did my best. Still, we all know I was a poor replacement. All I did was delay the inevitable."

She faced Deidra. "I will be residing at Swancott. Lord Ramscar's lands are to the east. We will be traveling to London for the season." Patience had yet to mull over her decision to accept the position with the Knowdens. For years, she had avoided London for fear she might encounter her family. It had been four years. Would her family even recognize the young lady she had become?

Her companion's eyes shimmered with tears. "We can stay at the inn a few more days. You might change your mind." Impulsively she hugged Patience, her movements awkward. It was the first show of affection Deidra had ever demonstrated.

"Perhaps." Patience did not want to make promises she had no intention of keeping.

Clutching her satchel, she walked over to Perry. "Farewell, Perry. When you think on this later, you will see the benefits to my leaving."

Perry stared at her mutinously. He was not happy with her leaving. In a very motherlike gesture, Patience lovingly pushed back a fallen blond lock of hair that obscured his vision and tucked it behind his ear.

"How so?" he asked.

She grinned at him. "Well, the profits will be split three ways instead of four."

"There is that," he said glumly, hugging her so strongly that she gasped. "I still say the man's a rogue. I heard one of the fancies saying he was one of them *les sauvages nobles*."

Patience wrinkled her nose at the French phrase. "The noble savages? What is it? Some sort of gentlemen's club?"

"Probably a vile one that lures young virgins to their doom," Link said gruffly, drawing her into his embrace.

"Well, then I have no worries," Patience teased, trying to lift the somberness of her departure.

Link smiled faintly at her misplaced sense of humor. "We will dally here for a few days. If this position is nothing but a ruse to procure a new mistress or something worse, then I want you to return to the inn. There is no shame in abandoning a scoundrel who has no honor."

Like I should have with Julian Phoenix.

She sighed softly. Patience had been too young to understand the sort of games a man like Phoenix liked to play. She headed through the door, only to pause and turn back. Despite their differences, she considered the troupe her friends. "If you find your way to London . . ." She said nothing else. The lump in her throat swelled to the point of pain.

By leaving the troupe she was finally free of Julian Phoenix. Lord Ramscar unknowingly was giving her a chance to start her life over again. Nodding farewell to her friends, she walked through the door to the carriage that awaited her return.

CHAPTER SIX

"I will not have a stranger underfoot in my household!"

Meredith was handling the news of Miss Winlow's arrival better than Ram had anticipated. Unlike many women in his past, Meredith had not succumbed to tears or thrown a single object at his head. Truly he was optimistic.

"Miss Winlow is joining us at my request," he said, giving Meredith a level stare. "You are mistress of Swancott. As such, I expect you to welcome her in a manner befitting your position."

His sister lowered her head and twisted the gold ring on her first finger. "*Your* Miss Winlow is not a visitor, Ram. She is a servant. Why should she be given any more courtesy than, say, the gardener or scullery maid?"

Ramscar was so stunned by Meredith's uncharacteristic viciousness, he just gaped at her. Any hope that his sister might concede to his dictates willingly vanished. Still, he was master of Swancott. "You are furious with *me*, Meredith. Do not shame me by focusing your ire on an innocent woman."

Meredith flung out her hands, appealing to the heavens. "Why do you not listen to me? I do not need a companion, for I will not be going to London with you."

Ram strived for patience, bridling his own temper. "We have discussed this several times, and I will not be denied. You are coming to London. There we will celebrate your twenty-fourth birthday with a ball that will serve as your introduction to the *ton*. As we speak, the preparations for the ball are being carried out."

His sister reminded him of a terrified, bristling kitten. One thing about cornered creatures, he thought, was they tended to lash out and bite those who underestimated them.

"Have your ball if you desire," she spat. "I, however, will not be in attendance. Let Miss Winlow take my place."

"It would be an honor, Lady Meredith. Regrettably, I would be a poor substitute for the Earl of Ramscar's sister," Miss Winlow said from the threshold.

Astonished they were not alone, both siblings whirled around to confront the newcomer.

The blonde demurely entered the room. "Forgive me, my lord, for interrupting. Your butler was kind enough to permit me to await you in the front hall. Nevertheless, I could not help but overhear your conversation."

"Congratulations, Ram," Meredith said, mockingly applauding him. "Not only is she breathtakingly beautiful but an eavesdropper, too. Well done."

"Silence!" he growled at his sister's flippancy. Pivoting, he addressed Miss Winlow. "I must apologize for my sister. The thought of journeying to London has her overwrought."

Meredith plopped into the nearest chair and crossed her arms. "Good grief! Knowdens never make apologies to the hired help. Have you dallied with cardsharps and courtesans for so long you view us all now as equals?"

His hazel green eyes flashed in warning. "That

remark was beneath you," he snapped. "Apologize to Miss Winlow."

Miss Winlow stirred, raising a hand in protest. "Lord Ramscar, there is no need—"

"I disagree," he briskly countered. Ram's gaze raked over her, resenting her interference. "Nor do I appreciate you overstepping yourself." He would bloody well deal with his own sister.

"Aye, m'lord," Miss Winlow replied, using a dialect one might hear on the streets of London but one he had never attributed to her. She did not even hold his gaze.

Meredith smirked at him. "Hear, hear, for the master of Swancott!"

Perfect. He had ruffled Miss Winlow's lovely plumage, too, with his temper. Ram pressed his fingers to his eyelids. His sister was determined to bait him until he reversed his demand that she join him in London. How had he been drawn into such a damnable awkward predicament? Ram scowled at both ladies. He had had enough.

He pointed his finger at his sister. "You are traveling to London, even if I have to bind you and stick you in a trunk." His heated gaze sought out the subdued Miss Winlow. She was not fooling him with that pathetic display of servile humility. "And you . . . you will remain and carry out your duties as my sister's companion. We have an agreement, you and I. I will not have you running back to your troupe just because you have belatedly realized that you are employed in a madhouse. There will be no talk of quitting!" he thundered. Without waiting for a reply, Ram stomped out of his sister's sitting room and slammed the door.

Patience pursed her lips in quiet contemplation. The earl had guessed correctly. Her first thought when she heard them arguing was to slip out of the house and return to the inn. Something had stopped her. Perhaps it was the fear and pain in Lady Meredith's voice that kept Patience from carrying out her plan. Instead of leaving, she had climbed the stairs to meet her new mistress.

"A troupe?" Lady Meredith asked curiously.

Patience had forgotten she was not alone. Reluctantly, she slowly turned around, prepared to face the woman's disdain.

Lady Meredith expelled a soft laugh. "So you are an actress? How marvelous. Ram gives me a stage strumpet for a companion. I must look more hideous than I thought if *you* are the best my brother could find."

Lord Ramscar shoved open the door to the library with his butler at his heels. What he needed was something strong to drink to wash away the bitter taste in his mouth. He despised fighting with his sister.

Comprehending his lord's needs, the butler seized the decanter of brandy and filled Ramscar's glass. Scrimm had been in the family's employ long before Ram's birth. He did not even know if Scrimm was the man's first or last name. He was simply Scrimm to the family and as ageless as Swancott. His carefully groomed hair had been white even when Ram had been a young boy. Of medium height, Scrimm's robust figure could be glimpsed bustling about the household. The smallest detail was not beneath the man's notice. His quiet efficiency and wry sense of humor had made him invaluable to Ram. Scrimm was always part of Ram's personal staff, regardless of his residence. From Scrimm's pained expression it was simple to deduce the man was troubled by what he perceived as a dereliction of duty.

His expression woefully apologetic, the butler handed Ram the glass. "My lord, I was not aware Miss Winlow had gone upstairs until the damage had been done. I distinctly told the young woman to remain in the front hall until she was summoned."

Ram sipped his brandy. Staring into the glass, he swirled the fragrant dark liquid as he contemplated the exchange that had taken place upstairs. "No apology is necessary, Scrimm. I should have let Meredith have her tantrum before Miss Winlow's arrival. My sister is usually a docile creature. Damn me, the lady has a set of sharp teeth, and she tested them on my arse. Would you like to see the marks she left behind?"

"If it is all the same to you, my lord, I shall deprive myself of that distinct honor," Scrimm said in his usual droll manner.

Ram laughed for the first time all day. There was little cause for laughter in this house, and that was something he hoped to change. He sobered as he thought of the two ladies upstairs. Had Meredith calmed after his angry departure? Miss Winlow was now under his employ, so he assumed that she would behave herself. Still, he had experienced firsthand her sardonic wit. He rubbed the back of his neck in agitation.

It had been a mistake to leave them alone.

"Guard the door, Scrimm." Ram swallowed the remaining brandy in two hearty gulps. "If Miss Winlow tries to flee, you have my permission to stop her by any means necessary."

"She will not get by me again, my lord. If drastic measures are required, I shall sit on her and await your return," the butler promised.

Oh, Ram could well imagine the elderly Scrimm tackling the fleeing Miss Winlow in the front hall and plopping down on her backside. Ram was certain that would confirm the lady's suspicions that the Knowdens were mad. Christ, what a quandary! Meredith was screeching like a harpy, and now he was likely to lose his new ally because he had made a muddle of things.

Handing the empty glass to Scrimm, Ram strode out of the library intending to put his house in order.

"A stage strumpet," Patience said, tasting the phrase with a contemplative frown. "I daresay no one has risked hurling that insult to my face before."

"I would think someone in your position would be quite used to having derogatory names and rotting vegetation thrown in your direction," Lady Meredith said, her expression one of scornful triumph.

"My position?" Patience politely replied.

"As an actress, of course."

"Oh? I could say the same of you, Lady Meredith," Patience said, crossing her hands behind her back and giving her a knowing look.

"I cannot fathom what you are about."

"Really?" She strolled closer to the young woman and gestured at a nearby chair. "May I sit?"

At first, she thought Lady Meredith might refuse out of spite. Suddenly recalling her manners, she nodded regally. "Of course. Please join me." She waited until Patience was sitting down before she gave in to her curiosity. "Now that the pleasantries are done, I insist you explain your earlier comment."

Lord Ramscar had warned Patience that the task of preparing his sister for London would not be an easy one. Lady Meredith viewed Patience as the enemy. This was nothing new to her. She was used to working beside people who merely tolerated her presence. Ram's sister would have to work harder if her goal was to discourage Patience. "You called me an actress. I simply returned the favor."

"You insult me?"

"On the contrary, Lady Meredith, I was admiring your efforts," she said, radiating sincerity. "Like recognizes like. You certainly had your brother fooled."

"You know nothing of me. What can anyone deduce from a few minutes of conversation?"

"Oh, quite a lot," Patience admitted candidly. "My profession has made me a student of human nature. Much can be deduced from inflection, expression, and posture."

Lady Meredith tilted her head in curiosity, and her lips parted as if she might ask Patience to elaborate further on her observations. Then the lady recalled the circumstances that had brought her new companion to Swancott, and mutinous rage doused any milder discourse. "My anger was not feigned, Miss Winlow. I resent your presence in my home. I do not want you here. My brother is wasting good coin in hiring you, because I have no desire to go to London."

Patience saw through the lady's anger to the heart of the matter. Her fears. Patience tried a different approach. "Oh, I would be foolish to contradict such a strong opinion. I actually was referring to your outlandish tantrum. It was quite a magnificent display and so contrary to your disposition."

The other woman choked with outrage. "What do you know— My brother spoke to you about me?"

She had gleaned enough from Lord Ramscar's tragic retelling of the fire and his sister's life afterward that Patience could make a fairly accurate presumption about the young woman's character. "Naturally, he would mention you, since we will be spending much time together. I would have thought it odd if he had not."

"You do not seem wholly surprised by my disfigurement. He must have warned you not to react to my scars," she said bitterly, her hand involuntarily rising to conceal her cheek.

Patience knew she had to tread carefully. Lady Meredith was hurt and troubled, but she was nobody's fool. If Patience pretended not to see what the young woman viewed as hideous scars, she would never earn Lady Meredith's trust. "Lord Ramscar told me that there had been a fire and that your twin sister perished. It was a miracle you survived."

Lady Meredith blinked, apparently not expecting the response she had received.

"A miracle," she mused, as if tasting the word. "I have never considered it as such. My death would have spared my brother the burden of hiring me a nursemaid."

Patience wrinkled her nose in disapproval. "You have two functioning arms, two legs, and some wits about you." She noted the lady's lips twitched. Perhaps they were making progress after all. "Why not pretend we are friends, and figure out the rest as we get to know one another?"

The defiance was back in Lady Meredith's pale face. "I do not want to go to London."

I am anxious, too.

Patience got up from her chair and knelt at Lady Meredith's side. "When your brother spoke of you, his love was so apparent. Such a gentleman would challenge anyone who dared to hurt you."

The young woman shook her head, wanting to deny her companion's words. "My scars—"

"Are inconsequential," Patience declared flatly. "I have some expertise in changing my appearance. There are things we can do to not call attention to your scars."

There was that glimmer of curiosity again. "How so?"

Patience grinned up at her. "Have you thought of cutting your hair? We can arrange your hair in a style that would conceal some of them. Perhaps a touch of powder also?"

Lady Meredith placed her hand over Patience's. Instead of anger or fear, she saw wary hope. "You could do that?"

"Not alone," she cautioned, needing the woman's cooperation if they were to succeed in this endeavor. "However, if we pool our intellect, I promise you that your brother will not even recognize you when you enter a ballroom."

"I do not believe you," Lady Meredith said flatly.

"Well, if I fail at my task, then you will have the pleasure of gloating about my spectacular blundering to your brother. Most likely, I will be unceremoniously sacked without references," Patience said pragmatically.

The notion of ordering her brother to sack Patience apparently appealed to the angry young lady. "So you are an actress?" Lady Meredith repeated her earlier question, though this time the mockery had lessened in her inflection.

Patience braced her hands on the arms of the chair and stood. "No. As of today, I am a lady's companion and your friend if you will have me." She held out her hand, half-expecting the other woman to refuse it.

Lady Meredith grasped Patience's hand. "We shall see, Miss Winlow. You know, I have never met an actress. I suppose you have all kinds of interesting tales of adventure."

If she only knew . . .

While Miss Winlow began regaling her companion with an amusing tale about a vicar and a goat, Ramscar quietly closed the door.

CHAPTER SEVEN

"You handled my sister with a level of compassion one does not normally expect in a stranger."

Begrudgingly, he had to admit that the little actress had dealt with Meredith's fit of temper much better than he had ever managed. The scene he had witnessed and Miss Winlow had dwelled in his thoughts for most of the evening. After he had departed the sitting room unnoticed by either lady, he had dedicated the rest of the afternoon to writing letters. He wanted the London town house ready for their arrival. The details for planning a small ball in Meredith's honor were sketchy, but he knew a few ladies who could assist him in that endeavor. Ram belatedly recalled Angeline Grassi. He absently wondered if she had found another gentleman to share her bed.

"Her resentment is normal, my lord. I believe—" Realizing she was overstepping her bounds again, Patience ruefully said, "May we speak frankly?"

"Yes, on the condition you will accept my apology." It was one of the reasons he had impulsively summoned her to the drawing room after Meredith had retired. Patience had cautiously agreed to his offer of hot chocolate and conversation. Her hesitation had made him feel brutish. "I regret chastising you earlier. My sister is not the only one who possesses the Knowden temper."

Amusement danced merrily in Patience's blue eyes. "I accept. You might not believe this, but I have been accused of having an unguarded tongue." She absentmindedly stirred her hot chocolate. "It is a failing I hope to improve upon while I am in your employ."

Charmed, he tipped back his head and laughed. He found nothing wrong with her refreshing arrogance, and neither did she. Ram had chosen brandy instead of hot chocolate to imbibe. Discreetly, he studied her through lowered lashes. His sister's opinion had been correct. Miss Winlow was beautiful. Her pale skin glowed with vitality under the candle-light. She had been a delightful and amusing companion at their table this evening, so unlike the quiet dinners he normally shared with Meredith when he was at Swancott. The swift molten heat of desire that struck him did not surprise him, but the aching intensity in his loins did.

Ram had never bedded anyone under his employ. It gave him a distinct advantage that he considered distasteful. Any lady he bedded was there of her own free will, not because she feared dismissal. What was he to do about his attraction for Miss Winlow? Pensive, he sipped his brandy.

"Is the chocolate not to your liking?" he asked politely, noticing she had barely touched her cup.

Appalled that she had insulted him, she said hastily, "Oh no, it is delicious." She brought the rim of the cup to her lips and sipped. Her eyes closed in bliss as she savored its rich flavor.

Ram shifted uncomfortably in his chair. The way she tilted her head slightly back with her eyes closed and her lips parted made his cock twitch in anticipation. Her reaction to the hot chocolate was so sensual, he wondered if it was deliberate.

Christ, he hoped so!

He groaned, and Miss Winlow's eyes opened.

Finally, aware of his intense stare, Miss Winlow set her cup aside. "You must think I am silly."

Silly? On the contrary, the lady was making him crazed. Oblivious to her effect on him, her tongue touched the corner of her mouth to catch a drop of missed chocolate. Ram resisted the urge to leap out of his chair and pull her down onto the floor. As far as he was concerned, the lady could put chocolate anywhere on her body and he would be happy to lick it off.

"It has been a while," she explained rather apologetically.

He heartily concurred. Usually, he was not so bothered by his bouts of abstinence. However, there was something about Miss Winlow that made him want to demonstrate to her why the *ton* called him and his friends *les sauvages nobles*.

She was Meredith's hired companion and under his protection, he reminded himself. Control. He needed to grasp it with both hands and cease fantasizing about bedding his little actress.

His.

"Lord Ramscar, are you ill?" Miss Winlow asked, her mouth pouting with her growing concern. "If you would rather continue our discussion tomorrow—" She started to rise, but she halted when he gestured for her to sit.

"I am fine," he said, wishing he had not made a damn fool of himself, mooning over this woman. "You mentioned that it has been a while." He prayed she would continue talking while he willed the slight swell in his breeches to abate.

"Yes, the chocolate. It has been years since I enjoyed a cup of hot chocolate," she said candidly. "You must think I am silly. I suppose if you were inclined, you could drink hot chocolate every night."

He had not considered what her life had been before he had met her at the Pownings'. "There is nothing ridiculous in taking pleasure in something you like. Your appreciation for the hot beverage is enchanting. Go on. Indulge." He motioned for her to sample more of the hot chocolate.

She smiled shyly at his flattery. Picking up her cup, she delicately sniffed the contents before drinking.

It was a near thing, but he stifled his groan. Ram watched her throat undulate with each swallow. He should have never invited her to the drawing room without Meredith. He had to think of something, anything, to distract him from the very bad idea of putting his hungry mouth to Patience's slender throat.

"You have been on your own for some time?"

The innocent question wiped the open pleasure from her face. Guarded, she cradled her cup with both hands. "Yes. Since I was fourteen."

She had been so young to be fending for herself. He was outraged on her behalf. "What of your family?"

A hint of sadness shadowed her blue eyes. "There is no one living who will claim me, my lord." Abandoning her hot chocolate, she hastily rose from her chair. Clearly, the subject of her family or lack thereof was not one she would willingly discuss.

It was his curse in life to be surrounded by prickly females.

"Lord Ramscar, I should retire."

" 'Ramscar' will do," he corrected her as he stood also. Fortunately, his unruly body had calmed somewhat. "Or 'Ram,' if you prefer."

She balked at his suggestion. "It does not seem appropriate."

"Oh, it is when you consider you have practically become a member of our family," he said, finding his reasoning sound. "We will be spending a great amount of time together. It creates intimacy, even amongst strangers."

Miss Winlow looked as if she was about to disagree. Wisely she resisted the urge to debate him. Instead, she nodded warily. "I bid you good night."

He was making her nervous. Ram did not mind. He wanted her to be aware of him. "Very well.

We will talk again soon. Pleasant dreams, sweet Patience."

Eros, the Greek god of love, must have visited her while she slept that first night at Swancott. Her dreams were dark and strangely erotic. Restless, Patience rolled onto her back, kicking off the sheet that was tangled around her legs. Visions of Julian Phoenix's face fluttered like pages of a book caught by a spring breeze. A bottle of laudanum suddenly appeared in her hand. Although it made no sense, she poured the contents over the book.

Stepping away from the book, she sensed Phoenix coming up to her, his arm snaking around her waist. She tensed against him, knowing what he wanted.

"Let me show you pleasure," her dark lover *whispered in her ear.*

His hand moved upward and cupped her breast. The dress she had been wearing melted away. Such was the magic and wonder of dreams. Patience moaned as he playfully pinched her nipple. She arched her back, teasing his rigid manhood with her buttocks. He gave her a good-natured swat on her backside for tormenting him. The Julian Phoenix of her dreams was different from the man she knew. She tilted her head to the side, exposing her neck. She smiled at his playful nip. This Julian, her magnificent dream lover, seduced her with his mouth and hands. His beautiful body was hers to command. She was free to explore him thoroughly in this realm; no request was forbidden.

I want to feel you inside of me.

She did not have to speak the words aloud. He sensed her needs almost before her. Patience slid her back down the front of his body, scoring his thighs with her nails.

"Get on your knees," he ordered huskily. *"I love taking you from behind."*

She did not mind yielding to this Julian. He never hurt her or forced her obedience when she defied him. This man was an inventive lover who only brought her pleasure.

Yes.

The background shimmered as the floor rushed up to meet her. When the mist cleared, they were in front of a hearth. She was now on her knees, and her fingers gripped the luxuriant animal pelt meant to protect her from the hard floor.

Her lover's warmth covered her like a warm blanket. Patience felt his hot breath on her right shoulder as he positioned himself. She wiggled against him. There was never any pain when he entered her. In her dreams, her body desired this lovemaking. In fact, she craved it.

Patience moaned at his forceful penetration. Julian

slid into her, burying his firm rod deeply. He flexed against her womb, his manhood throbbing. As always, her womanly sheath was wet, her desire for this union acute. His left hand splayed over her stomach possessively. Her toes curled in anticipation.

Please.

He slowly pulled out of her. Patience almost whimpered at the loss. Her lover was not about to leave her unsatisfied. He thrust against her, his rhythm energetic. She dug her fingers into the fur pelt, rocked against him, matching his tempo. Julian's hand slipped lower, seeking the cleft between her legs.

"Cry out for me."

He bit her shoulder to remind her who was in charge. The intense pleasure he could wring from her body was worth the surrender. Julian buried his fingers into the wiry nest of curls between her legs as he slammed his hips against her buttocks, over and over.

It was overwhelming. Lowering her head, she grimaced as the first wave of pleasure rolled through her. Her dream lover was relentless. His measured thrusts pummeled her, while she lay helpless and quivering. The maelstrom he had created had left her breasts sensitive and her body aching for more.

It was precisely what her lover had in mind.

Julian carefully withdrew his manhood and rolled her onto her back. Her eyes were still blissfully closed when he parted the tender feminine folds as he sought the heart of her. Patience smiled. The man was insatiable.

She opened her eyes, prepared to share her saucy opinion. Her lips parted in shock. The handsome face hovering inches above hers was not that of Julian Phoenix.

It was Lord Ramscar!

"Did you honestly think I was finished with you, Miss Winlow?"

He masterfully penetrated her before she could conjure a coherent reply. Her previous lovemaking had made her drenched sheath unbearably sensitive. One definitive thrust and she was lost.

Patience awakened sobbing, her hand pressed fiercely between her legs as the pleasurable rippling from her womb receded with her dreams. Confused, and more than a little frightened, she sat up in the bed.

She was alone.

It took her a moment to recall that she was at Swancott. She brought her clenched hand to her face and noted the subtle fragrance of her arousal.

It had been a dream.

A shudder she chose to view as relief gently shook her shoulders. She grabbed the blankets she had kicked off and pulled them over her bare legs.

There were tears on her cheeks.

Oh God, what was wrong with her? She rolled to her side and curled her knees to her chest. Since Julian Phoenix's death, she had endured these distressful dreams. He was always so tender in them, so unlike the man she knew. When she awoke, the recollection of their lovemaking had left her aching and guilty. Patience slammed her head against the pillow in frustration.

There was something truly wrong with her. She hated Phoenix. He had been a dreadful, inconsiderate scoundrel who thought only of *his* pleasure. Why was his handsome face the one her mind summoned? Why did she long for his touch?

Only this time, it had not been her old nemesis who seduced her so thoroughly in her dreams. It had been Lord Ramscar. She had willingly gotten down on her knees and had allowed him to mount her like a wild animal. If she had not awakened, he would have taken her again and again.

The writhing, aroused female in her dreams desired him. She would not have denied him. It was a chilling revelation.

It was only a dream.

Patience held on to the thought as if it was her personal talisman.

"Scrimm tells me that you took your breakfast with the other servants," Ramscar said, trying to keep the irritation from his voice. He had expected Miss Winlow to join him and Meredith at the table this morning. Miss Winlow's absence and his reaction had not improved his disposition.

"Yes, my lord. We did not get around to discussing my duties last evening. However, I assumed I would be taking all my meals with the other servants."

"You shared dinner with us."

She kept her gaze demurely lowered. "And it was generous of you to invite me. Still, it would have been presumptuous of me to assume that I would continue to join the family."

Ram heard two servants talking on the upper landing. There were too many people in this house for him to speak openly. "Walk with me." He did not wait for her consent. The air was crisp as they stepped outside. Before he had sought her out in the servants' hall, he had dressed for riding. Miss Winlow had swiftly donned a faded blue spencer over her dress and a bonnet so the temperature would not be intolerable.

In silence, they strolled down the long gravel drive. "Have I done something wrong, my lord?"

She had yet to meet his gaze directly, which he thought odd, considering her forthright nature. It was possible she had sensed his interest the previous evening and did not know how to respond. Was she embarrassed or intrigued? Ram would have paid her a small ransom for the truth.

"Only insulted me," he said teasingly. Her startled expression had him elaborating. "I must insist that you indulge me. The circumstances that have brought you to Swancott are unique. This trip to London is unsettling to my sister. I have added to her discomfort by bringing a stranger into our home."

"I understand, my lord," she said, staring out at the horizon.

The corners of his mouth lifted indulgently. "I believe I asked you to call me Ramscar or Ram. The familiarity will comfort my sister."

Patience halted and glanced at him, suspecting that he was teasing her. Satisfied with his innocent expression, she resumed walking. "Ramscar, you are master of an unusual household."

"You will become accustomed to the routines, Patience," he assured her. Politely, he placed his hand on her arm and guided her away from the gravel lane to a smaller path that disappeared into the woods. "And the master of Swancott."

CHAPTER EIGHT

Patience could barely look at his face without blushing.

Thank goodness, Lord Ramscar was oblivious to her discomfort. She would rather throw herself in front of a coach on one of London's busy streets before revealing her dark, intimate secret. Patience was struggling to understand why that scoundrel Phoenix appeared in her dreams. Now she had to contend with *him*. At least Julian Phoenix was dead. According to Lord Ramscar, she would be seeing him daily. How was she going to bear it?

"Is something troubling you?" he politely inquired.

"N-no," she stuttered, hating herself for babbling like a dimwit. "I was just—this position, it is so different than anything I have ever done. I pray you will not regret your decision." She hugged herself, silently chastising her lack of composure around this man.

"Life is too precious to waste it on regret, Patience," he said, after a lengthy pause. "How can anyone experience true happiness without taking risks?" His hazel green eyes swept over her. "Forgive me. You are cold."

"I am fine. I—"

Patience frowned as he removed his coat. Ignoring her protests, he slipped her arms into the oversized sleeves and tugged the front together.

"Better?"

She mutely nodded. Still warm from his body, the coat warmed her in ways she dared not contemplate. It smelled of smoke and the heady scent of its owner. "Thank you. I should have chosen something warmer to wear this morning."

From what she had seen, Swancott was a lovely estate. The wooded path widened, revealing a small pond. It looked natural, but a gardener had tamed nature by outlining the embankment with white stones. A wooden bench fashioned from a split log was positioned off to the right. Patience wondered how often Lady Meredith sat at the edge of the water, lost in her melancholy thoughts.

"Speaking of your attire . . . I do not mean to offend you by mentioning this; however, Scrimm commented that you arrived with one small bag. Should I have one of the footmen collect the rest of your possessions at the inn?"

Patience clutched the edges of his coat and strode over to the bench. For the first time in a long while, something akin to shame was crawling around in her insides, and she did not like it. The dresses she had packed were clean and presentable. Sadly, none would be considered by the *ton* as fashionable. She bit her lip, pondering this newest tangle.

"There are other dresses at the inn, but they belong to the troupe," she admitted reluctantly. "It did not seem right to take them, when Deidra will need—"

Lord Ramscar walked over to her and crouched down beside the bench. "Say not another word on the subject. My sister will need new dresses for London. We will order some for you as well."

A flicker of excitement flared to life at the thought of wearing something that was not a castoff, but she brutally extinguished it. There was a name for ladies who accepted intimate gifts from a gentleman, and it was not a kind one.

She rubbed her nose. "Oh, I could not. Perhaps, if I spoke to Deidra and the men—"

The earl took her hand, forcing her to meet his gaze. She saw a touch of amusement intermixed with sincerity in his hazel green eyes. "Let them keep the dresses. When I offered you the position, I had every intention of purchasing new wardrobes for both you and my sister. I hesitated telling you, because I did not want to offend you."

"But—"

"No arguments," he said with mock sternness. "You represent the Earl of Ramscar, and you will be fashionably dressed. A seamstress is arriving this afternoon to take measurements and begin the arduous task of getting you and Lady Meredith ready for the season. What cannot be accomplished here can be procured in London."

Agitated, Patience hopped off the bench. "It seems a lot of fuss and expense for a mere lady's companion," she protested halfheartedly. "Perhaps you can deduct the cost of the dresses from my wages."

Ramscar braced his hand on his knee and stood. He shook his head ruefully. "A few pretty dresses will not ruin me, Patience."

As he placed his hands on her shoulders, she could not help recalling her dream of him. He had been standing behind her when he grabbed her thusly. In spite of the warm coat, she shivered.

"You cannot deny it," he teased.

Deny what?

Was her reaction to his proximity so apparent? She was so aware of him, her breasts tightened in response. "I cannot?" she replied breathlessly. It was important that she remember that he was not the lover in her dreams. That man did not exist.

Ramscar inched closer. "Come now, Patience. Why fight it? Every young lady desires owning new dresses with matching slippers and gloves. Even you."

She really wished he had not used the word "desires." "I suppose a new dress or two would be nice," she said, looking away with feigned reluctance. "Thank you."

Lord Ramscar laughed at her obvious mischief. "That's the spirit!"

Impulsively, he picked her up and spun them both around. Even she was laughing when he lowered her back onto her feet. Panting slightly, Patience gazed up into his handsome face. The earl was unlike most gentlemen she had encountered over the years. He was confident, a tad arrogant, but there was a sweetness within him that people normally did not find in their superiors. True, Patience's connection to the Farnalys balanced the scales. Still, it was a fact he would never know. Never had she admired a man before for his ignorance.

Ramscar reacted to the subtle softening of her expression. In wonderment, he gently cupped her face. She felt herself weakening, and like the true predators most men were, he sensed it. Without breaking eye contact, he lowered his head until their lips lightly collided. Like the kiss, his hold on her was just as delicate. Patience could easily step away.

Step away.

She closed her eyes. Only in her dreams had she experienced such tenderness. It was only a simple kiss. Why should she walk away?

Ramscar nibbled her lower lip. Patience parted her lips and tilted her head upward, liking the sensation of his lips moving against hers. He responded by gliding the tip of his tongue over the sharp edges of her teeth. Emboldened, she tentatively tasted him. He growled his approval.

"Put your hands on me," he ordered gruffly before seizing her by the wrists and placing them on his shoulders. "Again."

There was no confusion in his intent. She had very little experience with kissing. Julian Phoenix had stolen a few kisses when he had been trying to coax her into running off with him. Once he had taken her away from the Farnalys, he had lost interest in such flirtations.

Without asking permission, Ramscar plunged his tongue into her mouth. Instinctively, she curled hers around his. Using his tongue, he retreated, drawing her tongue into his mouth and deepening the kiss. Patience moaned against his mouth. The earl tasted like coffee and wickedness. Her arms circled around his neck of their own volition. The hands poised on her waist moved to her back and then down the curve of her buttocks.

Cupping both cheeks, Ramscar pulled her tightly against him. It was as if he could not get close enough. It was a heady combination: that sinful mouth devouring her, while he created a delicious ache in her nether regions. How many ladies of the *ton* had surrendered their precious virtue just for a taste of his naughty play?

The question doused her ardor.

"No," she panted against his cheek. She placed her palms on his chest and shoved him away. The earl abruptly released her, causing her to stagger back. "Forgive me."

She dared not confess more. Her response to his kisses frightened her. She whirled away from him and returned to the wooden bench. If she had continued to allow him to take liberties, she feared he would have had her on her knees while he pumped himself into her willing body.

Just like my dream . . .

She trembled. What upset her most was that she did not know if she quivered from fear or desire.

Lord Ramscar cursed under his breath. "If anyone should be apologizing, it should be me. I should not have kissed you. I hired you for Meredith's sake, not to warm my bed," he said harshly.

Patience winced at his honesty. "I am to blame, too. I should have stopped you sooner." After a night of erotic dreaming, she had been curious to see if the man resembled her dream lover. It would have been better if Lord Ramscar had left her disappointed, instead of sensitive and aching.

"Do not leave me." Belatedly, realizing how she might misconstrue his words, he hurriedly added, "I need you to help me with Meredith. Without you, it will take a rope and mallet to get her to London." He smiled encouragingly.

Patience returned the smile, but it lacked sincerity. She was just too shaken to sort out her feelings. "Very well, Lord Ramscar. I will help you coax Lady Meredith to London."

A man like the earl belonged only in her dreams. In the flesh, he was just too tempting.

The days at Swancott passed swiftly.

Lord Ramscar was anxious to return to London. He had privately revealed to her one evening that he had tarried in the country longer than his previous visits for his sister's sake. Business obligations and his friends awaited him in town. Ignoring Lady Meredith's pleas, he had wielded his resources to hasten their preparations and packing. If one seamstress and her apprentices could not complete the dresses needed for both ladies, then he would hire a dozen. The expense did not concern him. For a lady who was used to living a frugal existence, the earl's blasé reaction bordered on obscene. Patience wondered if time would make her as jaded and extravagant.

Her days were filled with appointments with seamstresses, milliners, shoemakers, a furrier, several drapers, and even a jeweler. Some had journeyed all the way from London. Lady Meredith would meet the *ton* attired in the latest fashions. Her brother insisted on the highest quality for his sister and her companion. Patience had been so caught up in preparing and soothing her mistress that ten days had slipped by before she realized Perry, Link, and Deidra had likely moved on. She wished them well.

Scrimm caught her daydreaming in front of one of the drawing room windows. "Miss Winlow, there you are. Lady Meredith has requested that you join her upstairs in her private sitting room."

"Thank you, Scrimm." She moved to the door but hesitated at the threshold. "Is she dreadfully upset?"

"Nay, miss. Not any more than usual, I suspect,"

he said, giving her a wink. "Better for you to answer our lady's summons before the wind changes, I wager."

Patience smiled in response and dashed off down the hall and headed for the stairs. The Swancott butler had been initially aloof. She had defied his order to remain in the front hall and had blemished his spotless reputation. It would not do to have the man as an enemy, so after she had been dismissed by Lady Meredith, Patience had spent a few hours in the servants' hall in an attempt to repair the damage she had inadvertently caused. If she had learned only one skill as an actress, it was to charm even the meanest curmudgeon.

She was slightly out of breath when she entered the sitting room.

"There you are. I have half the house searching for you," Lady Meredith said petulantly.

"Only half?" Patience teased, smiling at her companion's exaggeration.

As she realized how foolish she must have sounded, the young woman's lips twitched. "Just. I thought you might have run off to flee this madhouse."

"Just your rotten luck I did not, eh?" Patience quipped, never forgetting that Lady Meredith was still searching for an excuse to convince her brother to abandon his notion of taking her to London.

Oh, truthfully, Patience had considered giving up and fleeing the Knowden household a time or two. Lady Meredith could be difficult when she wanted to nettle her new companion. And then there was the kiss Patience had shared with Lord Ramscar near the pond. Her reaction to his kiss had terrified her.

Fortunately, she was made of sterner stuff.

Patience had been wholly prepared to pretend nothing had happened between her and the earl, though generosity was pointless. Lord Ramscar spent his days either locked in his library or outside the house, not to be seen again until dinner. When she did see him, he was unerringly polite. Patience was beginning to wonder if the kiss had been part of her dream after all.

She had not been brought to Swancott to entertain the earl. It was Lady Meredith who needed Patience's guidance. "Abandon you, my lady? Perish the thought. I promised we would see this through together, and I keep my oaths."

In a display of affection she reserved only for close friends, Patience put her arm around the young woman's waist and gave her a brief hug. She ignored the rigidness in Lady Meredith's stance. "So what troubles you?" Patience nodded politely to the waiting seamstress who was holding out a very pretty dress. "Does the dress displease you?"

Lady Meredith blinked in surprise. "Why, no. It is quite beautiful. However, the dress is not for me, but rather you."

Awed, Patience walked over and reverently caressed the gossamer sleeves. She had never owned anything so fine. "No, you have made a mistake. This elegant dress was clearly made for you." Attired in such a creation, Patience could stand as Lady Meredith's equal and not her servant.

"No, this particular dress was fashioned for you. My brother insists that all the ladies of the *ton* will goggle at us with envy and curiosity when they see us in our finery," she said breezily. For the first time, there was a flicker of excitement in the lady's demeanor.

Until she noticed the tears in Patience's unfocused gaze.

Concerned, Lady Meredith awkwardly patted her companion's back. "Oh no . . . no, do not cry. If you hate it, Ramscar will order another to replace it."

Patience retrieved a handkerchief that she had tucked into her sleeve, and sniffed. How could she explain to Lady Meredith that she was simply overwhelmed by the generosity the Knowdens had shown a veritable stranger? Ramscar's sister had lived a very sheltered existence. She knew little of hunger, cold, or cruelty. New dresses were something even the reclusive young woman took for granted. The pleasure and extravagance of a new dress was an indulgence Patience had almost forgotten existed.

"There is no need for your brother to go to such lengths to please me, Lady Meredith. I am just being maudlin." Patience pasted a smile on her face to ease the lady's concerns. "It is a lovely dress. I have never dreamed of owning one as refined."

The distress in Lady Meredith's expression waned with understanding. "Well, this is the first of many. If you weep over each one, we will have to procure you another dozen handkerchiefs," she teased, taking the dress from the seamstress. "I summoned you here because Margaret wanted to assure herself of the fit. However, I have just been inspired by a grand notion. I want you to wear the dress at dinner this evening."

Dinner as alway had been excellent.

Cook had outdone herself with a succulent course of mutton, capon, and freshly caught eel. Steaming dishes of carrots, mushrooms, and parsnips were served next, and they enjoyed forced strawberries in thick cream for dessert.

It had been a long, tiring day. Ram left the house after breakfast. He had spent most of the day calling on his tenants and listening to their problems. When he had returned to the house, the stable master had approached Ram about an unmanageable mare. By the time he had washed up, he had almost been late for the evening meal.

The fatigue he had been feeling had vanished when Patience had entered the dining room arm in arm with his sister. The small fortune he had been paying the seamstresses was well worth the expense if the new dress Patience wore this evening was any indication.

After dinner, they had settled in the music room. Patience was seated at the pianoforte playing a tune that was as light and frothy as the charming confection she wore. Meredith sat nearby on the sofa quietly working at her embroidery, while he had chosen a book from the library. Ram read two pages and closed the book. A full stomach and the warmth of the room had made him lazy. Besides, he would rather study Patience's profile than peruse a dusty tome on the philosophy of war.

He thought about kissing her.

Often.

They had been carefully avoiding each other since the kiss at the pond. Ram had mentally listed a hundred reasons that he should not pursue this particular lady. Meredith was happier since Patience had joined their household, and dallying with his sister's companion would only lead to complications he would rather avoid. They were leaving for London in two days. Once they settled in the town house, he would seek out Angeline Grassi and satisfy his lustful urges. He was certain it was the isolation of Swancott that had sharpened his interest in bedding Patience Winlow. Returning to London would expose him to dozens of beauties and restore his perspective.

"Brother, I have been thinking," Meredith said, not looking up from her stitching.

Ram set his book on the small table next to him. "If you are preparing to argue another reason why you cannot join me in London, then do not bother."

"I am resigned to my grim fate," she said with the stoicism of a martyr. "However, it is not London I wish to discuss, but rather Miss Winlow's past."

Patience fumbled a few notes before continuing her flawless playing. "Should I leave the room, Lady Meredith?"

"Heavens, no," the young woman said, placing her embroidery onto her lap. "This concerns you, and your opinion on this matter equals our own."

"What matter?" Ram asked, drawing his sister's attention back to him.

What new machinations was Meredith concocting? She had seemed unruffled by Patience's theatrical past. In fact, Meredith had even seemed slightly awed by the young woman's worldly independence. If his sister thought she could find fault in her companion in order to delay their departure, she had sadly underestimated his determination.

Meredith tapped her chin as she scrutinized the other woman. Having gained both siblings' interest, Patience silenced the pianoforte. Her head high, she placed her clenched fingers into her lap. From her stoic expression, she also was anticipating Meredith's denouncing her.

"Are you well-known in London, Miss Winlow?" his sister asked gently.

Patience seemed momentarily flustered by the question. "No. Not at all. Our troupe preferred traveling the rural countryside. I daresay I am veritably an unknown as an actress. Why do you ask?"

"I mean you no offense, Miss Winlow. However, I am concerned about how you will be received in polite society if your past is revealed. In the weeks I have come to know you, I have come to admire your wit, ingenuity, and kindness. I will not have strangers abuse you for what they might perceive as a lacking in your character."

Pride warmed Ram's heart as he listened to his

sister. He knew Meredith was terrified that the *ton* would mock her imperfections. Despite her fears, she had given some thought to Patience's welfare.

"Do not fret, Lady Meredith. A hired companion is beneath the *ton*'s high regard, no matter how finely she is dressed," Patience said lightly.

Ram's keen gaze shifted to Patience. She was smiling at his sister, attempting to allay her concerns. Was that how Patience Winlow saw herself? A lady unworthy of polite society's notice? He wondered what scars the pretty actress hid behind her beguiling blue eyes.

"I agree, Meredith," Ram said, pressing his fingers together as he pondered a solution to their quandary. "Introducing Miss Winlow as a retired actress would only invite cruel speculation about her past."

Meredith was fretting that her new companion might be shunned by the *ton*. Ram did not have the heart to correct his sister. He had no doubt that Patience's beauty would garner the undesired attentions of every scoundrel in the *ton,* including his close friends Everod and Cadd. Damn those randy bastards!

This would not do at all!

"We could pretend she is our cousin," Ram's sister eagerly suggested, getting into the spirit of creating a clever subterfuge to fool the curious.

Ram thought it was an atrocious idea. Not only did Patience not resemble them in looks, but he had always claimed when questioned that Meredith was the only surviving family he had. Besides, if they turned Patience into a fictional cousin he would have to keep his bloody hands off the woman! He disliked that detail most of all.

"Calling her cousin might create a few problems for us later when Miss Winlow leaves us," he said, moving his hand with a casual wave of dismissal. "I recommend that we tell anyone who inquires that Miss Winlow is the daughter of one of Mother's old friends. Since this is your first season, Meredith, it would only be natural that you would want your dear friend at your side."

He leaned back in his chair, rather pleased with himself. To deter fortune hunters and other unsavory rogues, he would let it be known that Patience's family had fallen on hard times, so the lady was without a dowry. If the falsehood did not discourage his friends, then he would approach them privately.

"This is wonderful!" Meredith applauded his inventiveness. "A flawless plan, Brother. What is your opinion, Miss Winlow?" She slapped her hand over her mouth at her slip and giggled. "No, 'Miss Winlow' will not do. As my dearest friend, you will almost be family to us. From this day forward I shall call you Patience, and I will be Meredith to you."

Patience bit her lip, plainly worried about her fictional past. "Lady Meredith—"

"Ah." His sister waved a chiding finger at her. "If I must suffer the scrutiny of the *ton* with dignity, then you will do so at my side, friend."

She exhaled, her expression reflecting her impatience. "Meredith . . . Lord Ramscar . . . I am honored that you are willing to lie on my behalf. However, it is unnecessary, I assure you. I would not want either of you to suffer any humiliation if your trickery was uncovered."

"Oh, let Meredith have her fun, Patience," Ram said in a teasing drawl. His intentional use of her Christian name earned him a charming pout. "Our ruse harms no one. Can you deny the notion of making arses out of the very people who view themselves as your betters does not appeal to the actress in you?"

He had complete faith in Patience that she could hoodwink the *ton* into believing she was a noblewoman. Her refined manners, voice, and graceful movements perfectly mimicked those of any lady he had encountered at a ball. Meredith would do well to emulate her companion.

Patience braced her elbow on the polished surface of the pianoforte and rubbed her temple. She knew when she had been outmaneuvered. The question was whether or not she would surrender gracefully.

"Very well." She gave him a gimlet stare and muttered the words "amateur players" under her breath. "To keep things simple, I recommend that I remain Patience Winlow."

Society is now one polish'd horde,
Formed of two mighty tribes, the *Bores* and *Bored*.

—GEORGE GORDON NOEL BYRON, LORD BYRON
DON JUAN, CANTO XIII, STANZA 95

CHAPTER NINE

London, April 1810

"I cannot do it. I beg of you, do not make me," Meredith pleaded, gripping her hands together so fiercely that it had to be painful.

All in all, the two-day journey to London had not been as dreadful as Lord Ramscar had once predicted. Once when they were alone he had suggested pouring laudanum down his sister's throat, but Patience had curtly dismissed such an outrageous suggestion. She could not glance at a bottle of the opium tincture without thinking of Julian Phoenix and the vile plans he had for her the day he had died. Patience would rather endure hours of Meredith's hysterics than violate their budding friendship.

In the end, it was Meredith who had surprised them all, including herself. The first few miles of their departure had been tearful; however, once she had calmed, the young woman had begun to appreciate her new surroundings. Everything was a new experience for her, and it was easy to be caught up in her excitement. Patience had noted the flash of relief on Ramscar's face whenever he heard his sister's soft, hesitant laughter. The earl was aware he was gambling with Meredith's sanity by removing her from her precious Swancott. Fortunately, his instincts had been correct.

That was, until they had reached the Knowden town house. The earl had told her that this was not the town house Meredith recalled from eleven years ago. The house in which her mother and twin sister had perished had been sold off shortly after the fire. With the painful memories of his loss too fresh for comfort, Ramscar had purchased another house for him and his sister. Meredith had been too ill during those early months to appreciate his considerate gesture. Regardless, when the coach had halted in front of the house, the poor woman had been overcome with emotion.

Patience disembarked from the coach and held out her hand. "Meredith, you have nothing to fear. It is simply a house. Are you not curious to see where your brother lives?" Patience certainly was interested in exploring the town house.

Meredith placed her hands over her face. "Oh, you must think I am the biggest ninny to be fussing so."

"Oh pish! This is a homecoming of sorts, and what lady does not get a little emotional during these moments?" Patience said, feeling terrible there was nothing comforting she could utter that would ease Meredith's misery.

Ramscar marched toward them looking displeased. "Meredith, why are you still sitting in the coach? I want to introduce you to the servants and show you the house."

His sister placed her hand to her throat. "Something is terribly wrong, Ram. My limbs are frozen. And—and my lungs cannot seem to fill with air. I think you should summon a physician."

Patience met Ramscar's stern gaze and shrugged. They had gotten this far without Meredith succumbing to hysterics or a tantrum. A little fretting was expected during a very delicate and emotional situation. Her brother, above all, should understand.

When Ramscar moved closer, Patience stepped aside. Meredith was fortunate to have him as a brother. Patience had two younger brothers, Penn and Rawley. They had been away at school when she had run off. She wondered if they ever thought about her.

An abrupt screech from within the coach startled Patience from her wistful musings. She rushed forward, but Ramscar had control of the situation. Instead of coaxing his sister from the coach as Patience had expected, the brute had dragged his mulish sibling out of the compartment and tossed her over his shoulder as if she were a sack of onions.

"Put me down!" Meredith screamed as she pounded on her brother's back. Oh, she was in a fine fury.

Aghast by the earl's actions, Patience was uncertain what to do. "Ramscar? My lord, it is unseemly to carry your sister like she is—"

"A mouthy bit of goods?" he snapped at Patience. "I'll not have another word from you, Miss Winlow. I am perfectly capable of handling my sister." With an unwieldy burden, he marched up the steps into the town house. All Patience could do was follow them.

In front of the astonished servants, he bent down and released his sister.

"Welcome to London, Sister!" The idiotic man sounded rather pleased with himself.

Patience closed her eyes to briefly blot out the

awkward predicament Ramscar had created for his sister.

Completely mortified by the unwarranted attention, Meredith promptly burst into tears.

"Ramscar! About time you find your way back to town," Townsend Lidsaw, Viscount Everod, said, rising from a chair and giving him a swift affectionate hug followed by a wicked jab at his shoulder.

Ramscar grunted in reaction, but overall, he was pleased to come across one of his friends. He had decided for his first evening out to visit one of the popular gambling hells in town, called Moiria's Lust. Xavier, the proprietor, was temperamental about who sat at his tables, but he ran a fair establishment. Ramscar was not surprised to find his friend frequenting the hell instead of one of the fashionable gentlemen's clubs.

Lord Everod, known simply as Everod by his friends, was one of the more notorious of *les sauvages nobles*. The same age as Ram, his friend had earned the fitting nickname of Ever*hard* from several witty ladies of the *ton* who had shared his bed, albeit briefly. At six feet, three inches, his broad-shouldered frame was intimidating to the uninitiated. Ram thought his friend resembled a medieval warlord in looks and brooding temperament.

His shoulder-length glossy black hair was a stark contrast to his striking face. Exotic and beguiling, his eyes were the color of amber and edged with a thin outer dark ring of green. They were eyes that burned both hot and cold depending on the viscount's mood. The ladies seemed unabashedly fascinated by his masculine beauty and cynical wit, and Everod was swift to oblige his admirers.

In Everod's typical provoking manner, he seized a man passing by the card table and shoved him into his chair. Strangely, the man picked up the viscount's discarded cards and the game at the table resumed without him.

"What kept you? I expected to find you prowling about London a fortnight ago."

Abruptly, Ramscar's friend halted. He hooted with laughter and clapped Ramscar on the back. "Pray tell me you've enjoyed the winter snuggling up with that Amazon who couldn't keep her greedy fingers off your stiff poker?"

Ram had forgotten Everod had caught him and his mistress in the middle of what should have been a private encounter. Angeline had laughed when the unabashed viscount had suggested joining the couple later that evening. From Ram's point of view, it had been damned embarrassing. There were some things in life in which some might view him as a selfish bastard, and sharing his mistress was one of the more important ones. He left that particular carnal mischief up to Everod and Cadd.

"I remained at Swancott longer than expected," Ram explained, sitting down at an empty table. "Meredith has joined me this season."

"Meredith?" The viscount frowned, likely having forgotten that Ram had a younger sister. His next words negated that suspicion. "Your sister? Why drag her to town? She is a mere child."

"You should visit Swancott more often. My sister will be four and twenty at the end of the week," Ram dryly said. He smiled at the barmaid and quickly ordered two bottles of wine. "Fortunately, the Dowager Duchess of Solitea has kindly offered to hold a ball in celebration of Meredith's birthday."

"Damn me! The chit is practically a spinster, Ram," Everod said in his usually blunt fashion. He was not a cruel man, but he rarely censored his thoughts around his friends. "What were you thinking? You are six years too late if you hope to marry her off."

A plume of uninhibited anger unfurled within Ram. While he enjoyed the viscount's company, he, amongst all Ram's friends, was the wrong gentleman to be discussing the delicate handling of Meredith's fears. Solitea would have understood why

Ram had delayed bringing his sister to London. The duke had a younger sister, too. The impulse to coddle them was irresistible.

There was a hint of ice in Ram's hazel green eyes when he held the other man's gaze. "The fire scarred more than her face, Everod. Nor am I seeking to marry her off to some blackguard like you or Cadd—"

Everod looked offended. "Hey! That's mighty harsh, considering that we are your *friends*!"

"A man who is willing to tolerate a ruined face for a sizeable dowry." Ram shook his head, disgusted by the notion. He would rather keep his sister hidden away at Swancott than marry her off to a man who could not see Meredith's beauty.

Ram paused, recognizing that Everod had done nothing to deserve his anger. After all, had he not directed the same criticisms at himself? "Perhaps you are right. I should have brought her to town six years ago instead of capitulating to her tearful pleas to remain at Swancott. I am trying to remedy that mistake this season. I even hired a companion for her."

Ram silently cursed when he noticed the viscount's interest piqued at the mention of a hired companion. Everod had no shame when it came to seducing ladies, whether they were duchesses or lowborn milkmaids.

"A companion?" Ram's friend grinned, showing plenty of teeth. His amber eyes gleamed with admiration. "You clever bastard! Only you would figure out a respectful motive for having an unmarried wench in your house. Tell me, is she pretty?"

Unless Ram was prepared to ignore Everod the entire season, it would be next to impossible to keep him from meeting Patience. The lady was under Ram's protection. A small warning would not be construed as out of the ordinary.

"Heed me. Miss Winlow is seeing to my sister's needs, not *yours*," Ram said, unable to keep the steel out of his tone. The thought of Patience in his friend's bed made Ram want to slam his fist into Everod's cocky face. "We won't have a problem if you keep your breeches fastened and your language respectful."

"Oh, so she's very pretty," the viscount teased, satisfied that he had provoked the truth out of his friend. "I cannot wait to meet the beauty who has you issuing threats."

The barmaid returned with the bottles of wine and two glasses. Everod smiled up at her and patted her backside in a friendly manner. The comely wench flirtatiously nudged him with her hip. Ram was not oblivious to the signals the pair passed between them. He also knew Everod. The man was already thinking about how he could persuade the maid into neglecting her duties for a half hour so they might take pleasure in a brief tryst. In gratitude, Ram handed the barmaid a few extra coins for distracting his friend from pursuing the topic of Patience Winlow.

"Thank ye, my lord," the barmaid said to Ram, but her eyes were on the viscount. "If you have a need or two, just ask for Marjorie."

No doubt, Everod would be freeing his need especially for Marjorie in some private corner of the gambling hell later in the evening.

Ram picked up one of the bottles of wine and poured some into his and Everod's glasses. For a time Ram looked forward to forgetting about his personal problems and getting drunk with his friend. "So tell me of Cadd and Solitea. What news do you have of them?"

It was nigh past midnight when Ram heard the soft knock at the door. He had been expecting a visit from Meredith's champion. However, he had thought the late hour would discourage her from confronting him tonight.

"Lord Ramscar, are you awake?"

At the sound of Patience's low, husky voice Ram shut his eyes and tried to resist answering her summons. He was tired, edgy, and slightly drunk. The last thing he wanted to do was discuss his sister or his unpardonable behavior. When he had departed for the evening earlier, Meredith had still not forgiven him for his highhandedness.

"Ram, please."

Patience's quiet plea slipped under his weary defenses. Rolling out of bed, he padded to the door. For modesty's sake, he could have donned his discarded shirt. He refrained. A lady who dared to venture into a gentleman's bedchamber at midnight deserved to glimpse the ravenous beast she provoked.

Ram opened the door.

"Good evening, Patience."

He leaned his forearm against the door frame, admiring the young woman in front of him. This was a Patience Winlow he had yet to meet. Her long blond hair was down but neatly plaited into a braid down her back. She wore a simple white nightdress and kid slippers over her bare feet. A light green shawl was draped over her shoulders, preventing him from admiring her breasts.

"How many hours did you sit by the window awaiting my return?" he asked, giving her a wolfish grin. "If I had known, I would have told you it was a fruitless endeavor."

Patience was not immune to his near nakedness. Instead of looking away, she gaped at him, her expressive blue eyes taking in his bare chest and feet.

Dressed only in his breeches, he looked as if he had been about to indulge in a night of debauchery.

It was an outstanding notion.

"My apologies," she said breathlessly. "I had heard your return. I did not know you were already in bed. Please forgive my intrusion." She turned away, preparing to leave.

Oh, this would not do.

They had both been pretending the kiss at Swancott had not occurred. Now she was here at the entrance of his lair. Surely, her bravery should be rewarded.

"You must be cold. Pray, enter." He backed away and gestured her toward the fire. "We are both awake, and evidently you desire a private audience with me."

Ram glanced at his shirt on his bed and dismissed it. The sight of his half nakedness had rattled her composure, but she was too strong-willed to swoon. He joined her near the hearth and crouched down to tend the fire.

"Sit down," he called over his shoulder.

She gingerly sat down at the end corner of the small walnut daybed to the right of him. The long squab and head cushions were covered in dark blue velvet. The gilt headpiece had been carved into the fan-shaped plumes of a peacock. Despite its eccentricity, the daybed was a comfortable piece of furniture. Often he had fallen asleep near the fire with an open book splayed facedown across his chest.

"I suppose you have come to lecture me about my cruelty toward my sister," he said, setting aside the poker. Since she was poised on one measly corner of the daybed, Ram decided there was no reason not to enjoy the rest of it. She recoiled somewhat when he sat down and stretched his legs out behind her, but she did not seek a safer place to sit.

With her hands clasped together, she turned her head, and their gazes locked. "Is this where you tell me I have overstepped my position, my lord?"

"'Ram,' if you please, or 'Ramscar,'" he softly admonished, irritated that she was using his title to distance herself from him. "Remember our ruse. I should not view you as anything less than my equal."

She grinned triumphantly at his admission. "Then you do solicit my opinion regarding Meredith."

He grinned at Patience's arrogance. "No. I have been handling Meredith longer than you. While I admire your dedication to her, there will be instances when our methods for easing her fears will differ."

"You shamed her in front of the staff, Ramscar," Patience said, shifting so her knees were facing him. "Certainly, you must agree that your so-called *method* was autocratic and a bit cruel."

They might not have an audience, but his companion was attempting to shame him into extending an apology to his sister. And Patience thought he was bossy! Carelessly he used the edge of his thumbnail to scratch an itch just below his navel. Ram noticed her gaze had dropped down to his belly. A faint blush stained her cheeks.

Beguiled by her reaction, he decided that he was already bored with their discussion of Meredith. He would rather see what other responses he could provoke from the little actress. Still, the lady would be likely to leave him, disgusted by what she perceived as callous actions toward his sister. "How was Meredith this evening?"

"Calmer." Patience's soft sigh revealed it had been a trying day. "Nevertheless, she is very peeved with you."

"And her fears of the house or London?" He wiggled his brows knowingly at Patience.

Her lips parted in surprise. "Forgotten. Dear heavens, you deliberately set out to distract her, did you not?"

He grinned at Patience's accusation. "I understand my sister. She has a nasty habit of fretting over something until she works herself into a fit of hysteria. It seemed prudent to give her something new to concentrate on."

There was a quiet awe in Patience's expression as she stared at him. "Ramscar, you are a very wise gentleman," she said humbly. "I had not considered—Mayhap I owe you an apology?"

Ram straightened and moved closer to Patience until he was positioned behind her. Everod had believed Ram had installed her in his house for his own pleasures. While that was untrue, he was beginning to see the benefits of having her within arm's reach. "Why spoil your delightful arrogance with humility? It does not suit you." He caressed the long braid, admiring its subtle blond hues.

She stiffened at his touch. "I should go. I have kept you from your bed long enough." She clutched the ends of her shawl like it was a shield. If she grasped those taut ends any tighter, she was likely to strangle.

He reached around to her front and tenderly pried her bloodless fingers from the shawl. "Tarry a moment, Patience. There is one small matter I wish to address."

"Such as?" she whispered. Her mouth trembled when his fingers brushed under her chin.

She did not resist him as he guided her face toward his. "This."

Ram kissed her sweetly on the lips.

CHAPTER TEN

His kiss had not been an aberration.

With her hands shaking, Patience brought her fingers to his face and pulled him closer. Ramscar tasted like the brandy he preferred in the evenings. The beard stubble beneath her fingertips was rough and foreign to her. She wondered how that scratchiness might feel against her sensitive breasts, down her back, or along her inner thigh. Would the earl be scandalized if she expressed her question aloud or would he simply lay her down on the daybed and show her?

Egad, what was she thinking? Such curious musings would only lead to trouble. Although she had not wanted to humiliate Meredith further by revealing that she fully intended to chastise Ramscar about his appalling behavior, she now understood the risk of confronting him alone in his bedchamber. The friendly informality she and Deidra had shared with Perry and Link had lured Patience into believing that she and the earl could share a similar familiarity without the messy consequences.

Patience had made a grave miscalculation.

She had underestimated her attraction to the earl and overestimated the gentleman's restraint.

Ramscar nipped her chin and then proceeded to nibble the line of her delicate jaw until he reached her ear. "Just as I thought," he murmured, swirling his tongue around the inner spirals of her ear.

"W-what?" Leaning away to avoid his tingly torment, she bared her neck, giving him the access he eagerly exploited with featherlike caresses with his lips. She mentally willed herself to stand and walk away from the earl. It mattered little that his touch exceeded her wildest dreams. Oh, how he smelled? Intoxicating. Clearly there was no harm in a few kisses?

"Your scent reminds me of one of my favorite

desserts as a lad. Warden pie," he said, his lips sampling the juncture between her neck and shoulder. "I swear your skin has the subtle essence of clove."

It was the soap she used. Her sole private luxury, the soap was a pleasing aromatic mixture of cassia, clove, and lemongrass. "And this pleases you?"

Ramscar nonchalantly pushed her onto her back and crawled up her prone body until his face hovered inches above her nose. "It makes me want to devour you." He flipped the ends of her shawl away, exposing her thin nightdress. "Slowly. And most thoroughly."

She fought back the urge to giggle. Patience sobered quickly when he lowered his head to her breasts. Unwillingly, she arched her back at the teasing strokes of his hot lips over her right nipple. Even through the fabric of her nightdress, she could feel the moist heat of his tongue as he laved and suckled the swollen bud.

"So responsive," he murmured, kissing down her abdomen until he reached the juncture between her legs. "A man could become drunk on the power of evoking your unbidden passions."

Patience murmured a soft protest when Ramscar pushed up her nightdress, revealing the blond triangle of curls between her legs. Her hand instinctively moved to cover herself from his keen gaze. He lightly kissed the knuckles on each finger and nudged her hand away.

"Are you a virgin, Patience?" Ramscar asked, drawing his finger down her womanly cleft. The gathering wetness of her arousal allowed him to slip his probing finger deeper into her sheath. Before she could form a coherent reply to his brazen question, he shook his head. "Nay, you do not have to tell me. In truth, a lady's virginity or lack thereof means little to me."

Patience could not decide whether she was appalled or relieved by his statement. "You have a very tolerant view for a man," she said tartly.

She sensed his smile against her inner thigh. "You misunderstand. I value a woman's honest response in my bed more than her maiden's flesh." He pressed his fingers deeper into her sheath, and she bit her lower lip to keep from moaning. "A man would pay a king's ransom to savor the exotic flavors of a woman's passion."

To prove his point, Ramscar skillfully parted her womanly folds and *savored*. Sweet heavens! What a magnificent sensation! Her thighs quivered at the first flick of his tongue.

"Lord knows I should keep my hands off you," he murmured huskily, the heat from his breath melting her all the way through to her bones. "Troublesome business it is, tupping the help. Tell me to stop." His sensual actions belied his command. His nimble tongue was sheer wickedness, she thought as she clenched her teeth against the erotic onslaught. The serpentine motion of his tongue along her inner folds sent her heartbeat racing beneath her breasts. No other man had touched her in such a manner. The brief occasions she had been intimate with Julian Phoenix had been focused on her seeing to his needs. She had despised touching his stiff, ugly *thing*. Phoenix had only reinforced her hatred by causing her pain to gain her cooperation.

Ramscar moaned and inched closer as if he could not get enough of her. His actions perplexed her. What pleasure could a man receive by taking a lady in this manner? Patience reached forward and threaded her fingers into his long dark blond hair with the intent of stopping him. At that precise moment, he slid his fingers deep into her while his tongue circled the small, acutely sensitive nubbin at the apex of her cleft.

"Tell me to stop."

Instead of pushing him away, she impulsively pulled him against her.

Ramscar chuckled at her enthusiasm. He lifted his head and wiped his lips against his forearm. There was no hint of his amusement in his scorching hazel green gaze. The gleaming, feral intensity of his stare stole her breath. "I sensed there was passion in you, lady. I could only hope you would share it with me."

"You do not have to continue. Surely, a man does not find pleasure in the act," Patience said, although her protest was only halfhearted.

Ramscar gave her an incredulous look and shook his head at her foolishness. Suddenly, his eyes narrowed as a sly grin slid into place. With his fingers still buried deep in her sheath, he flexed them, ruthlessly surpassing his earlier penetration.

He thrust his fingers into her. Again. And again. The man was relentless. The muscles encompassing her stomach tightened as something not yet defined simmered in her loins. Patience freed her fingers from his hair and fell back against the daybed.

The sensation he was building within her was incredible!

Her right leg slid restlessly against his muscled side. The notion of Ramscar's manhood replacing his agile fingers was not so repulsive. In fact, she was beginning to crave more of him.

Except for her dreams, Patience had never experienced pleasure in a man's carnal embrace. The first time Phoenix had bedded her, it had hurt terribly. There had been other nights when he had climbed into her bed and taken his pleasure rutting between her legs. Although his carnal demands had no longer hurt her, there also was no pleasure in the deed.

Not like this.

"Ramscar," she said, saying his name as if it were a prayer.

The earl understood her soft plea. Licking her swollen nubbin, he began suckling it while his fingers continued their rhythmic thrust. Thoroughly. Deeply. Hard.

Patience gripped the sides of the daybed and screamed. The crest of an internal wave of pure sensation rippled through her entire body, only to reverse itself. An explosion of light burst in her head, blinding her. Small waves akin to raindrops striking the surface of a pond rippled everywhere. She had never experienced something so beautiful. Ramscar slowly withdrew his fingers from her still-quaking sheath. Patience did not have to glance at him to see the satisfied smirk on his handsome face.

A niggling thought intruded after the last lovely ripple faded. Pleasure gave him power over her. She had always been able to resist Phoenix in spite of his violent fists. What defense did she have against the man who could devastate her using only his mouth and hands? With her emotions so close to the surface, she covered her face with her hand and wept.

"Here now . . . What is this all about?" Ramscar crooned, gathering her up into his arms. His kindness only made her cry harder. "Did I hurt you, Patience?"

Patience fiercely shook her head in denial. "No! I had no notion I could feel—" She pounded her fist to her heart, frustrated that her words were so inadequate to the exquisite pleasure he had given her.

"Hush." The earl cradled her silently and let her sob against his shoulder. His arousal pressed insistently against her buttock, and yet he did not demand equal attention to his own carnal needs.

When the worst of her tears had waned, she hiccupped and used the edge of her sleeve to wipe the dampness from her cheeks. "Forgive me, my lord. I cannot account for my teary outburst. You have been quite wonderful throughout it all."

"Wonderful," he echoed absently.

Patience gave him a watery smile. Her fingers boldly reached for the buttons on his breeches. Abruptly, shaking off his lethargy, Ramscar seized her wrist and halted her efforts.

"My lord?" she inquired, fearing she had somehow offended him. He had given her a grand, exhilarating experience she would never forget. The least she could do was ease his apparent suffering. He had already proved he was a better man than Julian Phoenix had ever dared to dream of being.

"No, stop, if you please."

Lord Ramscar tenderly placed her back onto the daybed. He knelt in front of her while he pulled her nightdress down over her legs.

Men did not refuse a willing lover. Over the years, countless gentlemen had vied for her interest. Lord Ramscar's actions completely baffled her. "I do not understand. I thought you—"

"So did I," he replied grimly. "I was wrong."

What the devil was he talking about?

Oh God, she had done something wrong. Perhaps he had been repulsed by the dewy moisture that seemed to increase when he touched her. "You no longer desire me?" she said, detesting how pathetic she sounded.

His gaze jumped up to her face, and the hunger she noted in his piercing gaze silenced her. "You should return to your room. Do not forget to take a candle." He stood up and moved back to the fire.

"If I offended you by crying—" she began.

"It wasn't your tears," he snapped, speaking over her attempted apology. Ramscar scrubbed his face with his hand in agitation. "I was wrong when I told you earlier that a lady's virginity matters little to me."

He had been disappointed, after all, that she had not been a virgin.

"Oh, I see," she said, a feeling of shame stealing the residual joy she had experienced in his arms.

Ramscar broodingly studied her face. "Clearly, you do not," he said angrily. He marched over to her and hauled her against him. His mouth roughly claimed hers. She could not breathe as he greedily devoured her lips like a starving man. When he released her, both of them were panting.

"I want you, sweet, delectable Patience. So much that I will likely regret my decision on the morrow, so run while you have the chance." He braced his hand against the narrow mantel and stared into the fire.

The earl was making no sense. Perhaps she should leave. She edged along the daybed and backed away from him.

Without turning around, he said, "I once told my friend Solitea that a lady's virginity was akin to an affliction. That it was a man's sworn duty to relieve her from it." He paused a moment. "Christ, I was an arrogant bastard!"

Why was the man babbling on about virginity?

"Lord Ramscar, I did not come to you a virgin," she said soothingly.

"No, but you are an innocent." He finally turned and stared at her. "I did not know there was a difference until you laid your head on my shoulder and cried because of what I had done." He carelessly motioned at the door. "Leave. *Now!*"

His burst of temper spurred her into action. Grabbing a lit candlestick off the table, she rushed to the door and was gone.

Ramscar brought his hands to his face. He could

still smell the musky scent of Patience's arousal on his fingers. The haunting fragrance made his groin ache with need. So the little actress had been relieved of her virginity. Still, she had never experienced pleasure. It was only now that he understood his friend the Duke of Solitea's dilemma a year earlier when he had deflowered the lady he once believed was his father's former mistress. Neither Ramscar nor Solitea had had much experience with innocence to recognize the signs. Ram had been selective in choosing his lovers. Widows were ardent and amiable companions, and he had a partiality for actresses like Angeline Grassi.

And Patience.

He had wanted to ask her a dozen questions, and yet he did not have the right to demand the answers.

I gave Patience her first climax.

It was a staggering thought. The lady could not despise him for giving her pleasure. She might even crave more from him. An experienced lover only expected him to satisfy her carnal needs. An innocent would demand more than his body.

It was best for both their sakes that he stayed away from her.

Patience closed the door to her bedchamber and sagged against the hard surface. She was not worried that Ramscar would follow her and finish what he had begun. He seemed as spooked by what had transpired between them as she was. In the morning, she would awaken and have feelings of gratitude that he had ordered her out of his bedchamber.

Without a doubt!

Her legs were a bit wobbly as she walked over to her bed and sat down. She was not seeking a relationship with the earl. So she had had a few erotic dreams about the man. He was utterly gorgeous! Patience wagered many of the ladies of the *ton* sighed over the Earl of Ramscar each season. Besides, no good could result from taking him as a lover. To him, she was an impoverished unknown actress. She might make a fine mistress, nothing more. What if he learned of her connection to the Farnalys? Would it make a difference?

"Then he is not the man I believe him to be."

Some questions were best left unanswered.

CHAPTER ELEVEN

In hindsight, Ramscar realized that he should have warned his sister that she would be receiving a visit from the dowager duchess in the afternoon. However, Meredith had already been vexed with him the previous day and he saw no point in giving her a reason to hide in her bedchamber all day.

"Meredith, may I present Her Grace, the Dowager Duchess of Solitea," Ram said, using his brows to give his sister a silent signal to cease her open-mouthed gape at the older woman.

It was bloody disconcerting.

Patience was no help. When he needed her fiery spirit, the lady had chosen to play the role of the invisible servant. She quietly stood off to the left of Meredith and had yet to lift her gaze from the carpet. Ram was baffled. He did not know if she was angry because she had experienced her first climax with him or if her ire had something to do with him sending her away. Either way, he was damned, and Patience was planning to make him pay.

Ramscar shook his head over Everod's unexpected appearance. Was he drunk? What was he doing, acting as escort for the duchess? Christ, the man gave new meaning to "flirting dangerously." Solitea was likely to murder Everod on sight if he suspected the viscount was dallying with his mother.

Meredith roused herself from her stupor and curtsied. "Your Grace, you honor me. You must forgive my surprise. I confess, Ram was remiss and neglected to tell me that you intended to call on us."

"I will have none of this 'Your Grace' business from you, my dear girl. Ram is family to me and mine. That makes you family as well," the older woman chided with mock severity.

The dowager was the mother of Fayne Carlisle,

the Duke of Solitea. At eight and forty, the lady possessed a beauty that seemed timeless. Her daughter, Fayre, favored her mother in looks; however, both son and daughter were true Carlisles, having inherited the notable reddish brown hair. Sadly, the elder lady had lost her beloved duke last season. There had been rumors that the old duke had been rutting on top of his current mistress when his heart failed him. The family dismissed the suggestion as absurd, even though His Grace had been known by all as a faithless old rogue. The duchess had mourned the loss of her husband in her own fashion. She had spent the season and most of the summer in the loving company of two gentlemen who were young enough to be her sons.

Her son had been rather unsettled by it all. A private man, he had taken his father's death harder than most would have foreseen. Fortunately, he had his new duchess to distract him. There was nothing typical about the Carlisles. It was one of the reasons that Ramscar enjoyed them so much.

"And who is this lovely shy creature?" the duchess said, beckoning to Patience. "Another sister?"

Everod rudely snorted. "Mayhap Ramscar has taken to running a Covent Garden nunnery," he said, earning a menacing glare from his friend.

Meredith was too sheltered to understand that the viscount was referring to a brothel. Patience and the dowager, however, seemed to immediately grasp his insinuation. The duchess laughed, but Patience gave Ram a somber look that neatly cut him to the quick.

Irritated, he smacked Everod on the back of his head. Ignoring his indignant yelp, Ram strode over to Patience. He gently took her by the elbow and guided her over to the duchess.

"Your Grace, allow me to present Miss Winlow." He glanced at Meredith, and she timidly nodded. "Patience will be joining us for the season. I thought Meredith might be more comfortable having the daughter of one of our mother's cherished friends as a companion."

"Oh," Her Grace said, giving him a shrewd glance.

There was a wealth of subtlety in his statement. By revealing an intimate connection to his family, Patience's position had been elevated above that of a mere servant. On the other hand, the absence of her family implied a lack of social connections and wealth. Once the gossips circulated the particulars of her humble background, Ram was certain the news would discourage fortune hunters.

Patience gracefully curtsied. "Your Grace." She did not try to engage the dowager in conversation. Considering Patience's position, the introduction was enough.

Everod stepped forward. "Ramscar, I desire an introduction to Lady Meredith's attractive companion as well."

Damn that randy scoundrel!

Ram was reluctant to carry out the formal introductions. After what he had learned about Patience last evening, he was convinced she would be easy quarry for the viscount's practiced charm.

"Miss Winlow, may I present Lord Everod," Ram said brusquely. "Lord Everod is a notorious rake. Do not trust anything he says."

"You wound me, Ramscar," the other man said, seemingly annoyed by his friend. "Ladies, pray ignore Ram's malicious claim. I'm harmless."

Her expression enigmatic, Patience replied, "An honor, Lord Everod." She curtsied.

Everod bowed respectfully and then stepped back. "The honor is mine, Miss Winlow. Such beauty and captivating grace so artfully arranged. I cannot blame Ramscar for wanting to keep you for himself."

The duchess laughed gaily. Deliberately inserting herself between Patience and Everod, she said, "Beware of *les sauvages nobles,* Miss Winlow. Their devilry has broken countless hearts." The duchess escorted Patience and Meredith the short distance to the sofa and motioned for both ladies to sit.

"You are cruel, madam!" Everod retorted, nudging Ram to offer his defense. "You will scare these ladies with your flummery."

"If I wanted to scare them, I would merely have to repeat some of the tales I have heard about you, Lord Ever*hard*!" The duchess waved the gentlemen off. "Leave us. The ball is days away, my house is in utter chaos, and I have much to discuss with Lady Meredith and Miss Winlow. We cannot be bothered with your flirtations, you mischievous man. Now go!"

Before Everod could argue, Ram took his friend by the arm and physically hauled him out of the drawing room. Sometimes his compulsive need to seduce every female that he encountered was tiresome. It was best that they depart; else Ram feared they would come to blows.

Meredith would be fine without him. What could possibly go wrong, leaving his sister and Patience alone with the duchess?

As the door shut behind them, Ram heard the older woman ask, "Miss Winlow, you seem familiar to me. Do I know your family?"

Everod shook off Ramscar's fierce grip. "Does it pain you?"

Ram barely heard the question. He was wondering how Patience had responded to the duchess's

innocent query. Meredith was unused to subterfuge. She was likely to panic if Patience did not
keep her head. "Does what?" he asked absently.

"The stick shoved up your arse!" The viscount
seized Ramscar by his coat and backed him up until
he collided with the nearest wall. The mounted
swords clattered with the impact. "Since when do
you start cautioning ladies about my character—"
Everod's anger waned as a thought struck him like a
thunderbolt. He released his hold on Ramscar.
"Wait. This isn't about me. This is about you. You
want the blonde for yourself."

Ram tugged on his wrinkled coat. If he admitted
it, Everod would tease him mercilessly. He was too
edgy to trust his response to the man's taunts. "You
are wrong. Miss Winlow is simply under my protection. I will not have you playing your seductive
games with the young lady."

His friend sneered, unimpressed by Ramscar's
posturing. "Have you considered that Miss Winlow might desire my attentions?"

Ram went cold at the thought. If he was refrain-
ing from putting his hands on Patience, then Everod
could keep his bloody hands off her, too. Ram
stepped forward until his and Everod's faces were
scarcely an inch apart. "Cross me, Everod, and so
help me, you will feel the point of my sword."

"Oh, good," Holt Cadd, Marquess of Byrchmore,

drawled behind them. "It appears I have not missed all the fun, after all."

"I highly doubt that you have met my parents, Your Grace."

Patience and Meredith sat side by side on the sofa while the dowager admired the various knick-knacks in the drawing room as she conducted her interview. The older woman's questions were as subtle as the gaudy porcelain elephant she had clasped in her hands.

The duchess set down the elephant and gave Patience an arch look. "And why have you come to this conclusion, Miss Winlow?"

"Because my parents are dead, Your Grace," Patience said tersely. She did not react to Meredith's sorrowful cry of surprise. "These days they reside in loftier circles than polite society."

The next time Lord Ramscar decided to invent a respectable family history for her, they had best work out all the details beforehand. Her Grace, the Dowager Duchess of Solitea, was immeasurably curious about Patience's past. Meredith was offering no assistance. Patience's young friend was practically mute. Oh, how Patience wished she could throttle the earl for abandoning them.

The older woman smiled at Patience's spirited

retort. "I daresay I well deserved your sarcasm. Rudeness begets rudeness. Pray, forgive my curiosity, Miss Winlow. I am usually not one to pry. However, there is something about your face that brings to mind another . . ." She allowed her words to trail off. "Oh, bother! It will come to me one day."

Was the dowager duchess acquainted with Patience's parents? If so, her mother must have been thrilled to make such a connection. One's position in polite society took precedence over wealth in her opinion. If Her Grace knew of her mother, Patience would have to tread carefully as she moved through society. She might even be forced to abandon her post if the lady's memory improved with time.

Warily Patience watched the dowager duchess as she circled around the sofa until she faced her tense companions. "I have had enough of this house. What we need is some fresh air. Ladies, ready yourselves for an outing. I think a drive through Hyde Park is in order!"

"Blast you, Cadd! A few minutes more and Ram was going to oblige me by throwing the first punch," Everod said, his tone dripping with disgust.

At five and twenty, Cadd was the youngest member of *les sauvages nobles*. An inch shorter than Everod, Cadd wore his dark brown hair long and unfettered. When he was a youth, his good looks had a boyish prettiness that had placed him and his friends in the middle of countless fights. A broken nose at age sixteen had diminished his classical perfection, but the ladies of the *ton* did not seem to notice. There was always some unfortunate lady who found herself pursued by both Everod and Cadd. Over the years, the gentlemen's unspoken competitiveness had greatly amused Ram and Solitea. At least, it was comical until Ram or Solitea was forced to separate the fighting pair. Everod had a nasty habit of provoking the marquess at every opportunity.

At the moment, Everod's assessment of what their friend had interrupted was too close to the truth for comfort. Ram nodded at the marquess. "It is good to see you again, Cadd. Did you just walk through the door without waiting to be announced or do I have to reprimand Scrimm again for neglecting his duties?"

"Now you are picking fights with Scrimm?" the viscount said, coolly studying the tips of his nails on his left hand. "The man must be close to eighty. Who's next? His elderly mother?"

Ram took a threatening step toward Everod.

Sensing trouble, Cadd said, "I'll have you know that your man was dutifully at the door, watching over the ladies as they departed."

Ram forgot all about murdering his friend as he

switched directions and walked toward Cadd. He should have never left Meredith and Patience alone with the duchess. Like her son, the lady was unpredictable. "Ladies? All three?"

Cadd was baffled by the grimness in his friend's tone. "Naturally, unless you have a few others tucked away somewhere in the house. I greeted the duchess as she left the house with your sister and a Miss Winlow. Which reminds me, congratulations are in order. I knew that when properly motivated you would convince Lady Meredith to join you in London this season." He smirked at the viscount. "Everod, you owe me one hundred pounds."

Ramscar growled in frustration and marched by both startled men. "You actually wagered on my sister?"

"Cadd added it to the club's betting book years ago," Everod added provokingly. "I barely recall the particulars."

Cadd appeared affronted by the insinuation. "I wagered on your success. If you want to hit someone, focus your ire on Everod. Sadly, he did not have much faith in your abilities."

Disgusted with both of them, Ramscar headed for the door. Perhaps it was not too late to halt the ladies' carriage.

The young marquess followed in his friend's wake, unaware of his inner turmoil. "By the by, I must confess, the blonde accompanying your sister is a fetching creature. Where the devil did you find her?"

Ramscar gritted his teeth at the innocent query. He remained silent until he strode into the center of the empty front hall. "Scrimm!"

"Oh, so good of you to bellow, my lord. My ears, you know, are not what they used to be," the servant said, closing the door. "These days, such consideration is unexpected in the quality."

Despite his concern, Ram reluctantly grinned at the man's odd humor. "Did the duchess mention where she was taking my sister and Miss Winlow?"

"Her Grace was not inclined to linger for a visit, my lord. She prefers the young and stupid ones." The elderly man pointedly glanced in Cadd and Everod's direction. "Like those two. Is that all?"

"Yes. Thank you, Scrimm," Ram said, pressing his fingers against his eyelids.

Why had the ladies departed without a word? More important, he wanted to know how Patience and Meredith had fared in his absence.

Cadd struggled not to smile. "Ram, your sister and her friend will return to you unharmed. The duchess simply desired a drive through Hyde Park, and she thought the ladies, since they are new in town, would be thrilled by the outing."

"A drive in the park, you say?"

The marquess frowned in concern. "Nothing more. Why are you so upset?"

"I suspect the pretty blond wench," Everod revealed, clapping his hand companionably on Cadd's shoulder. "Ram was willing to run me through for speaking to her."

Cadd made a derisive noise. "Who could blame him? You'd bed anything wearing a skirt."

Recognizing where their conversation was heading, Ram removed the viscount's hand from the other man's shoulder, and they moved just out of arm's reach. "Ignore Everod," Ram advised sagely. "I am concerned about Lady Meredith. She has been distressed for weeks about returning to town, and you know that the duchess can be delightfully overwhelming. I do not want my sister thinking I have abandoned her to a stranger."

Although the subject of his sister rarely surfaced when he was in London, his friends were aware of Meredith's injuries and her preference to remain at Swancott. "I must confess I was taken aback when I saw Lady Meredith coming down the stairs. I almost didn't recognize her. Then I noticed the—" Cadd discreetly coughed into his fist.

Her scars.

It tore at Ram that the first and last thing any man noticed about his sister was her imperfections.

"Her Grace is holding a ball in Meredith's honor to celebrate her birthday. Have you received an invitation?" Ram asked, directing their discourse to more pleasant subjects.

"Most likely." Cadd shrugged. "I have not been in town long enough to glance at invitations."

Everod hissed. "Invitations. To what? Balls, fetes, and polite afternoons playing cards. Utterly boring." He clapped his hands and rubbed his palms vigorously together. "Since Ramscar has calmed down and no longer wants to fight me, you might as well tell us what delayed your return to London. Where have you been?"

Usually quite candid about his life, Cadd seemed noticeably ill at ease at the viscount's question. "Nothing specific. Or criminal. I tarried at my horse farm longer than I had expected. That's all."

"Well, stick with us, my lad," Everod said, clasping the younger man by the neck and pressing a loud smacking kiss to Cadd's forehead. "Your luck is about to improve."

Ramscar wondered if it was equally apparent to Everod that their friend was brazenly lying about his absence.

CHAPTER TWELVE

Despite Patience's initial reservations about leaving the house without first consulting the earl, the drive through Hyde Park was rather pleasant. The dowager duchess was an affable guide who seemed to know a frightening amount of gossip about everyone. Ladies and gentlemen waved and nodded cordially as they passed by the ladies' carriage.

Patience looked over at Ramscar's sister and fretted. She was unused to the curious stares. Sympathy for the young lady welled in Patience's heart when she noticed how Lady Meredith kept fussing with the right side of her bonnet every time a stranger passed them.

The older woman had noticed the telling actions, too. She reached over and patted Lady Meredith's hand. "My dear girl, you must forgive their rudeness. Ramscar has kept you sequestered away, so naturally many are eager to meet you."

"You are kind to say so, Your Grace," Lady Meredith mumbled, sitting with her shoulders hunched in an unflattering pose.

"Nonsense. Why would I bother complimenting a potential rival who bests me in both youth and beauty?" the dowager demanded. The not-so-subtle crispness had the younger woman straightening her spine and reluctantly earning Patience's respect. "Vanity, my dear girl, is a common flaw one encounters in the young beauties of the *ton* these days. It is a flaw I pray you will work to correct."

Her companion's eyes goggled at the notion that the elegant and beautiful dowager considered her beautiful. "Yes, Your Grace," Lady Meredith said demurely. When the next gentleman passed them on his horse, the young woman kept her hands clasped in her lap. She still looked miserable, but they were making progress.

Patience smiled, thinking Ramscar would be

pleased. Her smile faded when she noticed that the dowager was looking directly at her. With a slight tilt of her head, the older woman winked at Patience. With that brief intimate connection, she and the dowager had become silent conspirators in launching Lady Meredith into polite society.

Unbeknownst to the ladies, one of the gentlemen who had ridden by them earlier had changed directions and had guided his horse alongside them.

"I beg your pardon, Your Grace. It seemed rude to ride on without paying my respects," the dark-haired gentleman said, his brown eyes warming with pleasure when his gaze drifted to Lady Meredith.

Well, this was an intriguing development. Had she already found her first suitor? He looked older than Lady Meredith. If Patience were to guess, she would have approximated his age to be in his early thirties. Although he was not stunningly handsome like Lord Ramscar or his friends Lord Everod and Lord Byrchmore, there was something charming about his face that caught a lady's eye. Even if he had not known the dowager, the quality of his clothes and the manner in which he handled his horse indicated that he was a gentleman.

"Mayfield," the dowager addressed her coachman. "Lord Halthorn wishes to speak with us. Please pull us out of this traffic and rest the horses."

"Aye, madam." The coachman called out to the

team; his vocalizations were almost melodic, as if he was singing his commands to the horses.

The carriage slowed, finally halting with a quick jolt.

"Forgive me, ladies. I had no intention of disturbing your outing. However, it is a lovely day for it," Lord Halthorn said, confidently controlling his restless steed from shying away from the carriage.

"Handsome gentlemen are almost obligated to disturb the ladies around them," the older woman said flirtatiously. "You would have injured my feelings if you had not greeted me properly." Her calculating gaze shifted to her younger companions. "You would have also deprived me of introducing my new friends, Lady Meredith and Miss Winlow."

Lord Halthorn inclined his head. Something other than polite interest flared in his brown eyes when his gaze lingered on Lady Meredith's face. "Miss Winlow and Lady Meredith, welcome to London."

The Dowager Duchess of Solitea had also noticed the gentleman's reaction to the young woman. "Ladies, allow me to present Fenton Mitchell, Viscount Halthorn. Did I mention that Lady Meredith is the Earl of Ramscar's sister?"

The viscount grinned self-effacingly, catching on to the older woman's matchmaking. "No, Your Grace. You have been rather stingy with your knowledge of Lady Meredith."

The gentleman's face slowly began to turn red at his confession. Patience glanced over at her companion. Lady Meredith had recovered from her fascination with her shoes, and her expression gradually evolved from coyness into healthy curiosity.

Ramscar's expectations only involved his sister mingling with polite society. Patience wondered if the earl would approve of his sister securing a husband by the end of the season.

The sounds of female voices as they strode through the house heralded the ladies' return. Ramscar and his friends had moved outdoors to the back gardens. They had enjoyed the past two hours refining their fencing skills. The physical activity had taken the edge off his earlier frustration that the ladies had left the house without telling him. He had been sorely tempted to join the fashionable promenade of carriages through Hyde Park, but he did not want to embarrass his sister in front of the dowager duchess. Meredith was nearly four and twenty. If he continued to treat her like a child, she would never have any confidence to stand on her own. Besides, what harm could a drive through Hyde Park cause?

"Ram," Meredith said excitedly, walking as swiftly as her skirts allowed. Ramscar raised his hand, signaling Cadd to hold his position. "You should have joined us. We had a delightful drive through the park!"

It was on the tip of his tongue to remind her that no one had bothered to tell him of their plans, but the happiness radiating from her face silenced his complaint. Twenty steps behind his sister, Patience took her time closing the distance between them.

Lowering his fencing foil, he kissed his sister on the cheek. "Where is the duchess?"

"She had to leave us for another appointment." Meredith lowered her voice. "Did you know that she claims to have a lover twenty years younger? I confess, for a lady who is eight and forty she is beautiful. However, have you ever heard anything so outrageous?"

Cadd and Everod began choking on their laughter. It was well-known throughout the *ton* that Solitea's mother had a preference for younger lovers. There had been an occasion or two when she had collected them in pairs, much to the chagrin of her son and daughter. "The duchess was likely teasing you." He scowled at his friends to stifle their laughter.

It was hopeless.

"Miss Winlow, the shortest route across the turf is a straight line," he said, exasperated by her meandering. His barb had her squaring her shoulders as she strode toward them. From his perspective, the lady sat at his table, so there was no reason that she should hover in the background like an unwanted relative.

"Thank you for your advice, Lord Ramscar. Otherwise, I might have gotten lost in your expansive gardens," she said sarcastically. In comparison, Swancott's immense gardens could have swallowed up his town garden several times over.

"Miss Winlow, we meet again," Everod said smoothly, earning him a threatening look from Ramscar. "The next time you and Lady Meredith decide to ride in the park, I hope you will allow us to accompany you."

The randy scoundrel had already been warned off. Perhaps he needed a harsher warning that included pain. Ramscar took an aggressive step toward Everod, but Cadd placed his palm on Ramscar's chest and pushed him back.

"I am merely a—guest. I will leave the decision of all future drives in the park to Lord Ramscar and his sister, Lord Everod," Patience said, neatly defusing Ramscar's annoyance by acknowledging his authority. "However, I do thank you for the kind offer."

Ramscar turned his back on Everod and smiled at his sister. "I want to hear all about your afternoon with the duchess. Did she introduce you to anyone?" He had been disappointed that the duchess's daughter, Lady Fayre, had not joined her on this afternoon's visit. Three years younger than Meredith and married to a gentleman named Maccus Brawley, Lady Fayre had just arrived in town with her family and was still setting up her household. Ramscar hoped to introduce her to his sister the night of the ball.

Meredith glanced at Cadd and Everod. She was clearly uncomfortable having what she deemed a private conversation in front of Ramscar's friends. He was on the verge of suggesting that they go indoors when his sister blurted out, "The dowager introduced me to the kindest, most honorable gentleman!"

"The duchess spent the afternoon flirting and waving young lords to her carriage?"

Patience pressed her fingers to her brow. Hours had passed since Lady Meredith had made her innocent announcement of meeting Lord Halthorn, and Lord Ramscar was still brooding about it. The evening ritual he and Patience had started at Swancott of sharing hot chocolate and brandy while they discussed the day before they both retired had resumed in London. When Scrimm had told her of his lord's request, Patience had been tempted to refuse. She could think of only two reasons that he might summon her this evening. The first was to finally address what had happened the night she had come to his bedchamber. The second was to discuss Meredith and her attraction to the viscount.

Fortunately, Ramscar wanted to discuss his sister. While Patience was relieved that his ire was focused on the latter, she did not understand why the earl was so troubled.

"You know Her Grace better than I."

"Hence, my concern, Miss Winlow! Could you have not done *something*?" He gestured vaguely.

"Calm yourself, my lord," Patience said; her concern for him was visible on her face. Setting down her cup of hot chocolate, she stood up and walked over to the small table where he kept various decanters. Choosing the one he had used earlier, she returned to his side and refilled his empty glass. "Drink."

A soft noise of satisfaction vibrated in her throat when he complied with her order. She set the decanter down on the table beside his chair and returned to the sofa positioned across from him. "You hired me as your sister's companion—"

"I must confess, I am disappointed in your efforts this afternoon," he said, glaring at her.

The earl was worried about his sister. Patience bit her lower lip and privately vowed not to lose her temper with the exasperating man. Was it her fault that he had introduced his sister to the older lady? *No.* Apparently, from the earl's unreasonable reaction, the Dowager Duchess of Solitea had been rather humble about her exploits.

Composed, Patience clasped her hands and said, "As Lady Meredith's companion, I can assure you nothing untoward transpired, Lord Ramscar. We encountered dozens of people in the park. Ladies and gentlemen. Lord Halthorn was mentioned by name because he made a favorable impression on your sister."

The earl fell back into his chair. Tired, he wearily scrubbed his face. "I wish the duchess had warned me that she was running off with Meredith."

"Perhaps she thought you trusted her."

"I do," he snapped, goaded by Patience's insinuation. "It's just— Damn me!"

She had never seen him so conflicted. "You did the right thing bringing your sister to London, my lord. Truly. Your sister was not as happy as she had claimed living her quiet life at Swancott. If I may be bold—"

"Are you any other way?" he quipped, causing her to smile.

She had more in common with his sister than he would ever realize. "I believe you were so focused on bringing her here that you never considered what might happen once she arrived in London."

"Meaning?"

Patience sensed he knew the direction of her

thoughts but needed to hear them aloud. "You cannot hold on to her forever. Lady Meredith is awakening, Lord Ramscar. If she is fortunate, she will find a gentleman who does not see her scars, but only the beautiful soul within."

Delicately yawning, Patience stood. The ball was in a matter of days. She and Lady Meredith would be rising early on the morrow. "You sister will make mistakes." Patience laughed, thinking of the thousands she had made over the years. "Young ladies in love often do. We cry and we mend. She will survive, I promise you."

As Patience headed for the door, she heard him grumble, "She might, but what about me?"

CHAPTER THIRTEEN

The night had finally arrived for Lady Meredith's birthday ball.

As Patience stood off to the side, quietly observing Lord Ramscar and his sister greeting the new arrivals along with the Dowager Duchess of Solitea, she felt pride in her small part in this evening's festivities. When she had told the earl that Lady Meredith was awakening, Patience had struck upon the truth. The young woman was quite beautiful.

For her introduction into polite society she had chosen to wear a ball dress of green satin with epaulette sleeves. A white net was attached to the petticoat. It was flounced with a wide band of matching green ribbon with detailed white lace at the hem. Tiny pink roses adorned her waist and slippers. With the assistance of one of the maids, Patience had pinned Lady Meredith's hair at her crown and then curled the ends. Aware she was sensitive about her facial scars, they arranged the curls to conceal what they could.

"Since you are a friend of Lady Meredith's, no one would have been offended if you had stood beside her in the receiving line."

Patience stared at the young woman and tried not to gape. The woman was stunning, about Patience's age and height, but that was where the similarities ended. She looked like a fairy queen with her dark cinnamon tresses and otherworldly green eyes. The lady reminded her of someone. Patience glanced at the Dowager Duchess of Solitea and smiled. "You must be her daughter, Lady Fayre."

"Indeed. And you must be Miss Winlow," she said, greeting her as if they were equals in a world where rank was everything.

Patience wrinkled her nose. "I gather your mother mentioned me."

"Yes, she spoke highly of you."

This time, she did not hide her surprise, causing her companion to giggle.

"Did she try to intimidate you?" Lady Fayre shook her head. "My mother is a good judge of character. Ram had told Mama that Lady Meredith's friend would be joining his household for the season, but it remained to be seen if you were willing to help your dear friend or were here for your own amusements."

A protest formed on Patience's lips, but the other woman hastily added, "The duchess's concerns about you faded minutes after meeting you. My mother admires spirit, and she claims that you are an interesting addition to Ram's odd household. That is a compliment, coming from her."

Patience's gaze returned to Lady Meredith. Sensing she was being watched, the young lady looked back at Patience and waved. Several ladies in the line leaned to the side to see whom the guest of honor was acknowledging. Feeling sort of foolish, Patience waved back. Satisfied, Lady Meredith resumed her conversation with the lady in front of her.

"The duchess has been fretting about this ball since Ramscar wrote her asking for her assistance. Neither one was optimistic that Lady Meredith would attend, and yet there she is, smiling and greeting her guests. I suspect some of the credit goes to you, Miss Winlow," Lady Fayre said kindly.

Patience basked in the glowing praise. She had

done as Lord Ramscar had asked. Lady Meredith looked lovely, and more important, she seemed genuinely happy. "Perhaps a little," Patience said brashly, and then abruptly clapped her hand over her mouth in embarrassment when she recalled her surroundings.

"Good grief! That sounded terribly arrogant."

Both ladies simultaneously burst into laughter.

"Are you certain you do not want to join your friend?"

"It really is not my place. Besides, this is Meredith's special day."

Lady Fayre nodded approvingly. "Then come along. My husband, Mr. Brawley, is upstairs checking on our son. He is a new father, and takes his responsibilities very seriously."

The dowager had mentioned her son-in-law in passing. Obviously, she had great respect and affection for her daughter's husband. "I have not had the pleasure of meeting Mr. Brawley."

"I will be certain to introduce you to him later." Companionably Lady Fayre took Patience by the elbow and guided her toward the large ballroom. "For now, let me introduce you to one of my dearest friends, Lord Darknell. He is sinfully handsome, but you did not hear such praise from me. And over there is another good friend, Lady Lyssa. You will like her. Her family is pressuring her to make a match this season. Oh dear," Lady Fayre said as they watched a large-nosed gentleman attempting to pull the statuesque blonde toward the doors that led outside. "Let us go rescue her from Lord Wilberfoss's clutches, and then we can seek out Darknell."

Bemused, Patience allowed Lady Fayre to lead her into the ballroom.

"Heavens, Ramscar, let the girl have some fun," the dowager lightly chided him. When he saw Patience disappear into the ballroom, his instincts told him to follow her. "Miss Winlow is with my daughter. Fayre will keep her out of trouble."

Not likely.

The Carlisles were an eccentric, unruly clan. He was tempted to remind the older woman that Fayre had had a spot of trouble several years earlier when she was seduced by Lord Thatcher Standish. Their brief affair had caused a scandal. Later she made a bargain with her future husband, Maccus Brawley, in hopes of gaining revenge on the scoundrel who had seduced and humiliated her. She had stirred up the family with her mischief. Her brother and her father had thirsted for both men's blood.

Wisely, Ramscar held his tongue.

"When we have done our duty, you can go check up on your Miss Winlow," the dowager said, shrewdly picking up on his interest in Patience.

Ramscar had resisted touching her again since the night he had discovered that she had never known pleasure in a man's arms. Her contrary mix of innocence and worldliness confused him. He desired her, but she aroused his protective nature. Both sides had been engaged in an internal battle, leaving him surly and hungry for a woman.

"Good evening, Lord Ramscar." The warm accented voice literally purred his name.

A month earlier when he thought of easing his hunger in a woman's soft body, he had thought of this woman. Angeline Grassi. Belatedly, he realized he had not contacted her since his return.

He also had not invited her.

Ramscar stared at the dowager, who merely shrugged. "The invitations were sent out before your arrival." *Before she had met Miss Winlow.* "I thought you would be pleased."

Not above creating an embarrassing to-do in front of his sister, Angeline pouted. "I have not seen you in months. I have looked forward to resuming our friendship."

The suggestiveness of the throaty comment was not missed by anyone within earshot, including his innocent sister. He quelled any further comments from the actress with a hard glance. "Miss Grassi, allow me to present my sister, Lady Meredith. Meredith, Miss Grassi is a well-known actress in London."

His sister gave the blonde a measuring look. Whatever Meredith saw displeased her. "I am sure she is, Brother. Well-known, that is."

Ramscar's jaw dropped at his sister's waspish remark.

Angeline looked puzzled, uncertain whether she had been insulted.

The dowager duchess laughed gaily. The older woman was plainly enjoying his discomfort. "Miss Grassi, I saw you in a play last October. It was an admirable performance."

Grateful to seize upon anything that would end the awkward moment, the actress said, "Thank you, Your Grace."

"Let us not keep you from the revelry in the ballroom. Later, if you like, you can tell me about the new play you are rehearsing."

"*Sì, grazie.*" Angeline eagerly nodded. She stared at him hungrily, letting him know her next words were for him alone. "I shall look forward to *it.*"

She strolled off, confident everyone was observing her departure.

Immediately, Meredith pounced on him. "Is that vulgar Miss Grassi your mistress?"

The older woman snapped open her fan and concealed half her face while she rapidly fanned herself. "Yes, Ramscar, I would like to hear this one, too."

Ram suspected the lady was laughing at him. He

offered them both an aggrieved look. "No. Miss Grassi is not my mistress."

Not anymore.

"Satisfied?"

Meredith glared at the distant figure of Angeline Grassi and stiffly nodded. "I will be as long as she is *not*!" Meredith stomped off in the direction of the ballroom. Most likely she was searching for Patience.

Ramscar was about to order Meredith to return, but he and the dowager duchess were alone. They had greeted the majority of their guests. Irritated, he glowered at the lady beside him. "Do you want to comment on my former mistress, too?"

Still laughing, the dowager shook her head. "I believe I will let your sister have the final say on Miss Grassi. I recognize a superior exit when I see it."

Upset by the obscene manner in which that horrid woman had stared at her brother, Meredith stepped into the ballroom not really knowing where she was heading. Despite her brother's denial, she knew he had bedded the actress. The woman thought she had a claim on Ram. She had only accepted the invitation this evening so she could issue a private invitation of her own.

Horrible, greedy creature.

Meredith was extremely disappointed in her

brother. He was an intelligent man. Why had he not seen beyond the pretty mask to the ambitious woman underneath? Were all men so easily beguiled? A couple walked by her, nodding and smiling as they passed. Meredith noted the gentleman's gaze had lingered on her cheek.

Her scars.

She brought her hand up to her cheek. Changing directions, she stepped on a gentleman's shoes. Appalled, she looked up to apologize and immediately recognized the familiar handsome face.

"L-l-lord Halthorn," she stammered, letting her hand move away from her cheek and drop to her side. She took several steps back and curtsied. "I was not aware you had received an invitation."

"Her Grace issued me a belated one." He stared into Meredith's face, momentarily forgetting that he was in the middle of an explanation. He shook his head, giving her a beatific smile that warmed her all the way down to her toes. "Forgive me for my tardiness. I had a prior commitment that I could not decline. I came to see you—" He cleared his throat and tried again. "It is your birthday. I-I brought you something."

Curious and touched that he had brought her a small gift, Meredith quietly watched as he retrieved something that he had tucked into one of the small pockets of his waistcoat.

He opened his hand, revealing a small conical shell.

"This is for me? It is lovely." Meredith was not merely being kind. The delicate dark and light brown lines and dots created a pleasing symmetrical pattern.

He carefully placed the shell on her palm. "*Voluta musica Linnaeus.*"

Meredith giggled. The words reminded her of a love spell she had once read in a romantic tale. "I beg your pardon?"

"Its scientific name," he said, amused. "I have an extensive collection of seashells from all over the world. This particular one was found in Tobago."

"Really?" She cradled the shell with both hands, admiring it. "I have never been to Tobago."

"Neither have I," he confessed, his expression rueful. "A friend sent me this specimen for my collection. I have been collecting specimens since I was a boy."

"Oh no." She offered the shell back to him. "This was meant for your collection. I could not take it."

Tenderly, he closed her fingers over the seashell. "If I want another, I will sail to Tobago and pluck it from the water. This one is clearly meant for you."

Meredith had never seen a more exquisite shell. She stared at her precious gift and then into the brown eyes of the gentleman who had been thoughtful enough to bring it to her. "Thank you, Lord Halthorn."

Smiling brilliantly up at him, she forgot about her anger over Angeline Grassi.

"Are you enjoying your first London ball, Miss Winlow?" Lord Everod courteously inquired as they strolled away from the other dancers.

The viscount had been an excellent dance partner, but he had not been the first. The second son of a baron had approached her while she had been chatting with Lady Fayre and her husband. Once the first dance had ended, several other gentlemen had approached Patience. Lord Everod was her fourth dance partner for the evening.

"Indeed, my lord." Patience searched the crowded ballroom until she saw Meredith. She was sitting on one of the sofas positioned against the wall, conversing with Lord Halthorn.

"Am I a boring companion, Miss Winlow?" the viscount asked, grinning at her when she realized how rude her behavior might seem.

Sensing he was merely teasing her, she said, "You are a tolerable companion, Lord Everod. I was just looking for Lady Meredith. I would not be a proper . . . friend if I thought only of myself."

"Ramscar isn't a tyrant, Miss Winlow." Lord

Everod gestured at all of the people around them. Expensively attired, many were content to just circulate and chat with their friends. Others were taking part in the dancing or playing cards in an adjoining room. "This is an evening where everyone selfishly indulges in their own amusements. Lady Meredith is over there smiling at her admirer. She is content. Relax, my dear. I am at your service, and willing to indulge any whim," he drawled suggestively.

Lord Everod was charming—and unquestionably a handsome scoundrel.

If she dared to whisper an outrageous suggestion into his ear such as a whim to swim naked in the Dowager Duchess of Solitea's fountain just beyond the open doors, Patience believed the viscount would immediately have her out the door.

There was a subtle leer in his expression that revealed that the man rarely refused a challenge.

"I do have a small request, my lord," she said in a low, faintly husky voice.

"Anything."

"Would you mind frightfully if I asked you to get me some punch?" Patience glanced pointedly at the huge crowd blocking the tables displaying the various refreshments. "I am awfully parched from dancing. However, I loathe facing the hordes." She gave him a polite smile.

The keen interest she had glimpsed in his gaze

was abruptly leashed. Lord Everod was not going to pursue her unless she was willing prey. Relieved, she slowly exhaled.

"As do I," he said, casting a loathing glance in the direction of the crowd. "However, I will brave them for your sake, Miss Winlow." Offering her a bow, he turned on his heel and left her alone.

As she observed his departure, she could not resist admiring his lazy, graceful stride. Lord Everod was an exceedingly handsome gentleman. Still, she seemed immune to his masculine allure. His proximity did not make her heart race, nor was she anticipating his return.

Unlike . . .

As if almost against her will, she found herself searching the faces around her for Lord Ramscar. He had disappeared shortly after her second dance partner had escorted her away from Lady Fayre and her friends. Patience had hoped Lord Ramscar might approach her and request a dance as well, but he seemed determined to maintain a respectful distance.

Aha! There.

Patience spotted him on the other side of the room. Nor was he alone. An elegant blond-haired lady was laughing at something he whispered in her ear. She laid her gloved hand on his arm. The intimacy in the mystery lady's tiny gesture stole Patience's breath. The way the blonde leaned into him, boldly met his stare, and kept her hand on his arm revealed that they had been lovers. Patience was certain of it. Over the years, she had discreetly observed people, studying and mimicking their movements in an attempt to improve her portrayals of the various characters she played. That woman felt she had a claim on the earl, a silent declaration that was not objectionable to Lord Ramscar.

Suddenly, the ballroom felt a little stifling.

"You poor thing," an unfamiliar woman said as she and her two friends circled around Patience, effectively cutting off her escape. "All alone. Oh, this will not do, do you not agree, ladies?"

Her two companions concurred.

Patience had not been introduced to the trio, nor was she particularly interested in procuring an introduction now. There was something about their leader that seemed peculiar. Perhaps it was her light blue eyes. Whenever the lady's gaze touched her, Patience felt a distinct chill.

Where the devil was Lord Everod? She could use his timely rescue. "I am—"

"We know who you are," the dark-haired woman said, cutting off Patience's explanation that she was waiting for her escort's return. "You are Lady Meredith's little friend."

Well, she had certainly been put in her proper diminutive place.

The shortest of the three cocked her head in a manner that reminded Patience of a bird. "Miss Winlow, is that not correct?" she asked with a hint of a lisp.

"Yes."

"We have been told that your people are dead," explained their stout companion wearing a turban that was too large for her head. Each time it listed to one side, the lady was obligated to straighten it or navigate the ballroom with one visible eye. "Rumor has it that the Knowdens brought you to London because they hope you might secure a respectable position in town."

It was amazing how gossip circulated so swiftly about a room. However, Patience preferred their rumors to the truth.

The slender dark-haired lady stroked the necklace adorning her throat, drawing attention to the piece. "Lord Ramscar is a generous man. He is so tolerant."

If he ever returned, Patience had another request for the viscount. She wanted him to make these three ladies vanish from her sight. None of the animosity she was feeling, however, was evident on her face. "That is a lovely necklace, Miss . . . ?"

The other woman was not as skilled at hiding her feelings. Her dislike was as apparent as the overly sweet floral scent she was wearing. "*Lady*

Dewberry," the young woman said in a haughty tone. "May I introduce my companions, Lady Perinot and Miss Nottige."

Patience dipped respectfully into a low curtsy. "An honor to meet all of you," she sweetly lied. Her gaze returned to the exquisite necklace Lady Dewberry was unworthy of owning. "I compliment your husband on his exquisite taste in jewelry. The pearls seem authentic. Are the stones genuine as well?"

She was deliberately being provoking. Besides making her study the movements of others, Julian Phoenix had taught her to recognize the differences between an expensive piece of jewelry and those made up of cheap paste.

The woman's pinched expression revealed her outrage. "Naturally, the citrine and diamonds are genuine, and are of the utmost quality. The Countesses of Dewberry never wear cut glass! Of all the nerve," she sputtered.

"I have returned from fighting the hordes, Miss Winlow," Lord Everod said, handing her a glass of punch. "I trust you will forgive me for leaving you alone."

He was forgiven as long as he did not abandon her to the three harpies.

The viscount's cool sweeping glance had Lady Dewberry's companions taking a step backward.

"Ladies," he said, his smile revealing plenty of sharp teeth. "I promised my dance partner some fresh air. If you will excuse us."

Not bothering to wait for their consent, he took Patience by the elbow and guided her toward the doors. When they were out of earshot, she said, "Thank you."

Distractedly, he murmured, "The fault is mine. I should have warned you that you have already made enemies."

Patience blinked at him. "Enemies? I just met them. Why would they take an instant dislike to me?" Perhaps the three ladies were snobbish bullies who took pleasure in attacking anyone they considered beneath them.

"It isn't you, pretty Patience," he said, stroking her cheek with three fingers. Not wanting to call any more attention to them, he immediately withdrew his hand. "You are a beautiful unmarried lady who happens to be under Ramscar's personal protection. Certain ladies of the *ton* will despise you on principle, for you have achieved something they have not."

She took a sip of the punch the viscount had procured for her. It was too warm and sweet to quench her thirst, but it eased the dryness in her throat. "Such as?"

"His interest."

Patience made a scoffing sound.

"No, really." When Lord Everod offered her a genuine smile, she merely gawked at him. The effect was devastating, and she was positive the rogue knew it.

"Ram has not been exactly discreet this evening," the viscount said, shaking his head at his friend's inexcusable behavior. "I have caught him staring at you on numerous occasions, and I am certain others have noticed his telling actions as well."

CHAPTER FOURTEEN

It had been her first formal ball.

She had done well, Patience thought as she pulled the last hairpin from her hair and shook her blond tresses free from their confines. Rather pleased with herself, when she and Meredith had arrived at the house she had asked Scrimm for a small indulgence. A bath. The butler was worth his weight in gold. Within the hour, servants had carried into her bedchamber a small tub and buckets of hot water. Patience could not wait to soak her aching feet.

Oh, what an incredible evening!

She sat down on a chair and carefully removed her slippers. Pulling up her skirts, she untied her garters and slipped off her stockings. Lady Fayre had introduced Patience to so many people she would not recall their names when she awoke in the morning. Lord Darknell, as the lady had promised, was indeed sinfully handsome. He had even partnered Patience in a dance. As Lady Fayre had predicted, her friend Lady Lyssa had been eternally grateful to them for saving her from the drunken amorous attentions of Lord Wilberfoss. Both ladies had invited Patience and Meredith to explore the shops on Bond Street in the near future.

The incident with Lady Dewberry and her cronies had been unpleasant. For whatever reason, the young countess had taken an instant dislike to Patience. The brief exchange might have ruined the rest of the evening, if she had let it. Fortunately, Lord Everod had rescued her from their malicious clutches and restored her former good spirits.

Patience stood and gently tugged the edge of her bodice downward. While she had been waiting for the hot water, Meredith's personal maid had undone the back of Patience's dress and loosened the laces of her corset so she could undress without assistance.

The gorgeous, expensive dress Lord Ramscar had purchased for her slithered down her body and piled at her feet. The corset swiftly followed. Dressed only in her chemise, she stooped over and gathered up her clothing. Humming to herself, she acknowledged that she had never owned anything so costly. With loving care, she laid the dress out on her bed. Later, after her bath, she would put all her treasures away.

Her thoughts turned to Meredith.

The young woman had been incredible this evening. Only Patience and Lord Ramscar knew how difficult it had been for Meredith to smile and chat with the dowager duchess's friends. Patience had noticed on several occasions that Lord Halthorn had engaged Meredith in a private conversation. The viscount had given her a pretty seashell. Lord Ramscar had raised his brows when his sister showed him Lord Halthorn's gift, and thankfully resisted sharing his true thoughts. Nevertheless, Patience doubted a negative opinion would have deflated Meredith's enthusiasm. She was treating Lord Halthorn's gift like it was a handful of the rarest diamonds.

Ramscar had kept a respectful distance from Patience for most of the evening. He only approached her when other people were hovering around her. She had danced with his charming friends Lord Byrchmore and Lord Everod and Lady Fayre's husband, Mr. Brawley. Patience was not even aware of how deeply she had been anticipating an invitation from Lord Ramscar until her hopes had been utterly dashed. At the end of the evening, he had placed her and Meredith in the family coach and bid them a good night.

He had remained behind.

Patience crossed her arms across her breasts and rubbed away the slight chill she felt on her arms. She loathed admitting it, but she was still stinging from his intentional slight. It was because of the actress, Meredith confided to Patience on their drive back to the town house. Angeline Grassi. Lord Ramscar apparently had a fondness for actresses of the legitimate theater. Although he had denied it to Meredith, she was convinced the woman was his current mistress. The woman had sought him out this evening for an assignation.

He is with her now.

Oh, how it hurt! Patience had glimpsed him sharing secrets with Miss Grassi. Meredith was correct. The actress had touched him with a familiarity that reeked of intimacy. From the brief passion that had flared between them, she had deduced that Lord Ramscar was a virile, demanding lover. He obviously desired a lover who matched his voracious appetites, not an unskilled miss who had been coerced with pain into pleasuring her one and only lover.

Patience sighed. She leaned down, letting her finger trail along the surface of the water.

It was still warm.

Bending over, she grabbed the hem of her chemise and pulled the soft linen over her head. Wholly bare, she glanced at the door. Patience knew it was locked. She had seen to the task herself once the footmen had emptied the last bucket of steaming-hot water and departed the room with a ribald comment that it was a shame she was unwilling to share her bath. The footmen meant no offense. It was harmless teasing. Still, a sense of unease rippled through her. She glanced at the windows. The draperies were tightly drawn. Why could she not shake off the feeling of being watched?

Patience wrinkled her nose. She was being silly.

It was late and the servants had retired to their quarters. No one cared whether or not Lady Meredith's hired companion was indulging in a bath. Laughing softly, she stepped into the elegant tub. The warm water felt heavenly. She had never bathed in anything so lovely or whimsical. Hewn from wood, the tiny exterior of the tub was carved into the shape of a sea horse. A child would have been able to sit comfortably within it. Patience might have been able to squeeze into the narrow interior, but the thought of becoming stuck kept her from trying. A small ledge had been designed at the back so bathers could sit down while they washed.

Patience reached into the water and retrieved the large sea sponge. She held it high and squeezed. Water sluiced over her hair and face, momentarily blinding her. A muffled noise to her right had her whirling around and wiping the water from her eyes.

She was not alone.

Blinking rapidly to clear her blurring vision, she realized Ramscar stood off in the corner of the room, silently watching her from the shadows.

Even in the dim light, she saw the feral hunger burning in his hazel green gaze.

Her mouth went dry. Patience had nothing to conceal her nakedness from him. She would have to get out of the tub and move closer to him to reach the towels she had set aside. Her damp hair covered her breasts. She slowly lowered the large sea sponge to her sex.

"I locked the door. How did you get in?" she quietly asked. Patience was more curious than angry at his intrusion.

He stepped out of the shadows into the small ring of light the fire in the hearth and branch of candles on the table provided. He wordlessly stalked her, approached her in a casual fashion as if not to frighten her. "I was waiting for you."

It was a simplistic reply to actions that would complicate everything between them. When had he returned to the house?

"You stayed behind. I thought you were with—" She abruptly closed her mouth. Heavens, she was not about to mention his mistress. Patience was fiercely pleased he was not with Angeline Grassi. The thought of him pleasuring the actress with his hands and mouth, of him mounting her and finding satisfaction in her long, lithe body, was a disagreeable one. Then why was she resisting him, hesitating over what they could have together?

As he came up to the edge of the tub, Patience noticed his breeches did little to conceal his arousal. "Did you want a bath?"

Ramscar gave her a wry grin. "I want to share yours."

Patience glanced at the interior and giggled. "For once, you were rather shortsighted, my lord. If you desired to bathe with me, you should have commissioned a larger tub."

Admiring the way her puckered nipples were poking through her damp hair, he absently nodded in agreement. "I will have one commissioned tomorrow."

While he had been waiting for her, he had unknotted and removed his cravat. His coat had also been discarded. He had come to her room intent on seducing her. Her toes curled at the thought. "I was rather accommodating, was I not?" Patience stared down at her naked body. He had observed her as she had removed her clothing, and it had aroused him. She carefully sat down on the narrow ledge.

"Yes."

The scoundrel did not even try to lie.

Rolling her eyes, she threw the wet sponge at him. It hit him squarely in the chest. Ramscar caught it and tossed the sponge into the tub. "What would you have done if I had not ordered a bath?" she asked.

He pulled his shirt over his head. "The outcome would have still been the same."

The man's arrogance was truly insufferable.

She was tempted to throw the sponge at him again. "No."

"Protest if you must, my pretty lady." She looked away when his hands moved to his waist. "We both know this night was inevitable."

Patience was too stubborn to concede gracefully. She had suffered all evening because he had stayed away from her. Oh, when she thought of him smiling at that Angeline Grassi, while she prayed he would ask her to dance. She wanted to punish him for the misery he had inflicted on her heart. Closing her eyes, she listened as he removed his shoes, stockings, and, finally, breeches. Each item had a distinct muffled sound as it was discarded. She felt the searing heat of his body beside her.

"Has a man ever bathed you?"

Her eyes snapped open at his rude question. The way he was grinning at her, Patience could tell that he was deliberately baiting her.

"Dozens. Nay, legions," she brazenly lied. "This is the first time I have bathed alone in years!"

"I must respectfully disagree," he said, retrieving the sodden sea sponge.

Her right brow lifted quizzically. "Are you calling me a liar, Lord Ramscar?"

Ramscar shot up and nipped her lower lip before she could react. "No, Patience. I am just reminding you that you will not be bathing alone."

Patience was fuming and wet, but Ram thought she was the most beautiful woman he had ever been blessed to view naked. It took every ounce of his restraint to refrain from scooping her out of the tub and carrying her to the bed. Once he had her spread out beneath him, he would show her what they had been denying themselves.

She had looked so delectable this evening. As he watched her flirt and dance with his friends, it had taken all of his control not to separate her from the gentlemen she had partnered, throw her over his shoulder, and carry her off into the night. Instead, he had stayed away from her and brooded. He regretted that his coolness had hurt her feelings. At one point in the evening, Angeline had cornered him and Patience had seen them together. Even from a distance, he saw the hurt glittering in her blue gaze.

Angeline had whispered to him that she was willing to cast aside her new lover. She was repentant for her faithlessness. In her meager defense, she claimed that she had missed Ramscar terribly and it was a fit of anger that had provoked her to invite another man into her bed. If Ram left the ball with her, she was prepared to forgive him for ignoring her all these long months.

Ramscar's self-imposed celibacy and his unfulfilled desire for Patience had him briefly contemplating his former mistress's enticing invitation. Losing himself in a willing woman who would expect nothing from him except an expensive token of his appreciation the next day seemed preferable to spending another night denying himself the vulnerable lady who ensnared his senses and made him half-mad with lust.

Or it had seemed appealing, until he had seen Patience's woeful expression when he had escorted the ladies to their coach. In that moment, he knew it was not just a willing woman he hungered for; he wanted Patience.

Ramscar picked up the soap ball poised on the lip of the tub and rubbed it against the sponge.

She frowned at his benign actions. "What are you doing?"

Setting the soap down, he bent over and lifted her leg out of the water. "I thought I was being obvious. I am washing you."

Fearful that she would slip off the ledge, she gripped the sides of the sea horse–shaped tub while he scrubbed her leg. Her telling gaze lingered just below his navel. "Your actions are not the only thing that is evident."

Ram sighed as he glanced down. His cock was fully erect and primed for mating. There was little he could do to hide his present condition. With his cock jutting from its hairy nest, he could not blame Patience for assuming he would lunge for her. The instinct to take her simmered just below his civility. He released her leg and lifted the other one.

"A natural reaction to your proximity. Perhaps it will abate with familiarity," he said, his inflection hopeful, though he doubted his own words. "Stand up." He let go of her shapely limb.

"You cannot wash me *there*," she said emphatically, crossing her arms over her breasts.

If she needed coaxing, Ram did not mind in the

least. "Evidently, I am quite capable, and I am enjoying the view immensely. Now stand up so I can scrub your charming backside."

Patience rolled her eyes at him, but she stood, presenting him her back. He had not been exaggerating when he told her that he liked her back. Soaping the sponge again, he moved her hair to the front so he could appreciate her silky flesh. Ram pressed his thighs against the edge of the tub. His cock poked her in the hip. She did not screech or jump away, and he thought her silence was very telling.

He dipped the sponge into the water and rinsed the soap off her back. "You are still out of reach," he said, wanting to rub his arousal against the soapy cleft of her buttocks. Ram circled around to the back and straddled the tub. Gently he sat down on the small ledge. The tub might have been too small for them to share, but he had a mutually satisfying compromise. "Much better. Come closer, Patience."

She inched closer to him.

"Face me, lady," he ordered throatily.

After a moment's hesitation, she complied. "I can wash myself, Ramscar."

He surprised her by handing over the sponge. "Then show me."

Patience accepted the sponge and with brisk efficiency washed her face and both arms. She was doing her best to avoid gazing at his swollen cock, but he had caught her nervously peeking at it a time or two.

"Your breasts. It would be utterly criminal for you to ignore those beauties," he prompted when she hesitated.

Glowering at him, she washed her breasts with the enthusiasm of an elderly nun.

Was she mad? Why was she rushing? Patience undoubtedly did not appreciate her breasts as much as he did. Ram halted her brisk movements by resting his hand on her hip.

"Nicely done," he praised her, grazing his nails against the contour of her hip. "However, there are other, more pleasurable ways to go about the task."

Patience sensed Ram was no longer content to stroke her with his hungry gaze. A man like him was born to conquer, to take what he desired. The sponge plopped into the water forgotten. She leaned forward and kissed him softly on the lips. "Like this," she whispered against his mouth.

His manhood jerked in response. It heartily approved. "Show me again," he softly entreated.

She positioned herself between his legs and braced her hands on his shoulders. Her entire body tingled as her lips moved slowly, thoroughly, over his warm lips. Ramscar was a wondrous kisser. He knew the right amount of pressure to make her senses sizzle. The clever thrust and retreat he did with his tongue teased her to the point of mindless abandonment.

Ramscar cupped her breasts and kneaded the pliant flesh. Her nipples plumped like succulent raspberries as each rubbed against his palms. He broke away from her mouth and nipped her on the chin with his teeth. Drawing her in closer, he suckled her left breast. A pleasurable contraction caused the muscled walls of her womb to quiver. Her sheath tightened almost painfully in anticipation. Only Ramscar had touched her in such a manner. Phoenix had only been interested in having a lover who attended to his needs. The man in front of her thought only of building on her pleasure.

Patience moaned when his fingers stroked the cleft between her legs. Like her dreams of him and the night she had visited him in his bedchamber, the hot intimate feminine heat was slick with anticipation, the honeyed wetness permitting his fingers to penetrate her without discomfort. Her hand glided down his chest and shackled his jutting arousal. The hot flesh pulsed in her hand.

He flicked his tongue over her nipple. "No more flirtatious games, Patience. You have distracted me until I think of nothing but bedding you."

"You credit me with too much power, my lord,"

she said, closing her eyes when his fingers fluttered within her feminine sheath. "I wager no lady has held sway over you for long."

Ramscar did not seem to hear her. He was too intent on exploring her body. He withdrew his fingers from her snug sheath and tasted the moisture coating them. "Just as I thought. Your desire tastes like a spicy temptress's brew meant to ensnare a man's senses." He kissed her hip bone. "Consider me enslaved."

Without asking, he hooked his hand around her right thigh. Patience locked her arms around his neck while he silently coaxed her down so she straddled him. The position opened her, leaving her feeling awkward and vulnerable. She glanced down between their bodies and watched as the length of his manhood rubbed enticingly against her sex.

Ramscar threaded his fingers through her long damp hair, pushing her tangled tresses to the back. "Lift your hips slightly."

At her blank look, he grasped her by the waist and raised her high enough to position the thick head of his manhood over her feminine portal. Patience squirmed against the uncompromising pressure of his commanding penetration. She always disliked this part. This aspect of him did not resemble her dream at all. The earl was too big!

"You can," he said, deducing her panicked

thoughts. "Easy now." Adjusting his angle a degree, he eased into her sheath with tiny upward thrusts until she could wrap her legs around his hips.

Patience rested her cheek against his shoulder. His arousal stretched her, making her wholly aware of his invasion. There was no pain, but she could not fathom how to move. "I never dreamed that you were so large."

He smiled into her hair. "You dreamed of me? Of us as lovers?" He sounded pleased by the notion.

She nipped his shoulder with her teeth. The man's arrogance would not be contained if she confirmed his suspicions. "No. A slip of the tongue. I was thinking of another," she lied.

"Witch!" Ramscar swatted her backside. "I'll show you how to use that wicked tongue of yours properly." He fastened his mouth firmly to hers and devoured. He did not release her lips until they were both breathless. Panting, he said, "On the morrow, you will think of no other man but me."

CHAPTER FIFTEEN

Patience Winlow was a capricious creature. Part innocent, part temptress, the lady fascinated him. Ram tried to dampen his raging ardor by reminding himself that she was a skillful actress. She had had previous lovers and, perhaps, had practiced this blood-thrumming façade to perfection. She had succeeded in whetting his interest, and now he was fully prepared to reward her for her efforts.

The little actress would soon learn she was caught in her own sensual snare.

"You fit me quite nicely," he said, gritting his teeth as he helped her slide up and down his rigid cock. He had adjusted his legs and secured them against the exterior of the sea horse–shaped tub so he could better control their movements.

Patience sighed on a downward stroke and leaned closer to place little kisses along his brows. She continued across his cheek, her goal his ear. Ram turned his head to accommodate her. She bit his earlobe and then flicked the tip of her tongue over a sensitive spot just behind his ear.

A soft purr of contentment vibrated in her throat. "You are very cunning."

"I have always thought so," he quipped, not really certain why she thought him so clever. Nor did he care while he held her wet, naked body against him.

She opened one eye and studied his face. "You have placed me in a unique position."

He snorted at the politeness infused in her observation while his cock was buried so deep into her tight sheath that he could feel her heart beating. "When you tire of this one, I know several more that will amuse you."

Her brows furrowed at his boast. "Are they equally deceptive?"

"Deceptive?" He bucked up against her so she was aware of every inch of him. "I thought I was being extremely conspicuous."

She silently stared at him, clearly taken aback by his crudeness. "I was not speaking of *it*, you silly man!" She laughed and playfully shoved him on the shoulder. "I was referring to this position, me on top of you. I should be the one who has all the control, and yet—"

Ah, he immediately grasped what she was trying to explain. She seemed genuinely baffled by her predicament. As he had first suspected, her experience in carnal matters had been very limited.

"And yet you seem vulnerable to my whims." To prove his point, he ground his pelvis against her hard enough to make the tub rock and quake.

Patience dug her nails into his shoulders. She pressed her forehead to his. "Yes. Very much so."

Ram slid his hands over her firm buttocks, savoring the building tension he was creating in both of them with his relentless thrusting. He did not know if he could give Patience the control she was asking for. He had been born to protect and dominate those under his rule. His previous lovers had found him indulgent and creative in bed. However, there had never been any doubt that he was in charge.

"You'll learn," he murmured, nuzzling her throat and losing interest in the subject. Ram loved the way her breasts still slick with soap rubbed against his chest. Unfortunately, the tiny sea horse–shaped tub had never been designed for the rigorous demands of lovemaking. It rocked stern to bow with each shattering thrust. The water within slapped against the sides like a tumultuous sea.

"Oh, Ramscar! I feel—" Patience tossed her head back and cried out as her climax overwhelmed her.

Her glorious uninhibited abandonment was a siren's call for Ram's taut body. Quickening his movements, he sensed his own release was approaching. Their frenetic movements had made the small tub extremely unstable. It rocked in tempo, sending Ram deeper than he could have managed alone. Heedless of the potential danger, he buried his face into her breast and hastened his strokes.

"Oh-oh—Ram!" Patience cried out, another orgasm claiming her. She sank her sharp teeth into his shoulder as she mindlessly rode him.

His restraint shattered, Ram pulled her up tightly against him, his cock swelling in anticipation of the impending release. The subtle shift in weight capsized the small overburdened tub. Entwined with Patience, Ram fell backward. The back of his head and his back collided with the hardwood floor. He grunted at the impact as lukewarm water washed over them.

Horrified that he had been hurt, Patience crawled

off him and immediately began searching for injuries. "Good grief, Ramscar. Where does it hurt?"

Everywhere.

He could not answer her. The blasted fall had knocked the air out of his lungs. A pity the pain and lack of air had done nothing to quell his ardor. He curled his hand around his cock and rolled onto his side away from her. His body would not be denied. Ram clenched his teeth as his fingers squeezed the swollen head of his cock. To his utter mortification, he pumped his seed onto the floor.

Patience picked up a towel and returned to Ramscar's side. He was breathing heavily, and his body quaked. With his fist curled tightly around his manhood, she averted her gaze, realizing he was not as injured as she had initially feared.

She knelt at his side, facing his back. "I brought you a towel," she said softly. "We have made a real mess. I doubt Scrimm will grant me another bath."

Ramscar blindly reached for the towel she offered him. He pulled the cloth over his hips. "Christ, it was a debacle!"

Her lower lip quivered at his harsh statement. Until they had capsized the tiny tub, she had thought their lovemaking extraordinary. "My apologies, my lord. As you have just discovered, my experience in these matters is very limited. You should have accepted Miss Grassi's generous invitation if you desired a seasoned companion."

Despite the water pooling on the floorboards, Ramscar rolled toward Patience; his hot gaze lashed her. "I have no intention of discussing my former mistress with you," he said succinctly, rubbing the damp towel against his groin.

So Meredith had been correct about the couple's relationship, after all.

He carelessly tossed the towel aside. It was impossible not to notice the earl was still aroused. Oblivious to his nakedness, he climbed to his feet. "Furthermore, the only debacle is me! Ever since that day I kissed you by the pond, I have anticipated the day I would lay you down onto my bed and sate myself between your soft thighs." Thoroughly disgusted, Ramscar gestured at the watery mess at their feet. "And what do I do? I crack my skull and spine in one ruthless blow, and then hastily spill my seed as recklessly as a youth who has never glimpsed a woman's bared breast."

He stomped across the wet floor and pulled her up against his hard muscled body. "I did not want Angeline Grassi in my bed this evening. Whatever we shared was brief, and ended months ago." He lowered his head and rubbed his nose against Patience's.

"You were so beautiful this evening. I wanted to challenge every gentleman who approached you."

The coolness of the air made her shiver and snuggle closer for warmth. "You never asked me to partner you in a dance." Patience bit her lip, regretting her words. Now he knew how disappointed she was that he had not danced with her.

Ramscar roguishly grinned at her admission. His nails lightly scraped the length of her spine. "I was trying to be noble."

Noble? By ignoring her, yet speaking to his former mistress? Patience's eyes narrowed at his unlikely excuse. "Maybe we should mop up this water with a few towels."

"I was. Truly," he said, cupping her buttocks and maneuvering her closer. The length of his arousal pressed against her belly. "I had vowed to keep my hands off you. Each time I was close to you, I felt myself weakening. I knew if I touched your hand while we danced, all was lost."

The hurt she had experienced from the slight vanished with his explanation. A soft cry erupted from her lips when he scooped her up into his arms. "Did the fall addle you? Put me down."

"I will." Ramscar carried her over to her bed. He dropped her onto the bed. She bounced as she fell against the mattress. Covering her with the length of his body, he parted her legs and promptly slid his manhood into her until she gasped. "Our first time was a minor debacle, but I'm a gent who learns from his errors."

Imbedded to the hilt, he moved his hips against her and flexed. She threaded her fingers into his hair and moaned.

"Let me prove it to you."

After his first invigorating thrust, Patience forgot all about mopping up the water that was ruining the floor.

Patience awoke the next morning alone.

Shoving her tangled hair from her face, she sat up with a yawn. It was then that she realized she was naked. She glanced down at her body, viewing it differently than she had before Ramscar had stepped out of the shadows and offered to bathe her. As she had guessed, the earl was a virile, demanding lover. There was not an inch of her that he had not touched with his skillful fingers or tongue. The stickiness between her thighs reminded her of the hidden places he had eagerly plundered.

Ramscar had been quite thorough.

After he had carried her to the bed, he had proved to her that any doubts she might have had about his stamina or expertise as a lover were unfounded. Panting and sobbing his name, she had climaxed four times before he had sought his own release. Once he was sated, Patience had expected him to pull out of her body and leave her. Phoenix had always pushed her out of the bed once his needs had been satisfied.

Ramscar surprised her again.

He had rolled her onto her back and massaged her body, beginning with her feet. Grinning at the memory, she idly rubbed her finger over the two bite marks he had left on her breast. By the time he had worked his way up to her breasts, his love play had suddenly turned serious. Parting her legs, he slipped easily into her and rocked against her until they were both breathless.

Between the excitement of the ball and Ramscar's carnal demands, Patience had collapsed into a deep sleep. She had awoken several hours later. Rolling over onto her side, she discovered that Ramscar was also awake. Wordlessly, he pulled her leg so it hugged his hip, and gently coaxed his manhood into her. The frenzied passion of the previous hours had given way to tenderness. When she climaxed, she took him with her. The sensation of him pulsing inside her in tempo with her own release had been overwhelming and glorious. She had wept in his arms for the sheer beauty of it.

Her tears no longer seemed to worry him. He

had cuddled her against his side until they had both allowed exhaustion to claim them.

Patience retrieved her chemise from the floor. Pulling it on over her head, she winced when she noticed the dampness on the floor. Ramscar might not care about the condition of his floorboards; however, Scrimm would be very displeased with her once he learned of the mess.

She was not upset that Ramscar had left her while she slept. He was the Earl of Ramscar. Certain proprieties had to be maintained, not only for the staff but also for Meredith's sake. His sister had been upset that Angeline Grassi had been his lover. Would Meredith be equally distressed to learn he had replaced the blond temptress with Patience?

Did one night of lovemaking turn her into Ramscar's mistress? She was not exactly clear on the etiquette of taking a lover. However, one thing was certain—a gentleman did not install his mistress within his own household. It was expected that a gentleman would tuck his mistress away from prying eyes so he might inconspicuously visit her on occasion. Ramscar was not following the rules. Oh, how he must be crowing at his good fortune. As long as they were discreet, he could keep her in his household and summon her to his bed at a whim.

Patience glanced at the tiny bruise on her breast. She doubted she would be able to deny him if he came to her again. He had deliberately marked her as his. Strangely, she was not as unsettled by the idea as she should have been. She scooped up the wet towel he had discarded the previous evening and dropped the dripping cloth into the tub.

She froze at the soft knock on her door.

Patience cleared her throat. "Yes?"

"It is Meredith. May I enter?"

Patience stared at the door, appalled by the reasonable request. From her perspective, the rumpled bed and the carelessly discarded clothing were akin to a den of iniquity. "I have yet to dress."

"Very well. I will wait for you on the stairs," Meredith said through the door. She moved closer to the door. "You need to dress quickly. Something has happened. A man from Bow Street has been summoned and my brother is demanding your presence in the library."

It was not the friendly summons she had anticipated. Why had a Bow Street Runner been sent for? Hastily, Patience dressed. The answers she craved awaited her downstairs.

CHAPTER SIXTEEN

True to her word, Meredith had been waiting for Patience on the stairs. Sitting on one of the steps, Meredith had been admiring the seashell Lord Halthorn had given her. She stood at the soft sound of Patience's approach.

"What has happened?" she asked in a hushed voice.

"One of my brother's friends, the Duke of Solitea, entered the breakfast room unannounced. He mentioned that there had been a troubling incident at the ball, but he seemed reluctant to speak of it in front of me. They went into the library. My brother appeared an hour later to order Scrimm to send someone for a Bow Street Runner." Meredith took a deep breath. "And you."

The news did not bode well.

She touched Meredith on the arm, wanting to reassure her friend. "I am certain it is nothing."

Patience descended the stairs and headed for the library.

She squared her shoulders and lifted her chin before she knocked.

"Enter," Ramscar said, his voice gruff and unwelcoming.

If Patience had hoped to glimpse her tender lover, she was about to be disappointed. When she walked into the library, she was confronted by two stern-faced gentlemen who were used to getting answers. She curtsied. "My lord, you sent for me?"

Both gentlemen rose from their chairs as she entered the room. Lord Ramscar had been seated at his desk, while the Duke of Solitea had casually propped his hip against the edge of the desk. She had evidently interrupted a serious conversation between the two gentlemen.

"Miss Winlow, thank you for your promptness. My apologies for disturbing you after our late evening," Ramscar said as he gestured for her to sit. "May I present a good friend of mine, Fayne Carlisle, Duke of Solitea."

Looking up through lowered lashes, Patience demurely curtsied. In spite of his grim expression, the duke was another striking specimen of male perfection. His long cinnamon hair was a darker hue than his sister's and tied in a queue at his nape. Approximately the same age as Ramscar, he stood three inches taller than his friend. Lacking the flirtatious demeanor of his other friends Lord Everod and Lord Byrchmore, the duke observed her through unfathomable green eyes.

"Your Grace. I had the pleasure of meeting your sister, Lady Fayre, and her husband at the ball last evening. The family resemblance is quite noticeable," Patience said, pretending not to react to the tension in the room.

The duke's expression did not soften at the mention of his family. She swallowed thickly as she sat down in the chair the earl had offered. "Has something happened?"

Ramscar and the duke exchanged glances. It was the earl who answered her question. "Regrettably, yes. One of the guests had a valuable necklace stolen last evening."

Patience bit her lower lip as she digested the news. If the earl had placed his hand on her chest, he would have been alarmed by its hammering tempo. "It is terrible news. Was her coach robbed on the drive home from the ball?"

The duke's keen gaze was as unsettling as it was unrelenting. "The thief was brazen. He plucked the necklace from Lady Dewberry's neck."

Patience glanced away, wishing the victim had been anyone other than the Countess of Dewberry. The thief had superior taste. The necklace had caught Patience's eye as well. It was exactly the sort of necklace the troupe would have stolen. Her breath caught in her throat. Patience glanced at Ramscar, silently urging him to meet her gaze.

He ruthlessly ignored her mute plea.

It was then that the knowledge seeped into her chaotic thoughts.

Both men were aware of her brief altercation with the countess.

"Lord Ramscar . . . Your Grace . . . am I being accused of this theft?" she asked, clasping her hands so tightly together that her knuckles were bloodless.

"No," the earl angrily snapped.

The duke shot his friend an amused glance. The humor faded when the duke's green gaze fixed on her face. "Naturally, everyone is concerned about the theft. Anyone who spoke with Lady Dewberry is being questioned."

"Someone might have witnessed the theft or

noticed a stranger lingering near the countess," Ramscar added, Patience supposed as a belated attempt to ease her concerns.

Again, His Grace looked askance at his friend. "There is that possibility." The duke returned his attention back to her. "Miss Winlow, this is an awkward situation that has been presented to me. I regret that we did not first meet last evening. My sister spoke very favorably of you. Ram also vehemently defends your good character."

Patience's eyes became misty with tears. The earl's postures conveyed his annoyance about the entire subject. However, he had yet to glance at her. She blinked furiously at the stinging moisture threatening to ruin her composure.

"Neither of you has asked, but I will tell you. I did not steal Lady Dewberry's necklace," Patience said, retrieving her handkerchief. She delicately sniffed.

Slightly uncomfortable that he had upset a lady his sister liked and Lord Ramscar considered under his protection, the duke shifted his stance. "The countess claims that you had seemed inordinately curious to know if the stones were genuine or paste."

Patience shrugged negligently. "The workmanship was praiseworthy, even if its owner was not."

The duke's full lips twitched at her comment.

"Everod had mentioned the countess and her companions had greeted you warmly."

She crossed her eyes upon hearing Lord Everod's version of the incident. "Lady Dewberry sought me out, Your Grace. I personally wished she had not bothered."

Now more than ever.

Patience rose from her chair, her head high. "If I am not about to be hauled off to the magistrate in chains, may I excuse myself?"

The Duke of Solitea nodded. "My apologies for the intrusion, Miss Winlow. Dewberry has been pestering my mother since his hysterical countess realized her necklace had vanished, and naturally I was unwillingly pulled into the affair. When his lady pointed an accusatory finger in your direction, Lord Dewberry was determined to have an audience with you." The duke's expression revealed that he had done Patience a favor by sparing her from that particular ordeal. "For the sake of avoiding bloodshed, I thought it best that I act on his behalf."

"Then I wish you well on your hunt, Your Grace." Unsmiling, she inclined her head toward Ramscar. "My lord."

Patience left the library as swiftly as she could without arousing either man's suspicion. Oh, how she despised that hateful Lady Dewberry! If Patience *had* taken the countess's precious necklace, she certainly would not have so boldly admired it in front of witnesses!

"Patience, wait!" Ramscar called after her.

She was in no mood to humor him. How could he have treated her so coldly after the passionate night they had shared?

Curse him, and her stupidity for trusting him!

"Did you not hear me?" He grabbed her arm and forced her to halt. "I told you to wait."

Infuriated, she turned on him. "And I told you that I did not steal that rude lady's necklace." Patience poked her finger into his chest. "It appears neither one of us was paying attention."

Disgusted, and more than a little hurt, she shrugged off his grip and marched toward the stairs. Patience squeaked when Ramscar spun her around and tossed her over his shoulder. Her forehead bounced against his back. She glanced up to see Meredith staring openmouthed on the stairs. The young duke strolled out of the library in time to see Patience's humiliating position.

"Put me down, you heartless blackguard!" she growled.

"Christ, Ram," His Grace shouted at his friend's back. "That is no way to ease a lady's fears."

Ramscar failed to respond to the duke's casual ribbing. He carried her into another room and kicked the door shut behind them.

• • •

Solitea likely thought Ramscar had lost his head.

Ram lowered Patience to her feet. She immediately retaliated by kicking him in the shins. Her skirts hampered her efforts and she screeched in frustration. "How dare you? Of all the most disrespectful, arrogant—"

"You refused to listen to me!" he roared at her. He rubbed his forehead with the knuckle of his thumb. Ram had brought her into a small anteroom next to the conservatory because it gave them some privacy.

"Your sister was on the stairs," Patience hissed, and moved away from him.

Ram cringed. His actions of late could hardly be considered discreet. "I will explain my actions to her later. For now, I offer you an apology."

Patience looked like she wanted to kick him again. "I do not want it."

"Well, you have it just the same." Ramscar risked her wrath by putting his hands on her again. "Damn it, I do not think you are a bloody thief!" He had been as stunned as Patience had clearly been when Solitea had shown up and told him about the theft.

Her anger faded into hurt. It tore at his conscience. "Now who is lying? You could not even look me in the eye."

Truth be told, he had been livid when Solitea had

told him of Lady Dewberry's accusation. "After what we had shared, I felt like the heartless blackguard you accused me of being for even summoning you for questioning."

"Ramscar, I did not steal her necklace." Patience did not pull away from him, for which he was grateful. "Ask your friend Lord Everod. He will tell you those women—"

"Are cold, jealous bitches," Ramscar said fiercely, irritated that she believed his friend would staunchly defend her and he would not. "They sought you out, and cruelly reminded you of your inferiority. If you had told me what they had said to you, I would have ruthlessly ended their little games."

Patience wearily closed her eyes. A pang of guilt thrust into his heart. He had been too rough and demanding last evening. Once he had taken her with his body, he had only thought of doing it again. When he had awoken a little after dawn with her curled against him, his first thought had been to resume their lovemaking. However, he had noticed the faint shadows under her eyes and had let her sleep. Now he regretted not waking her from her deep slumber.

"Meredith told me that a Bow Street Runner has been summoned."

Ramscar's inquisitive sister must have been eavesdropping when he had called for Scrimm. Perhaps he should have a private chat with Meredith about her bad habits later. "At my request." Ramscar pulled Patience into his arms. "Listen to me. I know you are innocent. If anyone has the audacity to accuse you publicly, I will let it be known that I will consider it a personal insult. If that does not silence tongues, the offender will face me on a dueling field."

She shuddered and snuggled against his chest. She was aware that his father had died after a duel. It occurred to Ramscar that he might very well face his father's fate if the situation escalated.

"I do not want you risking your life over a spiteful woman's lie," Patience whispered, not bothering to conceal her distress from him.

It heartened him to hear her concern. Minutes earlier, she was behaving as if she had planned to shoot him herself. He kissed the top of her head. "I intend to hire a Runner to assist in tracking down the real thief. Never fear, he will be caught and I will insist that Lady Dewberry apologizes for her insult."

Patience's laughter was muffled against his chest. "Now that I will look forward to."

"Are you certain you wish to shop this afternoon?" Meredith said anxiously, following Patience as she headed for the shop.

"I have done nothing wrong, Meredith," Patience said, nodding at the gentleman who held the door for them. "Your brother and the duke have urged Lord Dewberry to silence his wife's tongue, but I fear the damage might already be done. If I remain at the house and cower in my bedchamber, I will only seem guilty of the theft."

"You are so brave," her friend said, her genuine admiration obvious. "I feel like a coward in comparison."

"Nonsense." Meredith was thinking of the years she had hidden from the world at Swancott because of her scars. "I am no different than you. Everyone rises to the occasion when the cause is just."

Meredith refused to let the matter rest. "I think you undervalue your abilities. You not only face your personal tribulation but generously shoulder the burdens of others."

Ill at ease with the young woman's undeserved praise, Patience pointed to a hat with three white downy plumes. "You should try that one on. I can think of three dresses that hat will complement."

Meredith studied the plumes with a contemplative frown. "Very well. I believe I shall try on the one with the lace, as well."

Patience stepped aside and watched as the store clerk eagerly moved in to assist her wealthy patron. As Patience had predicted, the hat with the white plumes was perfect for Meredith. With her shyly conversing with the clerk, Patience strolled over to admire a simple straw bonnet with light blue ribbons. It was a fine piece, but she had no intention of purchasing it. Thanks to the earl's generosity, her wardrobe rivaled that of his sister.

"No, no, this will not do," a feminine voice snapped with frustration. "Where is the proprietor? I must speak to him immediately if this is the best you can offer me."

"Mama, perhaps we should try another shop," a younger female calmly suggested.

"Our goods are made of the highest quality, Lady Farnaly," the clerk insisted.

Patience carefully set the bonnet she had been admiring down when she heard the woman's name. Dear heavens, after all these year, it could not be? Patience had not even recognized her mother's voice.

Fearing that he might be sacked, the clerk plucked the offensive hat from Lady Farnaly's hands and backed away. "I will summon the proprietor as you have requested. I am certain with his knowledgeable assistance we will find something that exceeds your refined tastes, madam."

Neither Lady Farnaly nor her young companion seemed to notice that they were being observed. It had been four years since Patience had glimpsed her mother and sister. Oh God, her sister! Deana had already celebrated her sixteenth birthday. What a beautiful young lady she had become.

And her mother. At eight and thirty, she was a handsome woman. Unlike her daughters, who were both blondes, Lady Farnaly had hair that reminded Patience of polished walnut. Lady Farnaly had given her husband four children, and yet she was nearly as slender as Deana. At the moment, her mother's lips were thinned with her displeasure and her expression was one Patience had experienced firsthand on countless occasions.

What if they recognized me?

The surprise of encountering her mother and sister had frozen Patience in place. Fear gave her the incentive to take a trembling step backward. With Meredith cheerfully chatting with the clerk behind Patience and the Farnalys ahead of her near the door, she felt her present and past were about to collide.

"Oh, Patience, you must come over here and try this hat on. It is absolutely frivolous," Meredith called out to her.

Lady Farnaly glanced at Meredith, who was giggling at the silly confection on her head. Unexpectedly, Patience's mother's gaze shifted to *her*. Patience stiffened under the cool, impersonal appraisal, unable to move. Her mother's irritated expression did not waver as her keen regard swept over Patience, assessing everything from her distraught expression to the quality of her shoes. It was fortuitous that the clerk assisting Lady Farnaly returned with the elderly proprietor. Patience's mother looked away and began chastising the gentlemen about a hat she had previously purchased.

If she had recognized Patience, Lady Farnaly had chosen not to acknowledge their connection. Still reeling from the incident, Patience strode over to Meredith.

"You must try on this hat!" Meredith said gaily.

"Another time," Patience grimly replied. She refused to look over at the Farnalys to see if the ladies were observing them.

Her friend's humor fled when she saw Patience's face. "Is something wrong? Did someone say something unseemly?" Meredith removed the hat from her head and exchanged it for the bonnet she had been wearing.

Patience had to get out of this shop before Lady Farnaly began to ponder her resemblance to her elder daughter. She took Meredith by the hand. "We must leave immediately."

"But—" Meredith glanced wistfully at the hat with the white plumes.

Surrendering gracefully, she allowed her friend to drag her out of the shop.

CHAPTER SEVENTEEN

Four days had elapsed since Patience had encountered her mother and sister in the shop. Day by day, Patience relaxed, eventually convincing herself that Lady Farnaly had not recognized her. When Meredith had questioned Patience about her strange reaction at the shop, she lied, claiming she had glimpsed one of Lady Dewberry's friends. Both Patience and Meredith agreed that Ramscar did not need to be told of the incident.

Their evenings had been filled with amusements. One night they enjoyed the theater. Thankfully, Miss Grassi was not one of the players. Another night, they ate boxed suppers at Vauxhall and watched the fireworks. The third night, Ramscar abandoned Patience and Meredith for an evening at one of his clubs. Her Grace, the Dowager Duchess of Solitea, took Patience and Meredith under her wing. They went to three balls that evening. Lady Fayre and her brother's wife, Kilby Carlisle, Duchess of Solitea, joined them on their adventures. At each engagement, the Knowdens and the Carlisles were silently showing their support for Patience. Their blind faith in her honesty humbled her. No one spoke out against her, not even Lady Dewberry, who had also been present at most of the balls Patience had attended. Of course, there had been a few speculative stares.

Especially when the thief boldly struck again and again. The villain seemed well acquainted with the *ton* and the various houses he managed to enter unnoticed. Although no one mentioned it, Patience had begun to notice a disturbing pattern. Many of the thefts occurred at balls Patience had also attended.

As for Ramscar, one might accuse him of being remiss in his duties as her lover. She had expected him come to her again, but their late evenings had kept them apart. Patience had been disappointed the previous evening when he had abandoned Meredith and her for one of his clubs. However, she was Meredith's companion, not his. It was not her place to complain.

This evening when Meredith pleaded exhaustion and expressed a desire to pass on a late supper, Patience was secretly thrilled when Ramscar told his sister to go home without them. She barely recalled what they had eaten, because all she could think about was that Ramscar was conspiring to spend a few hours alone with her.

Home at last, Patience climbed the stairs without checking to see if he was trailing after her.

"Come to me," Ramscar commanded huskily. His foot was poised on the first step.

Patience turned back. She leaned her hip against the railing and gave him a slow grin. There was something undeniably predatory about his gaze. A few kisses and an empty bed were not going to satisfy him this evening.

"Catch me," she replied saucily. Before he could react, she hopped up onto the stair railing and slid straight into his arms.

Ramscar caught her and gave her a hard shake. "You mad creature! What would you have done if I had not caught you?"

She slipped her fingers into his cravat and tugged.

"I would have been very, very cross with you, my lord," Patience said, smoothing out the long ends.

He tipped his head back and laughed. "Then I am a fortunate man, because the last thing I want is a troublesome wench in my arms." Ramscar nuzzled her earlobe and lowered her to her feet.

Patience unbuttoned the tiny buttons at his throat. "A pity. Troublesome wenches can be so *stimulating*." She rolled up onto her toes and kissed him full on the mouth. Dancing away, she ascended several steps. "If you are quick enough to catch one," she called back over her shoulder as she raced up the stairs.

Ramscar muttered something under his breath. "Slow down before you break your ankle." He charged up the stairs, a mischievous glint in his hazel green eyes.

She expected to lose this chase. In fact, she would have been disappointed if she had won. Laughing, she made it to the first landing, and as she had hoped, he was close at her heels. Seconds later, his arm hooked her waist and he dragged her backside to his front.

"Patience . . . Patience . . . what am I to do with you?" he whispered in her ear.

She turned her head to the side and caressed his jaw with her hand. "Why, anything you like, my lord," she whispered back.

His hand slipped into her bodice. He teased her left nipple until it puckered. " 'Anything' covers quite a bit of naughty territory, does it not?"

Patience wiggled her backside tantalizingly against his groin. "Depends, I suppose . . . on how quick you are on your feet."

She broke free and dashed up the next set of stairs, assuming they would retire to his bedchamber. Her room would not do because it was next to Meredith's. For some reason Patience doubted either of them would be inclined to subdued lovemaking.

She wanted to hear his guttural roar when his release vanquished the last of his control.

Ramscar's hand caught her ankle, forcing her to bend over and grasp one of the steps overhead. He expertly rolled her onto her back and dragged her toward him until she was positioned between his legs. His actions had pushed her skirt up to her hips, revealing her shapely legs.

He caged her with his arms. "Where are you going?" He glanced down and noted her exposed legs.

Slightly out of breath, she laid her head back against a step. "Your bedchamber." The edges of the steps were digging into her back, but the position was not the most uncomfortable she had endured.

His hazel green eyes looked almost black in the shadows. Even so, she could sense his amusement. "How very accommodating of you."

Patience grinned up at him cheekily. "I thought so."

Ramscar nudged her, rolling her back onto her stomach. He knelt beside her, his hand stroking from the back of her knee to the curves of her buttocks. "However, why should I deny myself when I could take you right here?"

She started to get up on all fours. He immediately pushed her back down. "Here? For heaven's sake, you cannot be serious?"

The rustling sound of him opening the flap on his breeches proved otherwise. Patience looked back and even in the dim light she could see that he was very aroused. "And you call me mad! What if someone hears us?" she whispered.

He moved behind her, taking a moment to push her skirt and petticoats higher. "I will try to resist shouting your name, but your delectable body tends to make me unruly," he murmured, guiding his manhood into her.

"Perhaps I like hearing your yell. Your bed—" Her breath came out as a hiss when he sank into her. No man had ever felt so good inside her. She could almost forget they were making love on the stairs.

"No." Not wasting a moment, Ramscar lifted her hips and moved with unhurried strokes. "I need you now, Patience. I refuse to wait."

She liked this eager, aggressive side of his nature.

Usually he was so restrained. The knowledge that she could shatter his control was an addictive aphrodisiac, much like his virile, handsome body.

"Faster," Patience quietly urged, pushing against him in an attempt to alter his pace.

"Greedy, are we?" Ramscar kissed her nape.

The hand on her hip slid diagonally to the front, seeking the curly nest of hair between her legs. She bit her lip to keep from crying out when he found the small hidden nubbin nestled within her feminine folds.

"Have I mentioned how much I adore your scent? A hint of clove mixed with the heady musk of your arousal. A faint whiff, and my cock stiffens in response. You were made for fucking, sweet Patience."

She was not offended by his crude carnal words. It only proved how aroused and reckless the earl was feeling. The revelation heightened her desire. That familiar warm heat she craved pooled in her belly. When she felt a gush of honeyed wetness from within her sheath it was Ramscar who softly groaned.

"That's it. Go on and sing for me, my little temptress," he said, punctuating his words with deep thrusts as his thumb worked its magic on her small, sensitive nubbin. "Just for me."

Patience buried her face into her sleeve to muffle any sound. Behind her closed eyelids, light blossomed like fireworks in her head, shimmering explosions of silver, red, and gold. The heat sizzled from her head down to her curled toes.

She was not alone.

Ramscar hugged her fiercely and began pumping himself frantically into her. Still highly sensitive from her release, she felt his manhood jolt as hot seed exploded deep within her womb.

CHAPTER EIGHTEEN

"You are worried about him."

Patience did not bother feigning confusion. She was concerned about Ramscar. "A natural reaction, do you not think? Especially since your brother has issued a challenge on my behalf."

Damnable savage! Why did all men believe violence satisfied all offenses?

She should have suspected something was wrong the night he had left them to visit one of his clubs.

He and his friends had been quietly taking care of the preparations for a duel. The next night he had deliberately sought an assignation with her. He had made wild passionate love to her on the stairs and then had carried her up to his bedchamber, where he spent the night devoting himself to the task of proving to her that his indifference in public was a flimsy attempt to dissuade anyone from accusing him that he lacked impartiality about Patience's connection to the jewelry thefts. In truth, he privately confessed to her, he had lost all objectivity where she was concerned.

He should have expected that he would not be able to keep Patience and his sister from hearing about the duel. Ramscar rarely felt the need to defend his honor on the grassy commons, so the news of his challenge and the reasons for it were hotly debated within the *ton*.

Ramscar refused to discuss the details of the duel with either Meredith or Patience. Tearfully, she had yelled at him that she did not care what anyone said behind her back. Her pleas for him to withdraw the challenge were ignored. Before he had retired for the evening, Ramscar had arrogantly ordered both ladies to leave the house the next day. They were supposed to conduct themselves in public as they would any other day.

Only this was not a typical afternoon. According

to Scrimm, Ramscar had left the house before dawn and they had not received a single note from him. Patience was worried. If he had been hurt, she would never forgive herself.

Opening her lilac-and-white-striped parasol, she idly twisted the long handle against her shoulder. "I do not understand why we are here at the park. What if your brother returns while we are out?"

Instead of going to the park, Patience and Meredith should have called on his friends Lord Everod and Lord Byrchmore. They likely stood as his seconds, so they would know Ramscar's fate. Perhaps they had carried him unconscious to one of their residences while a surgeon had been summoned. Patience's heart wrenched at the horrible thought. Needless to say, she did not share her depressing thoughts with her companion.

"I must confess I am not enjoying this walk any more than you," Meredith said, reaching up to adjust her bonnet as a couple passed them, so they did not notice her facial scars. The gesture was habitual rather than deliberate. "However, my brother has done so much for me and he demands little in return. If he felt us being seen together on a public outing was important, then I feel we must abide by his request. Even if it does seem absurd."

Patience thought that she understood what had prompted Ramscar into making the odd request. It had nothing to do with keeping up appearances, as Meredith believed. The earl did not want his sister to be at home if his seconds returned with his corpse. Their mother had been driven to madness by the sight of her dead husband. Ramscar did not want his sister to suffer needlessly. As usual, he thought only of protecting his family, not of himself.

Her thoughts tumultuous, Patience did not immediately recognize the couple approaching them. When the lady and her male companion held Patience's gaze and smiled, she realized she should have trusted her instincts and left London.

"Patience. My God, is that truly you?" Sir Russell said, crossing in front of Meredith and forcing her and Patience to halt.

The surprise and pain she saw in his expression made her yearn to embrace him. The vivid memory of his harsh rejection and her years of pretending to be anyone other that Patience Farnaly prevented her from moving forward.

Impulsively he reached out and touched her on the arm as if he was uncertain she was real. "When your mother told me that you were here in London, Daughter, I thought she was mistaken."

Meredith's wary gaze flickered from the older couple to her friend. "Patience?" Her friend obviously was recalling the afternoon when Patience had told the dowager duchess that her parents were dead.

"I fear, my lord, that your lady is gravely mistaken," Patience said, fighting to keep her expression perfectly blank. "I am not your daughter. Come, Lady Meredith."

Sir Russell was visibly staggered by Patience's rejection. "What's this? You deny knowing us?" Unshed tears gleamed in his eyes.

"Enough of this nonsense, Daughter," Lady Farnaly said crisply. "I do not fully comprehend the games you have been playing, but you will cease your mischief straightaway."

Playing games.

Was that how her mother had explained away her elder daughter's absence?

Four years had passed, and her mother had changed very little. So she had learned Meredith's name and her connection to the Earl of Ramscar. Patience was not fooled. Her mother was not eager to reacquaint herself with her long-lost daughter. Lady Farnaly desired an introduction to the Knowdens.

"I play no games, my lady. I am dead earnest in my denial," Patience said chillingly.

"Madam, your name if you please," Meredith spoke up before Patience could draw her away. "I am Lady Meredith. My brother is the Earl of Ramscar."

Patience closed her eyes, unwilling to watch the

life and friendships she had come to treasure shatter into useless wreckage.

"Forgive our rudeness, Lady Meredith," Patience's father said swiftly. "It was the shock of seeing our daughter again. So many years have passed without word from her that we feared her to be dead."

"I beg you to forgive my husband and our neglectful daughter. We are the Farnalys," Patience's mother interjected, since Sir Russell was still flustered by his daughter's presence. "This is my husband, Sir Russell. I am Lady Farnaly. And *you* clearly are acquainted with our daughter."

"A pleasure to meet you both." Meredith turned to Patience and whispered, "I do not understand. I thought your family was dead?"

"They are," Patience said grimly. She raised her chin and addressed her parents. "I am sorry for your loss, Sir Russell and Lady Farnaly. However, I am not your daughter. My last name is Winlow. I am an actress by profession. Of late, I am Lady Meredith's hired companion."

"Patience!" exclaimed her friend for deviating from the tale they had told the *ton*.

What tale they told no longer mattered. Patience's parents had ruined everything!

"I am no one of consequence," Patience said pointedly to her mother.

Taking Meredith firmly by the arm, Patience walked away from her parents.

"Ram!"

Meredith ran toward him, hugging him fiercely when they collided. "I was so worried about you! Patience and I followed your orders. We strolled for what seemed like hours at the park. However, when we returned to the house and there was no message from you . . ." She pressed the side of her head to his chest and listened to his beating heart. "I was beginning to think something tragic had occurred."

He stroked her hair, relishing his sister's unexpected show of affection. "Oh, sweetie, I told you not to worry. As I had guessed, Lord Bently was a coward. The gentleman hastily offered his apologies as soon as I demonstrated my abilities with a pistol. I was never in any danger," he lied, feeling she needed reassurance rather than the truth.

Ram had never questioned his skills. He was exceedingly competent with a sword or pistol. However, a nervous opponent was a dangerous one. There was always the risk Bently might have cheated or discharged his pistol by accident.

"Where is Patience?" Ram asked, carefully disentangling himself from Meredith's clinging embrace. He had thought of Patience often during the early morning hours. Her drawn, pale face and tormented blue eyes had haunted him. He could still hear her tearful voice pleading with him to withdraw his challenge.

"I beg of you. Please do not face him. I would rather face a dozen scandals than have your blood on my hands."

"Upstairs. When we returned from our walk, she asked not to be disturbed. This day was trying for both of us." Meredith moved away from him and glanced upstairs to confirm that they were not being overheard.

He scowled at her actions. "What is it?"

His sister returned to his side. "Something odd happened when we were at the park," she whispered. "A couple approached us. They introduced themselves as Sir Russell and Lady Farnaly."

"Their names are unfamiliar to me. Did they insult you or Patience?"

"No." Meredith paused, uncertain how to break the staggering news to him. "Ram, they claimed to be Patience's parents."

"Ridiculous. Patience told me that she had been on her own since she was fourteen. A gently reared lady does not abandon her family for the uncertain life of the stage. No father would permit it." On the other hand, Patience had fit into Ram's and Meredith's lives with such ease that it had been impossible for him to think of her as anything less than his equal. "How did Patience react?"

"Naturally, she denied knowing them. Even so, she was visibly upset by the encounter. She could offer no excuse for their outrageous claims, except that she must bear some resemblance to their dead daughter. When we arrived at the house, she pleaded a megrim and I suggested that a nap might restore her spirits. I promised to wake her on your return. She was very upset with you, and the chance meeting with the Farnalys added to her distress."

Was it merely mistaken identity or had Patience been keeping a few secrets from him? Ram needed to see Patience.

Immediately.

"Where are you going?" his sister asked, chasing after him as he swiftly climbed the stairs. "You cannot possibly believe that Patience lied to us. For what possible reason would she deny being a gentleman's daughter?"

"I do not know." Ram sensibly avoided glancing at the spot where he had shoved up Patience's skirts and had thoroughly plundered her soft, willing body. "I am certainly interested in hearing the lady explain away the coincidence of the Farnalys' daughter sharing her looks and her name. Aren't you?"

Ram pounded his fist against her door. There

was no reassuring sound to greet him on the other side. He knocked again. "Patience. Open the door."

Silence.

Meredith stared solemnly at the closed door. "Ram, she could just be sleeping."

He was not as optimistic.

Pulling on the latch, he pushed open the door and confirmed his bleak suspicions.

The room was empty.

For an independent lady, Patience was a wretched creature.

Wholly alone, she sat in the middle of the bed she had procured from the innkeeper for the night. Without a servant or protector, she had taken a risk asking for a room. The impertinent stare the innkeeper gave her confirmed that she might have trouble if she trusted only the lock. Bluffing, she told the odious man that her husband had been delayed because of the torrential rainstorm and that she expected His Lordship later. Once she was alone in the room, she had dragged a heavy chair in front of the door. If the innkeeper or anyone else thought she was easy prey, she had a knife in her satchel to convince him otherwise.

Patience sniffed, cursing the storm that had stranded her ten miles outside of London. The pretty

clouds that she had observed on her walk with
Meredith had overwhelmed the sky and darkened.
The rain had started to sprinkle when Patience
walked away from the Knowden house. A few miles
into her journey, lightning arced across the blackened
sky and the wind surged, shaking the cramped compartment of the stagecoach. Before long, the roads
had become impassable. Nearly blinded by the sheets
of rain falling from the sky, the coachman had
whipped the frightened team of horses, urging them
forward until the inn appeared on the horizon. Patience knew she should be grateful they had found the
inn at all. The alternative was not worth dwelling on.

This was not one of her grander escapes, she
thought gloomily.

Oh, slipping out of the Knowden household had
been ridiculously easy. Meredith trusted Patience.
She even seemed willing to believe Patience's claims
that she did not know the Farnalys. Poor, gullible
Meredith. By now, she and Ramscar must be wondering what had happened to their hired companion.

If he returned home at all.

Patience stifled the nagging fear. No, the earl was
fine. With all the weapons mounted on the walls of
his library, the man must have learned how to use
one or two of them. He loved his sister too much to
recklessly throw away his life for an unknown actress's tarnished reputation.

Blast it all, this was her parents' fault!

That day in the shop, Patience's mother had been content to forget she had an elder daughter until she recognized her companion as a lady of importance. Suddenly brimming with maternal love, Lady Farnaly was willing to forgive her wayward child? Why? Patience's lip curled in contempt. Her mother's change of heart had little to do with forgiveness or love. With a connection to the Earl of Ramscar, she finally discovered something redeemable in Patience.

"Well, not anymore, Mama," Patience said, ignoring the pain in her breast. "I will not let you ruin what I shared with the Knowdens."

No, she had wrecked everything just fine without Lady Farnaly's assistance.

Patience retrieved her handkerchief and blotted her eyes. In the distance she heard the low rumble of thunder. Several seconds later, she saw the flashes of lightning through the thin drapery.

Belatedly, she regretted that she had not left a note for Meredith to find. She might have told the young woman how much her friendship had come to mean to her. Of course, once Ramscar and Meredith realized Patience had lied to them, she doubted either one would think kindly of her. No, it was best that she did not bother with explanations. The wisest course was to disappear and never return to London.

Wise, mayhap, but why did she feel so awful?

Patience fell back and laid her head on the pillow. Squeezing her eyes tightly shut against the painful sting of tears, she rolled onto her side and brought her knees up to her chest. Her breath hitched as she thought about her weeks with the Knowdens. Meredith had slowly warmed to Patience's presence, and Ramscar, well, he had been wonderful. For a few weeks she had begun to believe that she could remain and be part of their family.

It all had been a frivolous dream.

Sobbing into her hand, Patience surrendered to the grief. What she mourned was never really hers to keep. After all, she was a young lady who liked to play pretend.

She jolted at the deafening clap of thunder. Lightning madly flashed as the walls seemed to vibrate from the storm's intensity. It sounded like the world was coming to the end. Although she had been annoyed at the coachman for refusing to continue their journey, she was thankful for his astuteness. The notion of enduring the worst of the storm within the small confines of the stagecoach was unacceptable, perhaps even perilous. She jumped as the deafening thunder heralded another vicious assault on the horizon. Simultaneously the door to her room exploded open, shooting out bits of debris and cracking the wooden frame as the door crashed into the small chest of drawers positioned along the wall. Patience screamed. The chair she had used to bar the door skipped across the floor and slammed into the wall. Clasping a pillow to her breasts, she forgot about retrieving the knife in her satchel when she recognized the man who nonchalantly sauntered into the room.

"A hellish night to be traveling, Patience," Ramscar said as his keen hazel green eyes swept over her. He nodded, satisfied that she was unharmed by her reckless adventure. "I have come for answers, and I won't leave until you give me the truth. Do you want to tell me why a baronet's daughter is pretending to be an actress named Miss Winlow?"

Meredith paced in front of the marble chimneypiece, her anxiety growing as the foul weather shrieked and rattled the window panes. It was an awful night for anyone to be outdoors.

Yet, her brother was out there in the night. Ramscar had left the house hours earlier to search for Patience. Meredith was confident her brother would eventually find Patience. Earlier, she had glimpsed Ram's face as he had quietly given orders to Scrimm. She had expected to see the underlying concern and determination on his grim features. What had surprised her was the revelation that her brother was in love with Patience Winlow. It was an intriguing development. Meredith idly wondered if Ram was aware of the depth of his feelings.

The sound of masculine voices approaching the closed door of the drawing room froze Meredith in place. Because of her machinations, Ram was not the only gentleman who had braved the foul weather this evening in search of a lady.

The door seemed to explode open, and Lord Halthorn strode boldly into the room. "Lady Meredith," he said, the relief that she was clearly unharmed evident on his face. "I received your note."

A disapproving Scrimm slowly joined them. "My lady, Lord Ramscar was quite specific in his orders this evening. Anyone calling on the family was to be turned away."

"We will make an exception for Lord Halthorn, Scrimm," Meredith said, feeling a little lightheaded now that the viscount was standing before her. "After all, I was the one who summoned him."

The butler squinted at her in disbelief. "Lord Ramscar will not be pleased."

Meredith silently agreed. However, Ram was not at home, so he could not send Lord Halthorn away, nor was he the only Knowden who had fallen in love. "Thank you, Scrimm. You may retire," Meredith said, ignoring the flutters in her stomach. "Lord

Halthorn will remain with me until my brother's return."

Ram was furious.

With fresh tears in her eyes, her shoulders slumped at his accusation. Instead of causing him to feel pity, her defeated expression only fueled his ire. How dare she run from him! If Patience had not looked so miserable, he might have paddled her for scaring ten years off his life.

"How did you find me?" she asked, refusing to look him in the eyes as she began pulling the blankets over her bare legs.

Ram was uncertain how to approach her. She was noticeably frightened, and he was too angry to trust himself not to accidentally hurt her. "It wasn't difficult. Since you left the house on foot and needed a conveyance to leave town, your choices of escape were limited."

Patience had taken a hell of a chance, wandering the streets alone with her saved wages in her reticule. She was tempting prey for any footpad who discovered her.

Ram privately wanted to throttle her for her carelessness. Instead, he shut the door. He retrieved the chair she had used to secure the door and shoved the high back against the latch. "Several gentlemen at the coaching inn in town recalled the beautiful blond-haired lady who traveled alone. If not for the thunderstorm, I would have arrived sooner."

He removed his sodden greatcoat and laid the garment over the chair. His frock coat had not fared much better, so he shrugged out of it and placed it on a chair closer to the small fire.

Patience hugged the pillow. "I suppose you bribed the innkeeper and he happily told you where to find me."

Ram smiled slightly at her waspish tone. "Honestly, no bribe was required. It seems my *wife* was anticipating my arrival." Ram wondered if she would fight him if he took the pillow she was using as a shield from her.

"I had to tell the man something. I hoped a husband would discourage him or any other man who thought to visit me uninvited." She sniffed disdainfully. "Clearly, such precautions were needed, since you are here."

"You have more courage than any other lady I know. Mayhap more than you should. Look me in the eye when you speak to me, Patience," he said harshly.

There was defiance in her blue eyes when she lifted her chin. An angry Patience was preferable to the defeated weeping girl he had glimpsed when he kicked open the door. "Why have you come, Ramscar?"

If she believed she was free to flit into his life and then leave without a word, Patience had sorely overestimated her abilities at guile. "I told you. For answers. What did you expect me to do when Meredith and I discovered that your room was vacant? You did not even bother to write a note explaining your abrupt departure. Meredith was upset, and I must admit I was struggling with a case of manly vapors at the thought of you running about London without protection."

Patience's lips twitched; she was amused by the notion of him suffering from any nervous condition. Ramscar did not return the smile. The lady before him had pulled him into the very depths of hell with her antics, and he was not certain he would fully recover.

He sat down on her bed and removed his boots and damp stockings. Ram gave her a considering look. "Patience, why did you run? Meredith mentioned that you both had encountered a gentleman and his wife, Sir Russell and Lady Farnaly, and that they claimed to be your parents. Were they telling the truth?"

She bit her lower lip and glanced away.

Ramscar growled in frustration. "Perhaps I am

asking the wrong question. Let's try this again. Has anything you've told me been the truth? Who are you? Are you Patience Winlow or Patience Farnaly?"

In a quiet voice she said, "Things would have been simpler if you had just let me go."

Let her go? Not likely.

"How fortunate for you I prefer the complicated over the simple," he replied, his temper not improving with her hedging. "Whatever your secrets, they will not damn you in my eyes. Give me the truth. Which name belongs to you?"

"You have been so generous with your time, Lord Halthorn," Meredith said after the viscount had thoroughly trounced her for the third time at Draughts. In truth, her mind was not on the game at all but on the handsome gentleman who sat across from her. "I feel guilty for squandering your evening."

"An evening with you is never squandered, Lady Meredith," Lord Halthorn said, a hint of gentle censure in his tone. "You are an amiable companion but . . ."

"But what?" she prompted when he hesitated.

He sighed as if reluctant to finish his confession. "You are perfectly horrid at Draughts."

After a few seconds of speechless bewilderment,

both the viscount and Meredith burst into laughter at his rude observation.

"How kind of you to notice, my lord!" Still laughing, she slid her chair away from the gaming table. Before she could rise, Lord Halthorn had jumped up from his chair and had positioned himself so he could help assist her.

He gently placed her hand in his. "You are worried about your brother and Miss Winlow."

Meredith nodded. "I am certain Ram has found Patience. Most likely they were forced to seek shelter elsewhere because of the storm."

"A sensible notion on such a foul night," the viscount concurred, stroking her fingers in a comforting manner. "While I regret the grim circumstances that pressed you to summon me, I cannot regret our quiet evening together."

There was something in his solemn gaze that quickened her pulse.

"Nor I, Lord Halthorn," she said breathlessly as their gazes locked. Meredith abruptly glanced away. "You have been so kind to me. I treasure your friendship, my lord. I . . ."

Slightly puzzled, he moved closer when she pulled away from him. "What is it? Have I offended you in some way, Lady Meredith?"

Meredith smiled at his question. "No, my lord. I just feel your kindness warrants a confession."

CHAPTER NINETEEN

"Both."

Ramscar stirred, his ominous expression hinting at his need for violence.

"Honestly, I can claim both names," she said hurriedly as he leaned menacingly toward her. "Though four years have passed since anyone has called me by the name Patience Farnaly. Truth be told, I would be content if I never heard the Farnaly name uttered in my presence."

The earl reached over and tenderly cupped her cheek. "None of this makes sense. You are the daughter of a baronet. Why have you been fending for yourself since you were fourteen? Were you mistreated?"

Lie. Gain his sympathy.

The urge to lie to him burned her throat. His protective nature would never allow the Farnalys to approach her again if he thought they had been cruel. With his hazel green eyes level and sincere, Patience wondered if he was prepared for the truth he demanded.

"Not mistreated." She took a fortifying breath. "Leastways, not in a manner that would warrant running away. There was a gentleman."

Ramscar let the hand cupping her face drop to the mattress.

The telling action stung. "What is the point in my speaking the truth if you are unwilling to hear it?" she demanded passionately. "If you recall, I did not come to you a virgin, my lord. Did you think my lack was a romantic tale of love and loss? What do you think happens to the sweet virgins you and your friends, *les sauvages nobles,* entice into bed and then, when you are finished, leave to move on to the next conquest?"

Her heated accusation cut him to the quick. "Christ, is that what you think? My friends and I may deserve the notoriety bestowed on us, but callously seducing virgins for sport is not one of them!" He felt insulted, and his eyes were like living green flame. "Is that what happened to you? Were you seduced by a gentleman and your family cast you out in disgrace?"

Patience laid the pillow she had been clutching flat on her lap and smoothed the wrinkles from its surface. "No. Perhaps you will think badly of me, but I left with Julian Phoenix willingly."

"I suppose this Phoenix was the worst sort of bounder."

"Yes," she said simply. "Although he called himself an actor, he wore the profession more as a mask to conceal his real talents."

"Which were?"

She allowed her hair to fall forward, concealing her face. Her shame. "He was a charlatan. Phoenix was very good at getting people to believe what he told them, and all the while, with the help of the troupe he had assembled, he was stealing their valuables."

The muscles along Ramscar's jawbone visibly tensed. "How did you meet him?"

At least Ramscar had not accused her of being a thief yet. She pushed her hair away from her face and tucked the strands behind her ear. "My father, Sir Russell, introduced us. Phoenix and his troupe were performing in our parish. My family attended one of their plays. At fourteen, I was enamored with the stage, and my father thought I would be eager to meet a real actor."

She sighed, wistful for her lost innocence. "I was. Mr. Phoenix was an impressive gentleman. Before I knew it, this beautiful man was begging to meet me in secret because he had fallen in love with me. I was flattered to have such a worldly gentleman praise my acting skills as well as my beauty. I was so infatuated by him, I never thought to question his claims of undying love. He suggested that we make a dash for Gretna Green. Afterward, as man and wife, we would share both a bed and the stage. Oh, he had painted such a lovely life for us."

"Bastard," Ramscar succinctly spat out the word.

The corners of her mouth lifted slightly. "I agree."

He glowered at her. "Phoenix had no thought of marrying you."

Ramscar had never even met the gentleman, and yet he had seen through Phoenix's ruse. A part of her despised that innocent fourteen-year-old girl who had willingly assisted in her own ruination. "None at all. Originally, he had paid attention to me in hopes that my father might notice and bribe Phoenix to leave me alone." She wrinkled her nose. "A sound plan, but Sir Russell is . . ." She searched for the appropriate word to describe her father.

"Dedicated to his inventions. He left any family business to my mother. I wager he did not notice Phoenix's keen interest until my mother had brought it to his attention. By then, it was too late."

"Why did the scoundrel keep you?" Ramscar scoffed at his ridiculous question. "Of course he would keep you. You were a beautiful child."

Her pulse fluttered at Ramscar's compliment. "In part. What appealed to Phoenix more was the raw talent he glimpsed within me. I had the makings to be an actress and a potential new member of the criminal class. I was young and trainable. It amused him and the others that they were turning a gently reared lady into a petty thief."

It was painful to admit her failings to anyone. She hesitantly told Ramscar about her harsh life with Julian Phoenix and the troupe. Her throat ached and her soft voice was ripe with suppressed emotion in the retelling. She spoke of her thoughts of escaping Phoenix's scheming guardianship and of her father's cruel rejection the one afternoon she had tried to return home.

"What's this?" Sir Russell glanced around as he descended from his carriage to see if anyone was witnessing his discussion with the daughter he had never expected to see again. Clearly Patience's sudden appearance and babbled apology had flustered

him. *"You think a pretty apology will absolve you. You arrogant chit! Your defiance was a betrayal, not only to me and your mother, but to your sister and brothers as well. How did you expect us to hold our heads high, once our friends and neighbors learned you ran off to become another man's whore?"*

Patience brought her trembling hand to her breast as if her father's words had scored deep furrows into her heart. She had expected, even deserved his anger. What she had not anticipated was the revulsion twisting his features into a cold, unfamiliar mask. "Papa, please—I beg of you—"

Sir Russell's hand lashed out and he slapped her hard across the face.

Both father and daughter seemed horrified by his violence.

Shaken, he curled the offending hand into a fist. "I have no mercy left in me, girl. If you must beg, beg on bended knee to God, though I doubt even He will listen to such a miserable, selfish creature as you. From this day forward, I want—I want nothing more to do with you."

Patience grimaced, banishing the unpleasant memory. Her gaze focused on Ramscar's face. He had remained silent for too long. Oh, how she wished that she could discern his thoughts.

Ramscar had not visibly reacted to her admission that she had been trained as a thief. His lack of reaction was disconcerting. Although he had assured her on numerous occasions that he had not believed her capable of thievery, she worried that her revelation might alter his view of her innocence.

"Ram?"

Slowly, he stirred from his stupor. "You must have loved him a great deal."

She was taken aback by his conclusion.

"Love? I despised him!" Patience tossed aside the pillow and hopped off the bed. She began pacing. "He took everything from me, and I—" She pounded her chest with her fist. "I *let* him!"

"You were little more than a child, Patience, when you ran off with this Phoenix," Ramscar said, rising off the mattress. He stepped in front of her and halted her frenzied pacing. Her eyes filled with tears at the humbling compassion she detected in his tone. It shattered her. "As for remaining with him, what choice did you have? Your family had cast you out. You were frightened and penniless. Phoenix offered you a substitute family and a means to support yourself. Many young ladies faced with your plight would have made the same decision."

"You are merely being kind," she murmured,

mentally shying away from the sliver of hope his words gave her. "I lied to you once. How do you know I am not lying to gain your sympathy?"

Ramscar rested his forehead against hers. He exhaled noisily. "I may dislike being lied to, Patience. Nevertheless, I am trying to understand your reasons."

She lightly touched his cheek and stepped away while she struggled to believe him. Most people were not so forgiving. The one time she had tried to approach her father in the hopes that he would save her from Julian Phoenix, he had callously rejected her. "Do you? Another man might wonder if my admission of being a willing accomplice to numerous thefts was proof that I stole Lady Dewberry's necklace the night of your sister's ball."

The corners of his eyes crinkled in his amusement. "Looking for a fight, are we?" he said, not bothering to agree or deny her charge. His hands slipped over both elbows as he roughly pulled her against him. "Poor, pretty Patience. You seem so determined to roil in your misery and past failings."

"Cease your mockery, my lord," she said crossly. He smelled of male musk, linen, and spring rain. She resisted the urge to press her nose to his shirt and breathe in his scent. "I am not claiming to be a martyr."

"Good." He tilted her face upward. "I have other plans for you."

Ramscar cradled her face in his hands with a reverence no other man had shown her. Light as a butterfly's wing, his lips teased her parted lips, quietly coaxing her into forgetting what awaited them beyond the closed door.

"You are so lovely, my hands tremble at the notion of touching you," he breathed against her cheek.

Patience arched her head back, giving him a mischievous glance. "Are you loving me, my lord?"

Ramscar was pleased that she wore only a thin nightgown. After she had tried to run from him, his feelings for this complicated, maddening woman were too close to the surface. He needed reaffirmation that she belonged to him, and he was impatient.

"Always," he vowed, nibbling her luscious neck. "You have slipped under my skin, Patience. Your very essence mingles like a fever in my blood." Ramscar gathered the fabric of her nightgown and pulled the offensive barrier over her head. He tossed it away.

Completely naked, she moved like a graceful cat. "You, too," she said, nuzzling her face against his chest. "I like the feel of you."

Not waiting for his permission, she pushed up the ends of his shirt, and he obliged her by removing it. His hands moved to the buttons of his breeches.

She circled around to his bare back. "You are the first man I have ever viewed naked. You are such a hairy beast. I never knew that such tantalizing pleasure could be had by the searing heat of your skin as you move against me or the delicious abrasiveness of the hair on your arms, chest, and legs. Julian Phoenix was a selfish boy in comparison."

Jealousy surged out of every pore, altering Ramscar into a full-fledged beast. The thought of another man intimately touching Patience was enough to make him hunt down the man and destroy him with nothing more than his bare hands. "Is he dead?"

Patience's fingernails dug into Ramscar's hips. She laid her cheek against him. He felt her warm breath tease the almost invisible hairs on his back. "Yes. There was an accident. His wounds were mortal."

Ramscar sensed there was more to the tale than a simple accident. Something she was reluctant to reveal. He had heard enough for now. Phoenix was dead, and Patience was his. He did not have to deny himself. "Good. Then I do not have to kill him," he said flatly, meaning it.

He turned until he faced her. Sweeping his arm under her legs, he picked her up. Patience clung to him, kissing him ardently. He blindly carried her to the bed. The violent need to protect the woman in his embrace worried him a little. It gave her power over him, and he was not the type of man who willingly surrendered to anyone.

In a display of great tenderness, he placed her down on the mattress. "Promise me that you will never run from me again." Belatedly he realized that he was slightly hurt by her actions. She had not trusted him to keep her secrets.

Patience eyed him impatiently, watching him as he removed his breeches. "Yes. How can I resist a man who clearly has the natural elements on his side?"

Ramscar chuckled. His cock was already swollen with need. Only Patience could give him the relief he craved. "Consider yourself fortunate the storms delayed your escape. If I had been forced to scour the countryside for you, I would have paddled your defiant backside for the trouble." He crawled into bed beside her.

"Oooh . . . issuing threats," she said, unimpressed with his angry posturing. "Who says you would have caught me?"

He grinned at her arrogance. For an intelligent

lady, she did not fully comprehend her predicament. "I do," he said, shifting his weight so that he reclined on his side. He playfully tousled the curly nest between her legs. "This eve or the next, the results would have been the same."

"A confession?" Lord Halthorn said, a frown marring his handsome features as he sensed her growing agitation. "Are you in trouble?"

"No." Meredith whirled away from him, attempting to hold on to the courage that she had possessed hours earlier. "I lured you here under false pretenses, my lord. I did not invite you here because I was so worried about my brother and Miss Winlow that I feared being alone."

His frown softened into bemusement. "You summoned me because you feared the violence of the storm, did you not?"

Meredith was tempted to seize the excuse he was innocently offering her, but she shook her head. "No. At the moment, all I fear is your rejection."

"My lady, I do not understand."

"I know," Meredith said, already regretting the heart-rending path she had chosen. "And your confusion makes me wonder if I have misunderstood your interest. Perhaps you should leave."

She started for the door, but the viscount's hand on her arm halted her hasty retreat. "Why would I want to leave when we are in the middle of a fascinating game called Confessions? Come now, Lady Meredith, this is not the moment to be cowardly. What was the true reason you summoned me?"

Meredith's tongue felt dry as she swallowed. She had spent a lovely evening with Lord Halthorn. What had compelled her to ruin it with the awkward truth? "Turn around," she commanded, unable to look at him directly.

"This is utter nonsense," he muttered in exasperation, yet he crossed his arms over his chest and complied.

Meredith also turned away so they stood back-to-back. Their bodies were so close, she could feel the heat of his body through her dress. Her body swayed and lightly brushed against his. Meredith trembled.

"Lord Halthorn, I requested your presence this evening because I had every intention of seducing you." At his soft intelligible oath, she closed her eyes and winced.

"It was a foolish notion. I see that now." Meredith clasped both hands and brought them to her chin. "If you are truly the kind gentleman I believe you to be, I pray you will forget I ever uttered such a ridiculous confession. I will never mention—"

"Lady Meredith," Lord Halthorn softly said her name, silencing the rest of her apology.

Meredith felt him turn around and his hands on her shoulders confirmed it. Slowly, she let him guide her until she faced him. As she stiffly stood in his embrace, she braced for his rejection.

When she was brave enough to look at him, she noted his expression was enigmatic. "So your plan this evening was to seduce me?"

Her eyes flooded with tears, mercifully blurring his face.

Disconcerted by her reaction, Lord Halthorn tenderly caged Meredith's face in his hands. "Oh no, my lady, do not cry." Leaning down, he kissed each tear as it rolled down her face.

Meredith flinched when his lips brushed against her scarred cheek. "Do not." She attempted to pull away but his hands held her in place. There was no possible reason why he should want to kiss her ruined cheek. Angrily she turned her face aside. "Please, my lord, stop."

"Why?" He did not sound angry at her; just curious.

Why?

"The scars are ugly and coarse. No man can find pleasure in touching them," she said sadly, her lower lip quivered at the confession.

Lord Halthorn gave her a lopsided smile.

"Meredith, you are too beautiful to be fretting over minor imperfections." He tried to resume his slow, sensual exploration of her cheek with his lips.

Meredith placed her fingers over his mouth. "There are scars, elsewhere. The fire—"

The viscount kissed her fingertips and moved her hand to his waist. "No longer matters. When I first met you, I sensed that you would resist any gentleman who tried to get too close. I had planned to court you slowly. Imagine my surprise, sweet beautiful Meredith, when you confessed that you hoped to seduce me this evening."

"You are not angry?"

Instead of replying, Lord Halthorn lowered his head and kissed Meredith. His light caress felt like a soothing whisper against her lips. She felt the impact of his kiss all the way down to her toes.

Pulling back, the viscount seemed equally dazed by the kiss. "Hmmm . . . I will be sorely disappointed if you abandon your plans to seduce me this evening."

Meredith tightened her grip on his frock coat. "I have never tried to seduce a gentleman before," she shyly admitted.

Lord Halthorn pressed his lips to her scarred cheek. This time Meredith did not flinch. "Really?

I suspect you will be remarkably adept at it," he murmured as he moved on to her neck.

Three hours later, Patience realized she had fallen asleep. Yawning, she pushed the stray blond hairs sticking to her face. If Ramscar's intent had been to make love to her until she was too weary to leave the bed, he had succeeded admirably. Parts of her body ached, but she was not complaining. The earl was a very thorough lover.

With a smile on her lips, she rolled toward him on the mattress. She half-expected him to be asleep. Instead, he lazily watched her with a heavy-lidded gaze. "Did you sleep?"

"I might have dozed for a few minutes," he murmured throatily. "Your snoring kept rousing me."

Patience sat up and punched him on the shoulder. He laughed at her indignant ire. "How incredibly rude! I do not snore!" she said, punctuating the last four words with a quick jab.

"Cease! I am defenseless against those sharp, boney knuckles," he said, his laughter belying his protest. "A pitiful lover you are. Instead of kissing me senseless like a dutiful lover should, here you are poking holes in me."

"Dutiful?" She straddled him and pinned his

wrists over his head. "Ha! Never. 'Dutiful' is a word a man reserves for his wife, not his mistress, Lord Ramscar."

He stilled. "Then marry me."

The walls closed in on her with those three calmly uttered words. Patience released his wrists and straightened. "Surely you jest?"

Ramscar captured her by the hips and prevented her from climbing off him. "Are you saying that I bungled my first marriage proposal? Now who is being rude?" he teased, though his hazel green eyes revealed his earnestness.

She blew at an annoying strand of hair tickling her nose. "You do not want to marry me," she said, the exasperation evident in her voice.

He lifted his brow in a lofty fashion. "You have the ability to peer into a man's soul, eh? Forget the stage or being a lady's hired companion, Patience. Any king would grant you your heart's desire to exclusively gain access to your unusual skills."

Patience stuck out her tongue. "Very witty. Such comments make your earlier proposal seem, oh, shall we say, shallow." She tried to slip away from him.

Ramscar grabbed her wrists and pulled her back on top of him. "Oh no. I'll grant you that you have a useful knack for twisting a man's meaning to your own purposes. You are as slippery as an eel when it suits you; however, I am on to you, Patience Farnaly."

Her mouth dried at the name she had vowed never to use again. "Pray, do not call me by that name. The lady no longer exists, even if you wish it."

She suddenly noticed the coolness of the room. Pouting slightly, she tried to tug the blankets around her. The way the earl was holding her made the task impossible, and he was not feeling indulgent.

"Ah," he drawled, ignoring her halfhearted attempts to climb off him. He gave her a considering look. "I believe I have figured out why you are hesitating to consent to my offer."

Her fingers itched to scratch the smirk from his handsome face. "Hesitating? Your arrogance is immeasurable, my lord. If I hesitate, I only do so to not injure your pride. If a swift answer is what you require, then you shall have it. I must reject your kind offer."

Patience blinked furiously, fighting the need for tears.

Ramscar had lost his indulgent expression when faced with her defiance. "Kindness has no part in this accord. Do you think I offer marriage out of pity?"

His grip bordered on pain. "No!" she exclaimed, feeling hunted. "I do not want you offering marriage at all."

He sighed, relaxing his hold but not his guard. "Then you must be the first woman born of Eve who has not wanted to bind a man to her, heart and soul."

Patience was not fooled by his demeanor. If she tried to lunge away from him, he would immediately cover her body with his. She pushed her hair back and gestured upward. "Why should we marry? You have been content with our arrangement."

He crossed his arms. "And what exactly is our arrangement?"

Heat burned her cheeks. It was awkward discussing these matters with him. "We are lovers. More specifically, I suppose I am your mistress." He grimaced at her indelicate word choice. "Oh, do not be coy, Ramscar. I know you have kept mistresses, or have you so quickly forgotten Angeline Grassi?"

Ramscar scrubbed his face in agitation. He did not like the unpleasant reminder that Patience was painfully aware that she had not been his first choice for a lover this season. "There is a distinct difference between you and Angeline Grassi. I have asked you to be my *bride*."

Patience closed her eyes and tried to envision herself as his countess. All she saw was her mother staring back at her with an ambitious gleam in her eyes. How could she think of marrying him with the lies that had been told? What of her unsavory past with Julian Phoenix? "Marriage would muddle things. Besides, I would not make you a good wife."

"Perhaps." He chuckled when her eyes narrowed at his quick agreement. "Then again, I may not make you a good husband, Patience. It is a risk all people take when they pledge themselves to another person. Come now, you are not one to behave cowardly."

He knew the appropriate thing to set fire to her temper. Ramscar chose to see only the benefits of their union and not the problems. "I have been on my own since I was fourteen. I have done things that shame me when I reflect on them. Your title and personal honor require a lady who—"

"Is a paragon?" he interrupted her; a challenge lit his eyes. "Can increase my wealth? A milk-skinned virgin with the pedigree worthy of my noble seed?"

He was poking fun at her fears. "No," she said tightly. "I highly doubt anyone in the *ton* would view *les sauvages nobles* as virtuous. I have heard some of the tales whispered about you and your friends."

"Exaggerations, I am certain."

It was ridiculous to be jealous of a past she had no part of, but it was disconcerting when she thought of him pursuing other women. "They call the four of you wicked, pleasure-seeking scoundrels—"

Instead of denying it, he had the audacity to grin. "Why is pleasure-seeking a sin? I, personally, would recommend all and sundry to engage in the practice daily." He slid his hand up her and gave her buttock a playful squeeze.

Patience shook her head. "You and your friends have family, titles, and wealth to protect you. The rest of us cannot afford your recklessness."

He frowned at her. "You, my dear love, happen to be one of us."

She glared back at him. He was being deliberately obtuse. Her ties to the Farnalys did not pardon her from the life she had led since she left the protection of her family.

"That is what I have been trying to tell you. I am not one of you," she said, sneering at the absurd suggestion. "Patience Winlow is rebellious, opinionated, and known to lie when the occasion warranted. She is a struggling actress and a former thief. Go ahead and ask your friends. I would wager they would tell you that my sterling qualities would make me a fascinating mistress but a terrible countess."

Ramscar wearily sighed, not disguising his disappointment. "So, you not only speak for me but my friends as well?"

He was not being fair. She was trying to save him from an ill-fated decision. "Be practical, Ram," she pleaded with him. "Given time, you would come to your senses and regret your impulsive decision."

"I disagree," he said curtly. Ramscar wiggled up and braced his head with his arm. "For you see, I have fallen in love with you."

Her lips parted at his declaration. Speechless, she gaped at him. Gentlemen had whispered that feverish vow into her ear while they pressed wet kisses onto her mouth and attempted to fumble for her breasts. Their intent had been to seduce her into bed with sweet flattery. Ramscar had already claimed her body on numerous occasions. Patience had remained in his bed of her own free will. He gained nothing by wedding her, except trouble.

The tempo of her heart increased at the realization that there was one detail she could not disregard. She laid her hand over her chest, almost afraid to speak the words aloud.

Ramscar was in love with her.

Her stunned silence pricked his pride. He scratched the back of his head and glowered at her. "I can see my honorable declaration has cudgeled you senseless. The next time I want to silence you, all I have to do is tell you that I—"

Patience lunged forward and cut off his tirade with a hard kiss. When he parted his lips, she smiled against his mouth, knowing that she had his complete attention.

On a growled oath Ramscar seized her by the arms and pushed her back. "What game are you playing, Patience?" He gave her a little shake.

"None, my lord," she said, fighting back the urge to giggle. "I was just rewarding you for having the astuteness to love me."

Wariness and anger simmered just beneath the surface of his calm façade. "When a man declares his feelings for his lover, mocking him is a dangerous business."

Patience hugged him. She pressed a reassuring kiss against his temple. "Oh, Ram, I am not ridiculing you. Your sincerity has always unsettled me."

Ramscar stroked her cheek with his knuckles. "Be truthful. Are you telling me that you cannot love me in return, Patience?"

She shook her head and rested her forehead against his. "No, you misunderstood me. In the past four years, there have been other gentlemen who have claimed to have loved me." She pulled back and stared into his beautiful hazel green eyes. "Not one of them meant it. Until you."

Grasping her by the back of the neck, he pulled her closer and leisurely kissed her. "Give me the words I hunger for, Patience," he said, nibbling her lower lip. "I need to hear them."

If she revealed her true feelings to him, her

protests would fall on deaf ears. Ramscar would view her declaration of love as binding as if she had spoken the words in front of a vicar. He was not considering the trouble her past or her parents might bring him. If she allowed herself to be vulnerable and he cast her aside later, she was not certain she could survive the loss. Patience leaned closer until her lips brushed his ear. "Your feelings are wholly returned," she whispered into his ear. She grinned as his aroused manhood bumped her buttock.

His eyes reflected his frustration. "Patience—"

She lightly bit his earlobe. "Hush." Moving down his body, Patience sat back on her heels. "When words seem inadequate, an affectionate demonstration is required."

She lowered her face and slowly curled her tongue around the swollen head of his arousal. Ramscar's entire body jolted at the moist caress. Phoenix had schooled her in the arts of pleasuring a man in this fashion. Years earlier, it had seemed like a demeaning, unpleasant task. However, she had preferred using her mouth on Phoenix instead of having him violate her body.

Patience swirled her tongue against Ramscar's smooth heated flesh and deepened her teasing strokes.

"Christ, you have a wicked tongue, lady!" Ramscar's breath came out like a hiss between his teeth. He lifted his hips, encouraging her to take more of him.

Her nipples hardened in response to his low moan. She was slowly becoming aroused, and she was amazed by the discovery. In the past, she had never taken pleasure in touching a man thusly. Ramscar was different. There was little that she did not like about him. To prove it, she cupped his testicles, and the earl was at her mercy. She used the flat side of her tongue to measure him from his salty tip down to the soft sac in her hand.

"Patience!" His fingers threaded through her blond hair, urging her to take him back into her mouth again.

Patience heeded his silent demand. He was close to his release. She could sense it, could taste the subtle change in the dewy moisture that collected at the tip. Holding on to his hips, she glided up and down.

His fingers in her hair tightened almost painfully as his manhood convulsed against his powerful release. An almost inaudible gasp erupted from Ramscar. She did not pull away. Rather, she continued stroking and milking the swollen head of his arousal until he went limp on the bed.

Patience lifted her head, wondering if he had passed out from the pleasure.

Sated, he gave her a heavy-lidded glance. "You were right," he said huskily. "There are times when words are not adequate. You have convinced me. We shall marry as soon I can arrange it."

CHAPTER TWENTY

"I hear congratulations are in order," Meredith said, smiling as she greeted them in the front hall. Adorned in a white muslin dress that was edged with pale blue bows, she looked freshly scrubbed and slightly out of breath.

Ramscar could not quite decide what had changed in his sister's demeanor since he had said farewell to her. As he watched Patience and Meredith embrace, he noted that she exuded a quiet confidence and radiant joy that he had never glimpsed in the past.

"How did you know?" Patience asked, dazed by her friend's enthusiastic greeting. Patience glanced at him and frowned. "Good grief, did you have the banns posted in my absence?"

Patience was chafing against his possessive claim. If he pondered the life she had led, he assumed her reaction was not surprising. First, she had been bullied by an abusive lover, and after he had died, she had been mistress of her own fate. In time, she would calm down and settle into the life she and Ramscar would build together.

"If you hadn't run off, I might have accomplished the task," he mildly retorted. "Though, I confess, I was admirably compensated for your defiance."

"Behave yourself, Ram," Meredith scolded; the pink hue on her cheeks was a slightly darker shade than that on the cheeks of his bride-to-be. "If I was Patience, your vulgar speech would have me dashing out the front door again." His sister turned to address her friend. "Despite my brother's boldness, he did not share his intentions with me. The depth of his feelings was there for me to see when he learned that you had left us. He was so determined to bring you home and keep you, I half-expected him to carry you off to Gretna Green."

If his sister harbored any resentment toward the match, she was concealing it amazingly well. Not that her disapproval would matter to him. He intended to marry his lady. However, Patience was skittish, and she was not above using Meredith as another reason that they should not marry.

"I thought I would never hear the end of it, if we had excluded you," he said dryly as Meredith stepped into his embrace. He kissed her on the cheek. "Since the duchess did an excellent job launching you into polite society, I recommend that we petition Her Grace for her assistance once again."

Patience paled at his suggestion. "I would not want to intrude."

"Nonsense!" he said, surprised that she was intimidated by the dowager. "For the duchess, attending a merry celebration is second only to being in on the planning of one. When Solitea and his new wife eloped, Her Grace had them marry again in her gardens. She will know what is required for us to marry quickly, while I secure us a special license."

"Perhaps we should go over the details again, before we involve others, Ramscar," Patience said, sending him a meaningful look.

He was about to dismiss her suggestion when he sensed that they were not alone. Turning his head,

Ramscar froze when he noticed Lord Halthorn standing near the stairs.

"Good morning, Lord Ramscar. Miss Winlow. When Lady Meredith did not return, I feared she had received troubling news," the young gentleman nervously explained.

"Troubling" seemed a strangely apt description for this astonishing development.

Suddenly the subtle change Ramscar had noted in his sister became quite clear. "Meredith, you did not tell me that you had a visitor."

"Ram will call him out. Oh, this is entirely my fault," Meredith said, staring at the closed door as if her fate were being decided within the library.

Actually, it was, but Patience did not have the heart to call attention to that fact.

"Credit your brother with some discipline. He is not likely to pull down one of his treasured weapons from the wall and slay Lord Halthorn where he stands," she said, wishing she believed her assurances. "Forgive me for prying, Meredith. Did His Lordship seduce you?"

Ramscar might have a liberal view of a lady's virginity; however, Patience suspected he was downright traditional when the lady was his beloved sister. Oh God, Meredith was correct. Ramscar would likely kill Lord Halthorn for touching Meredith.

"Seduce me?" Her friend wrinkled her nose at Patience's erroneous conclusion. "Heavens, no. Halthorn is too honorable to besmirch a lady's reputation."

"Good," she said, visibly relieved. "The man might survive his private meeting with the earl, after all."

"I was forced to seduce him."

Patience was certain she had misunderstood her friend. "I beg your pardon?"

Meredith covered her mouth with her hand and giggled. "Oh, dear heavens, I have shocked you. If you could only see the look on your face!"

It was not her expression that troubled her. Patience was more concerned about what Ramscar would do to the young lord when he learned that his sister had taken on the role of a seductress.

"I have ruined your sister."

Ramscar seized Halthorn by the front of his frock coat and threw him toward a plum-colored lacquer coffer. The viscount bounced rather nicely against the side, but Ram was not finished. He picked the man off his feet and slammed his backside onto the flat surface of the chest.

"Give me a reason why I should not end your life, Halthorn," he said, wishing the man would at least fight back. Ram wanted an excuse to pummel the gentleman senseless.

Halthorn clearly thought he deserved whatever punishment Ramscar deemed appropriate. Panting slightly, Halthorn clutched Ram's wrists. "I was weak. I should have resisted touching her—"

Wrong answer.

Ram drove his fist solidly into the viscount's belly.

Apparently, Ram really did not need an excuse for violence, after all!

He heard the library door open with a bang. Scrimm must have given his sister the key. Damn the man for his interference. Ram just wanted a few more minutes alone with his sister's vile seducer.

"Ram! Dear God, do not hurt him!" Meredith cried out, both she and Patience rushing toward them. "He is an honorable gentleman and has done nothing that you yourself have not done."

It was the wrong thing to say to him, considering all the things he had done to Patience since he had discovered her at the inn. He thumped the back of Halthorn's head against the hard surface of the coffer. "Name your seconds," Ram hissed, enraged that he had not protected his sister from the bounder.

"For a man who abhors dueling, you have been

rather busy issuing challenges these days," Patience said wryly. She did not make the mistake of stepping between them.

"There is no call for violence," Halthorn said, staring over Ram's shoulder at Meredith. "I will marry your sister. Most willingly!"

Meredith placed her hand on his arm. "Halthorn awaited your return so he could formally ask for my hand. I think an autumn wedding would be lovely."

Halthorn's sappy expression might have been comical if the man had not confessed to ruining Meredith.

"Might I suggest a late September wedding?" the viscount said, momentarily forgetting his perilous position. He blinked and focused on the man he needed to convince. "That is, if we have your brother's blessing."

Ramscar glowered at the prone man. They were opposites in many ways. An intellectual, Halthorn preferred lofty books of antiquities and frequented literary circles and science lectures. Good God, the man did not even gamble or drink. There had to be something wrong with him. No gentleman could be so utterly wholesome. Ugh, the man was a damn puppy! Ram wanted to hit the man again on principle.

Then again, Halthorn had also claimed to have fallen in love with Meredith. A gentleman who was so blinded by Ramscar's sister's gentle inner radiance that he did not notice her facial scars was a man he could learn to like.

"He thinks I am beautiful, Ram," his sister disclosed solemnly. The joy twinkling in her eyes when she gazed at her beloved was her brother's undoing.

Disgusted his younger sibling could mollify him so effortlessly, Ramscar lowered his head in defeat. He held out his hand to the viscount and pulled him into a sitting position.

"Halthorn, I recommend that the next time you have news to share with me, you lead with the good. The judicious measure will spare you from getting your jaw broken," he said, shaking his head at the way his sister was fussing over Halthorn's wrinkled coat.

"Omnia vincit amor," Patience said, coming forward until she stood next to Ramscar.

Love conquers all.

Virgil. While she preferred to pretend she was not born of Ramscar's world, she made use of her education. "Aut vincere aut mori," he murmured for her ears alone.

Either conquer or die.

For once, Patience did not have a witty retort.

CHAPTER
TWENTY-ONE

Patience awoke trembling and confused. She pressed her fist to her damp forehead. It was a dream. Still, she could not shake the unease that someone had watched her while she had slept.

Ramscar?

Instead of enjoying the fete that was being held in honor of her and Ramscar's upcoming nuptials, Patience had slipped away from the well-wishers and had gone upstairs to her bedchamber. Exhausted,

she had fallen into a restless sleep filled with unpleasant images of Julian Phoenix and her disapproving mother.

When Ramscar realized Patience had disappeared, he would likely gather a hunting party for
his errant lady. Covering her indelicate yawn with
the back of her hand, she stretched out the other
arm. Her fingers connected with a blanket draped
over her legs. Well, this proved someone had come
into the room, she thought as she sat up. She had
not covered herself with a blanket.

Smiling at the sweetness of the gesture, Patience
lifted the corner of the blanket and tossed it aside.
She nearly fainted. Underneath was a small fortune
in jewelry! She tentatively picked up an elegant citrine, diamond, and pearl necklace that she recognized as Lady Dewberry's. It was a truly exquisite
piece. The young countess was still upset about her
loss. Another trinket glinted up at Patience from her
lap. The sapphire and diamond bracelet belonged to
Lady Dewberry's friend Lady Perinot. There were
several unfamiliar pieces that Patience had never
seen before, but she recalled Lady Oliff wearing this
gaudy diamond and emerald choker.

I am in trouble.

Patience dropped the jewelry as if the glittering
gems had burned her.

"No," she whispered, terrified of the erroneous

conclusion everyone would come to when they saw the stolen jewelry in her possession. "I am still asleep. This is just a horrible nightmare. I did not steal from those ladies."

The magnificent pile of jewelry made a silent mockery of her fervent denial.

Coming to a decision, she began gathering up the stolen jewelry. "I did not do this," she muttered, her stomach roiling and twisting until she feared that she would be sick. "Ramscar will believe me. He will know what to do."

Someone had gone to a lot of trouble so she might be blamed for the thefts.

With the jewelry clutched to her breasts, she slid off the bed and rushed to the door. Her only frantic thought was to find Ramscar. She ran down the hallway and down the stairs. Everyone was outdoors, enjoying the festivities. If she could just find Ramscar and signal him to join her, no one would ever have to know that the stolen pieces had briefly been in her possession. He could give the jewelry to the Bow Street Runner he had hired after Meredith's ball. The thefts had mystified the police, and the Runner Ramscar had hired had not turned up any suspects. Patience glanced down at the jewelry. Maybe if the stolen items were returned to their owners that would be the end of things.

It was a futile wish.

Someone had deliberately slipped into Patience's bedchamber. That person had taken the time to arrange the jewelry on her skirts and concealed their mischief with a blanket so it was Patience who first discovered the stolen pieces.

A warning?

Possibly. It appeared her upcoming marriage to the earl had displeased someone.

Clutching the jewelry in one hand, Patience opened the door to the back parlor. The room should be empty. With a little luck, she hoped to spot Ramscar from one of the windows facing the gardens. The door opened and Patience came face-to-face with Lady Perinot, Miss Nottige, and Lady Dewberry. The trio seemed equally startled by Patience's unexpected presence.

Patience jerked the door partially closed, using it to hide her precious burden.

Lady Dewberry, the boldest of the three, looked arrogantly down her narrow nose at Patience. "My dear, Ramscar has been searching for you. Naturally, he was concerned by your absence."

Patience belatedly realized that she had not combed her hair or changed her rumbled dress. With her face flushed with excitement, she had the look of a lady who had just come from a passionate tryst.

"I clearly have I interrupted a private meeting.

Since Lord Ramscar is searching for me, I shall seek him out immediately," Patience said, edging backward out of the room with the jewelry clasped in one hand and the door in the other.

Miss Nottige raised her hand to halt Patience's awkward departure. "Miss Winlow," she said, giving her companions sideways glances as if needing their support. "There have been some rather interesting rumors of late regarding your parentage. I have heard conflicting stories. One of the more shocking accusations claimed that you were the daughter of an illiterate butcher and a French prostitute." There was a calculating, malicious gleam in the lady's eye that was troubling.

All three ladies closed in on Patience.

Patience turned slightly, attempting to conceal her costly burden from her companions. She backed up a step. The opening in the doorway was narrowed by an inch. "Miss Nottige, you should know better than to believe the gossips."

Lady Perinot hastily added, "Another made the outrageous boast that you were the missing child of Sir Russell and Lady Farnaly. Their daughter had reportedly been kidnapped by smugglers."

Of all the ridiculous suggestions . . .

The three ladies tittered. Apparently, if they had to choose between the two tales, they considered the rumor about her being a baronet's daughter the more absurd one.

Lady Dewberry frowned at her. "Is there someone with you?"

Patience paled at her assumption. "Of course not!" she said crossly. "Now if you will excuse me, ladies, I must find Ramscar—"

"What are you hiding from us?" Lady Perinot demanded. Without warning, she tugged the door from Patience's fingers.

All three stared at her with varying degrees of mute amazement on their faces.

"Well, well, you are full of surprises, Miss Winlow. Where did you get that jewelry?" Lady Dewberry said, being the first to recover. "Did you steal all of it?"

"No. I found the pieces upstairs on the bed," Patience cradled the jewelry protectively to her chest, not wanting the other ladies to peer too closely at the stolen treasures. "I need to speak with Lord Ramscar. Where is he?"

Lady Perinot pointed an accusatory finger at her. "Lady Dewberry, is that not your citrine and pearl necklace?"

"It is!" the countess cried, snatching the necklace from Patience. She made a crooning sound as she examined her property for damage. "I was so heartbroken when I realized it was gone. I never thought I would see it again."

"Lady Perinot, I believe that is your bracelet," Miss Nottige said, ever the helpful twit.

As Lady Dewberry lifted her gaze up from her necklace, her expression was blatantly hostile when she stared at Patience. "Well, it appears we have succeeded where Bow Street has not, ladies. We have found our thief."

"Give me back my bracelet," Lady Perinot whined.

"Lady Dewberry . . . Lady Perinot . . . you must believe me, I am not the thief. I just found the jewelry on my bed," Patience tried to explain, knowing it was futile. None of these ladies were particularly friendly toward her when she was merely Lady Meredith's companion. She had literally handed them a reason to vilify her.

"An improbable tale." Miss Nottige sniffed with disdain. "Why would anyone leave a fortune in jewelry on *your* bed?"

Why indeed.

Patience could feel the panic rising from her chest to her throat. The muscles constricted painfully when she swallowed. "I can offer you no explanation for the thief's actions. All I can tell you is that I did not steal your blasted jewelry!"

"Thief," Lady Dewberry sneered. "Poor Ramscar.

Beguiled by a pretty face. I am certain he had no notion that he was harboring a criminal in his household."

The other ladies made concurring wordless sounds.

Patience's entire body was trembling. "Please, you must listen to me," she begged.

"Thief!" Lady Perinot echoed her friend, and pried the bracelet from Patience's numb fingers. "You will hang from the gallows, Miss Winlow. I will personally insist that you are punished for your crimes."

"Someone should summon the authorities," Miss Nottige suggested, and Patience was ready to strangle the young woman for her encouragement. "And one of the earl's weapons. There is no telling what her sort will do when cornered."

Fearful they were facing a desperate criminal, all three ladies screamed.

"Help!" Lady Dewberry cried out. "Please do not hurt us!"

Patience was too overwrought to worry about calming them. Besides, they were not likely to believe her anyway. Afraid that the ladies' cries would draw more unwanted attention, Patience pushed the jewelry into the flabbergasted countess's hands.

"Here. Take it all. I do not want it. Nor am I

your thief," Patience said, her voice catching slightly as she sobbed.

She turned and ran. No one saw her as she flung open the front door and dashed into the street. Patience whirled around. The street was congested with the carriages belonging to Ramscar's guests. Which direction should she go? Where should she go? Ramscar could no longer help her. There was enough evidence in his house that she would likely hang for her supposed crimes. Lady Dewberry and her friends were likely telling everyone that they had caught the future Countess of Ramscar with the stolen jewelry.

There would be a terrible scandal.

Everyone would begin to speculate that she had been the clever thief all along. It was her upcoming marriage to Ramscar that had convinced her to give up her criminal ways, or worse, she had been caught by Lady Dewberry and her companions before she could hand over the booty to an unknown cohort.

I am going to hang for something I did not do!

With her thoughts racing to a dire conclusion, Patience picked a direction and ran. She wanted to get as far from Ramscar's house as swiftly as her legs would carry her. Once he heard the accusations he would understand why she had left him and wonder if she had lied to him. Her heart lurched painfully in her chest at the notion he might come to believe the accusations.

A man stepped out from between a carriage and an enclosed coach. Espying him too late, she collided into him. The man staggered backward, but he kept them both from falling onto the filthy street.

"I beg your pardon, sir," she panted, so winded that she could barely speak. "I—"

Patience glanced up and froze in the stranger's arms.

No. It could not be . . .

Grinning down into her horrified face was Julian Phoenix. "Miss me, my little pigeon?"

Something hard connected with the back of her skull. Patience saw a bright flash of light and then saw nothing at all.

CHAPTER
TWENTY-TWO

The foreign taste of blood awoke Patience from her slumber. Confused and with her eyes still closed, she licked her lips. Her mouth was sore. She must have cut her lower lip when someone or something struck her from behind. Considering the immense throbbing pain radiating from her skull, she was wagering it was a wagon laden with barrels of ale. She raised her hand and realized someone had tied her wrists together.

Julian Phoenix!

"So you are finally awake," Phoenix said from somewhere behind her. "I was afraid that your thick skull had been cracked from the blow."

Patience slowly opened one eye. The nausea and headache she was suffering from made even the dimmest light unbearable. She tried not to whimper. Men like Phoenix preyed on the weak. She would not give him the satisfaction of revealing how badly she was hurt. "You are supposed to be dead," she said tersely.

He had brought her to a small theater. Opening both eyes, she glanced about. He had carried her up to the second tier and had placed her in a private box close to the stage. She did not recognize the building. The interior smelled of dust and stale air, so if the building was still being used, any occupancy had not recent.

Phoenix circled around until he was facing her. "Such fiery defiance. Once, I tried to teach you that there are instances when you should accept your defeat gracefully. This is one of those moments. You have undeniably been outwitted and there is no chance of escape." He knelt down in front of her. "What do you have to say for yourself?"

Her swollen lip gave her the appearance of pouting. Giving him a sullen look, she said, "I was careless. I should have stabbed you through the heart with the hay fork to ensure that you were dead."

The ire in his eyes was her only warning to his intent. Drawing back his arm, he slapped her. Her head snapped roughly to the side. Her cheek stung like he had seared his palm into her flesh. She brought up her bound hands and lightly touched her face.

"Bloodthirsty little wench! I nearly perished from your first thrust," he said, glowering at her as he stood. "However, much like the mythological bird that is my namesake, I was reborn into the man you see before you."

Patience flexed her fingers. He had tied the rope around her wrists so tightly her fingers were numb. "It was an accident. If you recall, I wanted to summon help, but it was too late, or so you said. I hate to be rude, but why are you not dead?"

His mouth curled up into a feigned smile. "Oh, I was quite convinced death was close at hand. An icy lethargy had deadened my limbs and each breath became shallower than the next. I could barely hear the words you were screaming at me as my vision dimmed to blackness."

Patience felt a pang of guilt. She had been so upset that afternoon in the barn. Had she seen only what she had wanted to see? "I thought you were dead," she said contritely. "If there had been a chance to save you, I would have gone for the surgeon." She had tried to go for help, but Phoenix had only taunted her for causing his death.

"You had done enough," he said waspishly. "When I awoke, an angel hovered above me. While you left me to rot beneath a moldering pile of hay, the lady who discovered me, bloodied and unconscious after your heinous attack, unquestionably saved me from a certain death. She cleaned and bandaged my wounds, bathed my feverish brow, and remained by my side day and night until the shadow of death was banished from my sickroom."

His final words and death had haunted Patience for two years. Although she had not deliberately sought to harm him, she had been burdened with the sin of killing another person. She had lied to people she had thought were her friends and privately endured the shame of her omission. Why? Phoenix could have spared her years of misery if he had revealed himself.

"Deidra, Perry, and Link were concerned when you failed to appear at the inn. Why did you not send your angel to us, and tell us that you lived?" she demanded angrily.

Why did you let me think I killed you?

He leaned nonchalantly against the façade enclosing the private box. His eyes gleamed in merriment. "I was not ready to reveal my miraculous recovery. Besides, you told the troupe that I had abandoned the lot of you. No one was grieving my death, my pigeon, except for you. And you did mourn for me, did you not?"

Hate rose within her breast for Julian Phoenix. She would never forgive him for taking something precious from her. Oh, not her virginity but her innocence. It was difficult to trust anyone. Her days with Ramscar and Meredith had softened the prickly exterior Patience presented to other people. Nonetheless, she was still struggling to give Ramscar the trust he offered unconditionally.

"Of course I mourned you. Unlike you, it is not my nature to harm others. I regretted what had happened in the barn—"

"And yet you ran away and lied about my fate?" he taunted, sounding disappointed in her.

Phoenix made her actions to protect herself seem monstrous. "I was not the one intent on pouring a bottle of laudanum down my throat so Lord Grattan could violate me while you got rich from my pain! Though I regretted what had occurred, I was not going to hang on your behalf!"

He slowly grinned and glanced upward. "Do not be so certain."

Although it pained her to tilt her head in any direction, she could not resist looking up to see what had captured his interest. Overhead, a hangman's noose was suspended from the ceiling. The rope was low enough so that if she stood, the noose could be fitted around her neck.

She bit her lower lip and then winced at the pain. "Must I point out that you are alive, sir? You are not righting any wrong by hanging me."

"Oh, I have no intention of hanging you, my duplicitous little protégée," he said cheerfully. "You will carry the task out for me."

Something Phoenix had revealed earlier troubled her. "How did you know that I had lied to the troupe? Unless you were following us or had someone spy . . ." She trailed off.

He crossed his arms and waited for her to figure out how close he had been to her all this time.

No!

"Deidra," Patience said with grim confidence. "She was the angel you had mentioned, the lady who saved you?"

"I was surprised that you never guessed. Deidra detested you. Yet she remained by your side, supporting you when Link and Perry chafed under your authority. Did you never wonder why?"

Deidra was a better actress than Patience had guessed. The other woman had never been overtly friendly toward her. Their alliance had been borne of necessity to keep their small troupe together. Deidra never concealed the fact that her loyalty would always belong to Julian Phoenix. In hindsight, Patience realized that her friend had never doubted that he would return to them one day.

God, she had been such a fool!

"Yes," Phoenix said, slowly nodding his head as he let the unpalatable truth sink in. "Deidra was always rather protective of me. When I told her to remain at the inn with the others, while you and I drove out to Lord Grattan's estate, she naturally followed us. The poor dear always disliked the intimacy between us."

"She loves you."

"Ah, yes," he sighed. "Love. Such a useful emotion. In the proper hands, it can be wielded as a warrior manipulates his dependable sword or shield." He moved away from the façade framing the upper tier and stood over her. "She arrived just in time to see you stagger out of the barn, sobbing and cursing my name. After you had climbed into the wagon and driven off, she entered the barn and found me," he said, fingering several curls near Patience's left temple. "As one might expect, she wanted to return to the inn that very night and slay you while you slept for what you had done to me."

No doubt Phoenix had embellished the retelling of the tale so Patience was the villainess of the piece. She had lived the last two years believing she was finally free of Phoenix's machinations. It was a bitter realization to acknowledge that she had been his pawn all along. Sullen but not defeated, she stared at him. "So I am here because Deidra demands revenge?"

"For Deidra?" He chuckled softly. "No."

He abruptly hauled Patience onto her feet. She cried out as daggers of pain exploded in her skull. "No—no," she said, attempting to avoid the noose. The extensive length of the rope hinted that he intended to throw her over the façade. Her own weight and gravity would eventually strangle her. He roughly pushed aside her bound hands, and the hemp circled her neck like a hideous necklace.

"You are facing *my* retribution, little pigeon," he said, tugging on the knot at her nape. "You know I can be most thorough when it comes to my plans. When I leave this abandoned theater, you will most certainly be dead."

"You are the thief," she said, wetting her dry lips. She had to keep him talking. It was not a difficult task. Phoenix was too enamored by his own genius to refrain from gloating. "For weeks, jewelry has been disappearing throughout the *ton*. When I awoke this afternoon and found the stolen pieces on my bed, I finally understood that someone was awfully determined to have me blamed for the thefts."

"Isn't it wonderful?" he said, reveling in his cleverness. "I am the talk of the season! I've enjoyed reading the papers and laughing as they tried to speculate when and where the dastardly thief would strike next."

The weight of the hemp rope felt like a thick iron chain around her neck. She cringed, fighting to keep her composure. "I applaud you. It was a laudable scheme. While you plucked the *ton* of its pretty treasures, you gave Ramscar's Bow Street Runner a likely suspect. Me."

Phoenix gripped her arm firmly to prevent her from removing the noose. "Deidra has been a valuable accomplice. Disguised as servants, it was not difficult for us to gain entry into a busy household. There is always extra staff underfoot during a ball, so we were rarely questioned. On a few occasions, we changed our attire again by borrowing clothes from our host and hostess and then reappeared as guests. No one suspected. Not even you," he purred triumphantly

Patience frowned. The night of Meredith's birthday ball, there had been a moment when a sense of foreboding had overwhelmed Patience. She had shrugged off the sensation, assuming she had been suffering from a case of nerves. Everyone had been staring at her and Meredith that evening. Patience would never have guessed that Phoenix had been stalking her while he plotted her downfall.

"Why stop?" she wondered aloud. "The season

has not ended. You could have continued plundering the *ton*, and waited until someone made a formal accusation against me. If I had been convicted, I would have been hanged."

"Regrettably, certain recent developments have forced me to alter my original plan," he said defensively. "I should have anticipated that you would unwittingly ruin my lucrative scheme. You have always been troublesome baggage, Patience. Although, I must confess, you are highly entertaining. I have enjoyed watching you over the years as you desperately tried to prove to yourself and others that you are at heart an honest woman. While that was amusing, I have long anticipated the day when I would rid myself of you."

Patience dug her fingers into his coat when he nudged her closer to the ornate façade. If she was going over the balcony, she intended to take him with her. "You do not have to do this," she said, every cell in her body rejecting the notion of bargaining with the devil. "Lord Ramscar is wealthy. You could ransom me!" She twisted in Phoenix's embrace.

He snorted at her naivety. "The moment you were safely ensconced in the earl's custody, you would tell him I was responsible for the thefts."

She shut her eyes, striving for sincerity. "I will not. I swear!"

Phoenix shook his head. There was no feigned regret to soothe her feelings. "Even if it meant you would face the magistrate for the thefts? I do not believe you. You would tell me anything to avoid going over that edge."

He was correct. She would tell him anything to stop him from carrying out his plan. "Ramscar loves me. I-I could convince him not to pursue you," she said, truly believing for the moment that after she was released she could sway Ramscar into not hunting down Phoenix and Deidra. "You could have the ransom and your life."

With the back of his hand, he gave her cheek a downward caress. He gripped her chin and tipped it as he studied her face. "I have no doubt you have wiled your way into the earl's heart. A man in love is likely to do anything for the lady who holds his affections. Of course, there is one small problem with your logic."

"What?"

His handsome face contorted into an insolent sneer. "Lord Ramscar became my enemy the night he lied on your behalf to discourage the speculation that you were the *ton*'s mysterious thief. I confess, I had not anticipated his protectiveness so soon. Did you offer him your body to gain his loyalty?"

She almost sputtered at Phoenix's assumption. "There was no reason to barter my body for his protection. I *was* innocent of the thefts!"

"I might have been content if you had been charged with my crimes as I had planned. However, your lover thwarted me, so I have decided to return the favor of spoiling his plans. Specifically, his marriage to you." Phoenix grabbed the hair at the back of her head and cruelly tugged. Patience cried out. Her poor head had been too sorely abused for her to conceal her discomfort.

"Oh dear, did you really think I would permit you to become his countess?" Phoenix taunted, constricting his grip until she cried out again. "Not while I live, my sweet pigeon. I hope Ramscar is present when your cold corpse is being cut down. On your behalf, Deidra wrote a touching note in which you confessed your heinous crimes and begged the earl's forgiveness for shaming him. To avoid further scandal, you told him, you planned to kill yourself. He naturally will find your tragic note too late for him to save you from your desperate act."

"He will never believe I willingly killed myself."

"It matters little to me. I will be gone, and you will be dead. If it amuses him, the earl can spend the rest of his days in quiet contemplation, wondering if you truly took your own life or if you died by foul means. A fitting punishment, do you not think?"

Patience peered closely into Phoenix's face. What she saw terrified her. There was no madness gleaming from his brown eyes. No, Julian Phoenix was quite sane. In his cold, manipulative mind he had reasoned that she had goaded him to this mortal conclusion. His dispassionate expression revealed he was indifferent to the task. No plea for mercy or cunning lie would persuade him from his goal.

He grabbed her upper arms from behind and tried to slowly walk her to the ornate façade. Patience stiffened in his arms. She was not some docile lamb who would blindly accept her captor's dictates. He had called her a troublesome baggage. She did not want to disappoint him. Flailing her bound arms wildly, she fought back, knowing her life literally depended on her actions.

"Damn you!" he growled; her vigorous disruptive movements were throwing him off balance.

Unfortunately, Phoenix was heavier and stronger. Despite her efforts, he was inching her forward. The rope around her neck became tauter as they neared the front of the box. "No. No!" she screamed, kicking at his legs.

She did not want to die. The man seemed impervious to her attacks. One foot connected with the façade, and in a desperate attempt to free herself from his hold she pushed off the paneled surface with her leg, sending them stumbling backward.

The rope was jerked hard and she choked against the sudden constriction. Fighting to keep her balance, she slipped her fingers under the rope and pulled. The noose widened with surprising ease.

There is not much time. . . .

Bumping against Phoenix, she struggled with the noose, hoping to ease it over her head before she lost her advantage.

"No." As soon as he realized she was succeeding in freeing herself from the noose, he seized the rope and tried to pull it back down. "Damn your eyes. Stop! You are not escaping me so easily."

It was a battle she refused to lose. She worked one side of the loop over her head before he could decrease the diameter of the noose. The moment the rope was away from her throat, she deliberately went limp and dropped to the floor.

Phoenix was suddenly grappling with rope and empty air.

"No!" he roared in fury. "Cease this defiance, you silly bitch! You cannot win. You are going over the façade even if I have to pick you up and toss you over the side."

"Patience!" a male voice echoed from below.

Ramscar.

A sob bubbled in her throat. Crouched down, she had never been so grateful to hear his voice.

Julian Phoenix turned away from her as they

heard the sounds of other people entering the building.

Patience did not hesitate. Rising up like a vengeful Fury, she used her entire body to shove Phoenix. Her thighs slammed against the façade, halting her momentum forward. Julian Phoenix reached and found only air. She heard the outrage and denial in his scream until his body smashed onto the floor below, silencing him abruptly.

She peered over the edge. There was a chance he could have survived the fall. The awkward position of his limbs and the odd angle of his head revealed that he had managed to break his neck. A bright red pool of blood expanded around Phoenix's head, eerily reminding Patience of a halo.

She turned her back on the scene below.

"Patience!"

Ramscar charged at her and scooped her into his arms. He hugged her so fiercely she could not speak. "Do you have any notion what you have put me through? Christ, I thought I lost you!" He pressed a harsh kiss to her mouth.

Oh, how it hurt! Her lip was too tender for his rough, affectionate kiss. Nevertheless, it was pain she would gladly endure.

Everod appeared behind them. "Is she hurt? Should I send someone for a physician?"

Patience touched the side of Ramscar's face. "I am

a little bruised, but I am fine. Please," she pleaded softly, "can we just go home?"

Not trusting his unruly emotions, Ramscar abruptly nodded. With her cheek resting on his strong shoulder, he carried her out of the theater.

CHAPTER
TWENTY-THREE

Ram carried her into the town house. Although Everod had good-naturedly teased Ram for his budding romantic inclinations, Patience had not protested. Perhaps, like him, she had been so shaken by what had almost happened that she loathed to be parted from him.

Scrimm greeted the trio at the door. "I see you recovered your lady, my lord. I trust you will not be so neglectful next time."

At his butler's harmless ribbing Ram winced. He was partly to blame for what had occurred. If he had not been distracted by his friends, she would not have been able to slip out of the house unnoticed.

Patience stirred in his arms, prepared to offer him a defense.

"Do not bother," he murmured into her ear as they crossed the foyer to the stairs. "It won't help."

The fete had ended the moment Lady Dewberry, Lady Perinot, and Miss Nottige sought him out with an outrageous tale about Patience strolling about with a small fortune in stolen jewelry cradled against her bosom. He had stared at the glittering evidence in their hands and refused to believe their lies.

"Ram! Patience!" Meredith took the stairs at a quick pace. Lord Halthorn followed in her wake.

She gave both Ram and Patience an unwieldy embrace. "I am so pleased my brother found you before Mr. Phoenix could have harmed you. If another minute had passed, I vow I would have collapsed into a fit of vapors!" Belatedly, Meredith took a closer look at her friend's bruised face. "Oh dear, Patience . . . your face . . . does it hurt much?"

"Hardly at all," she lied bravely for Ram's sister's benefit.

On the journey back to the house, Patience had told him and Everod what had transpired between her and Julian Phoenix. They had arrived at the town house before Ram had had the opportunity to explain how he had learned her whereabouts in such a timely fashion. It was simple to deduce by her slight frown that Patience was baffled by his sister's knowledge of Julian Phoenix. They still had much to discuss.

A soft feminine cry had everyone glancing up to the next landing. With tears in her eyes, the Dowager Duchess of Solitea applauded the earl. "Hurry, my darlings," she called out to the others in the drawing room. "Ramscar has returned!"

Solitea appeared next to his mother, holding his sleeping daughter in his arms. His duchess peeked from behind her husband and grinned. "Well done, my lord."

"Where is Cadd?" Everod asked, continuing to climb the stairs.

Lord Halthorn responded to the viscount's query. "He has yet to return from his errand." Halthorn glanced meaningfully at Patience.

The lady in Ram's arms was a trifle overwhelmed by her homecoming. Unwilling to let the others see her tears, she pressed her face into his neck. A lady who had long believed that she was alone in the world, whether she wanted a family or not, she had been adopted by the odd characters that made up his family.

"Ram, the poor girl is simply done in," the dowager duchess said. Patience's battered and rumpled appearance had roused her motherly instincts. "What she needs is some fortifying tea."

"And something to eat," Meredith added as she reached out and smoothed her friend's tangled blond tresses. "Are you hungry, Patience? Or would you rather just rest?"

"Oh, Ram," Patience whispered despairingly against his neck.

He appreciated everyone's concern, but Patience needed some privacy if she was to regain her composure. "Duchess, tea sounds heavenly. I will leave the refreshments in your competent hands. We will join you later in the drawing room, after Patience has had a chance to change into a clean dress."

Solitea nodded approvingly. "Do not hurry on our account. See to your lady. Now that Everod has returned, he can regale everyone with his most recent exploits." The duke disappeared in the direction of the drawing room. Ram could hear the dowager making faint cooing noises at the sleeping infant.

His friend's petite duchess eagerly pounced on the salacious topic of the viscount's love life. "Everod, you wicked man, are the rumors true?"

"Is what true?" Everod tersely replied.

Not offended by his insolent tone, she looped her

arm through his and led him away. Over her shoulder, she winked at Ramscar. "Oh, someone told me that you have been included in the memoirs of a particular lady. The gossips go on to say . . ."

Her Grace's voice faded as the distance between them increased. A minute later, Everod's booming laughter echoed throughout the halls.

Damn it all, what new mischief had Everod gotten himself into?

Lord Halthorn placed a possessive arm on his future wife. "Come, Meredith. I find myself curious to hear the rumors circulating about Everod, too."

When everyone had departed, Patience lifted her face from Ram's neck and met his steady gaze.

"We have unfinished business between us, Miss Winlow."

Dressed only in her chemise, Patience sat demurely on her bed while she watched Ramscar twist a sodden cloth over a washbowl. Since he had carried her out of the abandoned theater, he had been gentle and understanding. She knew him well enough to know the chaos of emotions simmering just below the surface.

She was prepared for his anger.

Ramscar returned to her and sat beside her on the bed. "Tilt your chin up." She complied and he pressed the cool cloth against the colorful bruise along her jaw where Phoenix had slapped her.

"You promised you would not run from me again, Patience," Ram said, grimacing when she hissed as he touched an extremely tender area. "Imagine my surprise when Lady Dewberry and her friends came to me with a crazy tale about you being the thief Bow Street has been searching for and you, my sweet bride-to-be, had conveniently vanished to add credibility to their story."

While she had expected and deserved his anger, she was not braced for the hurt she had caused him. "Lady Dewberry and Lady Perinot despise me. Miss Nottige is their loyal sycophant. I knew they would gleefully run straight to you with a—"

"Damn it, Patience, why didn't *you* run to me?" He pulled away from her and returned to the washstand. She listened to the musical sounds of water droplets as they struck the surface of the water in the bowl. "If you had come to me and told me what had happened, you would have never walked into the trap Phoenix had set for you." Just thinking about the perilous position Patience had placed herself in was enough to ignite his fury again.

"I was so frightened when I awoke and recognized the jewelry. Honestly, my first thought was to find you. I went into the informal parlor to see if I could signal you from a window, but I encountered

Lady Dewberry and her cronies—" Patience forgot all about her explanation as his statement penetrated her practiced defense. "What do you mean, a trap?"

"I am referring to your good friend Miss McNiell. You introduced me to the lady at Lord Powning's house, if you recall," Ramscar said snidely. Despite his harsh tone, when he sat back down and continued his ministrations, his touch was gentle. "Scrimm prides himself on personally knowing his staff. When he noticed an unfamiliar maid slipping into one of the rooms, he was suspicious. With the help of several footmen, he detained the maid so I might question her."

Phoenix had mentioned that he and Deidra had been slipping in and out of residences all season as either servants or guests. Patience closed her eyes, unwilling to meet Ramscar's gaze. As usual, Phoenix's plan had been flawless. He had sent Deidra into the Knowdens' residence. When Patience had retired to her room for a short nap, the young woman had seized the opportunity. While Patience had slept, Deidra had placed the stolen jewelry on the bed and covered the evidence with a blanket. Just as the couple had anticipated, Patience had panicked when she saw the jewelry. Had Deidra observed her from a discreet distance and gloated? Her stumbling upon Lady Dewberry and her snobbish companions must have seemed like providence to her former friend, because it was the impetus that sent Patience blindly fleeing the house and into Julian Phoenix's malevolent embrace.

"For two years, I have lived with the guilt that I was partially to blame for Julian Phoenix's death," she said, wiping a stray tear from her cheek. "It was an accident—"

"So you said the night at the inn. Fortunately, Miss McNiell provided me with the unsavory details that you had carefully omitted from your story. I know that Phoenix had planned to sell you to a Lord Grattan and there had been a fight. You impaled him with a hay fork and ran off, believing he was dead."

She gasped at Ramscar's accusation. "I did *not* impale him. If you must know, he impaled himself on the hay fork when we were struggling." She abruptly ceased her defense. "Oh, what does it matter? Now I am responsible for his death."

Patience could not deny that she had intentionally pushed Phoenix off the balcony. Ramscar and Everod knew the truth and viewed her actions as a last desperate attempt to save herself. Perhaps they were right. Phoenix would have taken both himself and Patience over the edge, rather than surrender to the authorities.

She said nothing for a few minutes, allowing Ramscar's admission to sink in. He knew *everything*. There were no more secrets between them. It was a liberating sensation.

Finally, she said, "For someone who had been caught trespassing, Deidra was awfully chatty."

"Miss McNiell was impressed with my considerable charm," he said dryly. Ramscar dabbed the cloth against the slight swelling on Patience's lower lip.

His not-so-subtle evasion only heightened her curiosity. Deidra was immune to a gentleman's charm, unless he had the proper coin to entice her. Patience wondered what threats Ramscar had used to gain Deidra's cooperation. She highly doubted the young woman had regretted sending Patience off to her death.

Another thought occurred to her. "By the by, where is my dear former friend?"

"Explaining her part in Phoenix's schemes to the magistrate," Ramscar replied, not particularly concerned about the lady's fate.

Patience gave him a shy, hesitant glance. "I suppose you are angry with me for running off."

"It would have spared you the colorful bruises you have on your face," he said, tossing aside the damp cloth.

A disheartened Patience felt her lower lip become more pronounced.

He tipped her chin up so she met his level stare. "No. That is not quite true. You believed the man had died from his wounds. Even if you had told me the circumstances surrounding Phoenix's death, neither one of us would have considered a dead man was behind the thefts. Nor would the truth have stopped Miss McNiell from baiting the trap with the stolen jewelry."

Patience leaned against him, savoring his warmth. His calm acceptance of what she considered one of the biggest debacles of her life was a balm for her soul.

Ramscar waited several beats before adding, "That said, I am slightly annoyed with you for not having faith in me. I would have taken your secrets to the grave."

Patience sighed. His calm acceptance was inordinately brief.

"I know it now. I cannot say that I did yesterday. You have to understand something about me, Ramscar," she said, holding his hand. "I have been looking after myself for so long I do not—"

"Want a man fussing and coddling you. My protective nature threatens your independence," he said bitterly.

"Wrong!" Patience turned to him. Very tenderly she framed his beautiful face with her hands. "I crave it. I just did not trust myself. If I became dependent on you, and then you cast me aside, I was not certain I could manage on my own again."

Or survive losing his love.

She let her arms drop at her sides. Her eyes filled

at the thought that her fears might push Ramscar away for good if she did not learn to manage them.

"Cast you aside? I want to marry you, lady!" he roared at her.

Patience had the strange urge to giggle. She was an odd creature to find comfort in his bellowing.

"Hear me well, Miss Patience Rose Farnaly Winlow. I see you clearly, flaws and all, and I still want to marry you. I love you."

Her nose itched and burned from her welling tears. "I love you, too."

Ramscar nodded arrogantly. "I have waited an eternity for you to say those words and mean them. Will you marry me?"

She smiled and then groaned at the pain. "Yes. I would be honored to marry you tomorrow."

"Today."

Patience was appalled by his suggestion. She looked hideous. "I beg your pardon?"

He grinned down at her, reminding her of a hungry wolf. "You heard me. I don't want to wait."

Patience thought of his friends and family waiting for them in the drawing room. As she grew suspicious, her eyes narrowed. "You planned this all along?"

Ramscar looked sheepishly at her. "Not exactly. The idea struck me earlier while I was out in the gardens. I was waiting for you to appear and, I realized, was impatient to start my life with you. I've already procured the special license, so I asked Cadd to find a clergyman willing to perform the marriage ceremony this afternoon." He grimaced and rubbed his jaw. "Of course, I had not anticipated that my bride would run off and have her life threatened by an old enemy. Nor could I have guessed that Cadd would have to ride to Cornwall to find a willing clergyman! It was a simple request. Only Cadd could turn it into an afternoon quest."

Oh, how she loved this man. She was certain he would disagree, but he had his flaws, too. His high-handedness about the wedding was a perfect example. Nevertheless, she felt no inclination to change him. "I am certain your friend has a reasonable explanation for his delay."

"He usually does," Ramscar said gruffly, tenderly kissing her on the lips.

"Your friends and family are waiting for us to join them."

"*Our* friends and family," he corrected, softening the chastisement by nipping her chin. "You are not alone any longer."

She understood what he was telling her. Whether he liked it or not, only time would allow her to believe it. "What do you propose we do while we wait for Cadd?"

He licked her ear and she shivered. "I have several scandalous suggestions."

"Do tell," she purred. The spark of passion was swiftly doused when he laid her back onto the bed, jarring the nasty bump at the back of her skull.

"Regrettably, you are too bruised for anything energetic." Rolling her onto her side, Ramscar molded his body against hers. "I have another suggestion."

"Go on." His proximity made the dreadful pounding in her head ease slightly.

"Why don't I just hold you for a while?" he murmured sleepily against her ear.

Patience sighed and snuggled closer. "Sounds heavenly."

It was a perfect beginning to the wondrous life they would plan and build together.